MW00604338

MYSTERY AT HEATHER HOUSE

A CASSIE ASHCROFT MYSTERY

LINDA RAWLINS

MYSTERY AT HEATHER HOUSE

Mystery at Heather House
A Cassie Ashcroft Mystery

By Linda Rawlins

Copyright © 2023 by Riverbench Publishing, LLC All Rights Reserved.

E-Book: 978-0-9600549-6-1
Paperback: 978-0-9600549-7-8

Discover other titles by Linda Rawlins at
www.lindarawlins.com
All rights reserved. No part of this book, or parts thereof, may be reproduced or transmitted in any form or by any means, electronic or mechanical, including scanning, uploading, photocopying, and recording by any information storage or retrieval system, without permission in writing from the copyright owner.
This book is a work of fiction. Names, characters, places, and incidents either are the product of the author's imagination or are used fictitiously. Any resemblance to actual persons, living or dead, business establishments, events, or locales is entirely coincidental.

ACKNOWLEDGMENTS

It was such great fun writing about Wexley Village, a fictitious place in England. It takes a village to produce a book and I'd like to take a moment to thank everyone who has helped me. First to my mother and my husband who helped me research my village in Wexley, England. Hours and hours of enjoyable research were had by the three of us. To Joyce for help with direction and editing!

To my husband Joe for keeping the world spinning in the right direction. A special thanks for making my special coffee each day!

To the real Joe Duffy – my favorite Chief Constable of the medical world. Thanks for letting me use your name!!

To my team of first readers – Joyce, Lorraine, Anita, Sandi, Krista, and Cathy S. You constantly bring suggestions and find errors that remain elusive to me. I appreciate you all so much!!!!

To the team of Riverbench Publishing – for everything else! Especially Matt for fantastic covers, website, social media, marketing, and publicity. To Krista for blurbs and creativity. To Ashley for creativity and all the bits and pieces that need to be done.

To my readers, fellow authors, librarians, booksellers, and friends (here and abroad). You are certainly the best and I'm so happy to call you all family! Thank you for reading and sharing my books in person and on your social media. I love hearing from you. You inspire me to continue to write!

I have a legion of friends and the best ones are my immediate family, which is very cliched but true.
   - John Nettles aka Tom Barnaby

1

"England? What do you mean, England?"

"Just what I said. You're going to England to research your book." Evie looked at Cassandra with a smile. "Isn't it wonderful?"

The silence was thick for a few seconds while Cassandra swallowed hard. "For how long? I can't just up and leave America. I have responsibilities here." Cassandra Ashcroft stood up and held the back of her chair as she stared at her agent and friend, Evie Thompson.

"For as long as it takes," gushed Evie excitedly. "Think about it. The London branch of the publisher is all in. They're willing to pick up the cost of a cottage if you send in frequent updates."

Cassandra laughed. "There's more to it than that. Publishers pay close to nothing these days. What are they getting out of it?"

Evie hesitated for a moment but decided to be truthful. "I thought the same thing and after having lunch with the VP of Acquisitions, he finally caved. It turns out the publisher signed a contract for a non-fiction book about the organizational structure of a police department in Wexley, England, and the writer for that project pulled out. Well, he didn't exactly pull out, more like he had a heart attack and died."

"That's horrible," Cassie said with a frown.

"Coincidentally, you're a best-selling author, writing a blockbuster fiction novel in the same setting, so...," Evie rose, walked around her desk, and sat in the chair next to Cassandra. "It was suggested we kill two birds with one stone. They pay for you to be in England for however long it takes to research their book while you're writing your own novel. Take whatever time you need. They'll hire a ghost writer to finish their project but give you credit as well. A win-win situation."

"I don't know if I want to go to England. Ethan won't be able to go with me."

Evie laughed. "That, my dear, would be a triple win. You may owe me for that in the future. We'll see. I know this may seem indelicate, but it's time to ditch that man. You're a whole different class of sophistication." Evie reached out and touched Cassie's arm. "Honestly, honey, he's bringing you down."

"He's a successful attorney," Cassandra protested lightly.

"He's a bore who doesn't pay you the kind of attention you deserve."

Cassandra didn't want to admit she had already decided to break up with Ethan. He was all about show and clearly didn't understand a writer's life. Hell, she didn't understand her own life.

"I don't know, Evie. Let me think about it."

"Think fast. Do you realize I managed to have a major publisher give you a research position as well as a contract to publish and market your fiction novel. Believe me, it is a rare and very coveted agreement and quite frankly, I wouldn't publicize this arrangement until the books are out. I know it's a lot to process all at once, but I did promise I would give an answer by Monday."

"Let me get this straight. The publisher gave you one weekend to convince me to up and leave America, maybe for a year, to work on my novel while doing research for them."

"Yes, that's basically it. Be reasonable. Do you know how many writers out there would kill for this opportunity? You'll be compensated by writing your book in the location where it takes place. I'm sure they would also offer a lucrative marketing package considering your name is attached to the other project as well."

"Evie!"

Evie put her hand up in Cassandra's face. "Not another word. I'm serious. You go home to your empty apartment. Look at your desk, cry, do some thinking. You don't have a family, a pet, or a plant to worry about." Evie watched as Cassandra's face dropped and immediately reached out to hug her. "All I'm saying is you don't have anything to physically tie you here, to New York. I know the city is your zone, your jam, your familiar place. I know how important stability is to someone. But don't let inertia stop you from accepting an amazing opportunity. You know, the whole destination is the journey type of thing. Don't ever make a decision without sleeping on it. I'll call you in the morning and we'll talk. By then, I'm sure you'll have made a list of positive and negative reasons to stay in America. We can talk about all of them during brunch over a good bottle of wine. Now go ahead and get out of my office. I have a lot to do before I can celebrate the fact that it's Friday night." Evie turned Cassandra around, placed her purse in her arms, and walked her to the door. "Sunday morning, 11:00 a.m. You and I are having brunch at the Waldorf. I will pick you up and we'll talk. Now, go home and think."

2

Cassandra blindly wandered down the lush hall to the outside of her agent's building. She was struggling to tamp down the panic rising within her. She'd always wanted to be a writer and fumbled for years trying to finish a book. Cassandra followed advice by joining writing groups and taking classes while working her daytime job as a medical tech in a large hospital. She submitted query after query and had a large pile of rejection letters memorializing her efforts.

Then one day, she was working in the emergency room, when Evie Thompson was rushed in after a serious injury. Evie had been walking down a sidewalk in New York when a car lost control, swerved onto the sidewalk, and hit her. The driver never stopped. Evie was sent to trauma while the police checked security cameras in the area to see if they could get a license plate or description of the vehicle.

Evie Thompson was one of the most coveted agents in the publishing industry. Cassandra recognized her name immediately and was nervous when she found she was assigned to be her medical technician. Her job was to observe and keep Evie calm and occupied while they waited for the various emergency scans and lab to return.

Not having a topic to discuss, she told Evie about her struggle to become a writer.

"I'm sure you can't go out in public without someone throwing a manuscript in your face," Cassandra laughed.

"You can't even imagine, honey," Evie said as she tried to speak against the collar surrounding her neck. "What's your name?"

"My formal name is Cassandra, but everyone calls me Cassie."

Cassandra neatly folded what was left of Evie's clothes and placed her belongings in a bag on the side of the room. "I'm sorry, your designer outfit was ripped when the EMT's brought you in, but your lovely shoes are still intact."

"No one will give two cents about what I was wearing if I don't survive." Evie paused. "Now that I think about it, that may be the first question from the paparazzi. What was she wearing when she was plowed over by the hit and run driver?" Evie's voice broke as she spoke the words prompting Cassandra to take her hand. Evie whispered, "I'm scared. The doctor said they were looking for internal bleeding and I may need surgery."

Cassandra smiled as she tried to gently frame her words. "They're having trouble managing your blood pressure, so the doctors are checking to see if you have internal bleeding. If they can find the problem, they can fix it. You're alert and talking, so that's good. The best surgeons and trauma teams are in this hospital. You're in good hands, Evie. Have faith that all will be well."

"You won't leave me?" Evie's tears fell harder as she spoke. "I don't have any family. Hell, I don't have many friends. The higher you climb, the more people hate you." After a few sobs, she whispered. "I don't want to die alone."

"I'm right here and I'll be with you the whole way. I promise. Try not to worry until they have results."

"Then distract me, Cassie. Talk to me about something." Evie laughed as tears and snot congealed on her face. She squeezed Cassandra's hand harder. "I never thought I would say this. Not that I'm a snob but you have no idea how many people are on me. Tell me about your best book. What's your elevator pitch?"

Cassandra spent the next ten minutes discussing the plot of her book. The passion in her voice was unmistakable as she outlined the story, but she noticed Evie was drifting off. "Is the plot that boring?"

Evie answered in a weak voice. "No, I like it. I think it's got great potential but I'm not feeling well right now. I'm tired and dizzy."

Cassandra loosened her hand and rechecked Evie's blood pressure. It had dropped to a dangerous low. She immediately called a code to get emergency personnel involved at the same time a trauma surgeon rushed in to say they'd found a bleed. "I'm going to scrub. She needs to be in the OR in three minutes or less. She'd better be ready when I'm gowned."

A weak thready voice asked, "What's happening?"

"Evie, they found something on your scan. You're going into surgery now, but I'll be with you in spirit and as close as I can be. You concentrate on having faith."

"Cassie, you promise I won't die alone?"

"I promise I'll be with you all the way. Stop talking about dying. You trust me?" Cassandra's gut wrenched as she realized she had no idea if Evie Thompson would survive, but she knew it was not the time to outline her chances. They had her sign a general consent when she arrived so she would be in the operating room as soon as possible.

"I'm going to trust you, Cassandra." Evie's grip loosened on Cassandra's hand as her pressure continued to drop.

For reasons unknown to Cassie, she choked up. She wanted Evie to survive. She willed her to survive. As the trauma calvary burst into the room, they moved en masse to the operating suite.

3

"C'mon, I don't want to be late," Evie said as she waited for Cassandra to get into the limo.

"I'm moving as fast as I can," Cassie said as she slid into the back seat next to Evie. The driver ensured she was comfortable and closed the door before he moved around to the front.

Evie grasped Cassie's hand. "I can't tell you how excited I am about this deal. It's going to be wonderful for you, me, and the agency."

"Evie, I haven't agreed to it yet."

"You can't possibly pass up this offer," Evie shook her head to emphasize her words. "I know you're nervous, but we'll talk about everything at brunch."

"Nervous? You know how I panic."

"It's the funniest thing because you're always solid as a rock for everyone else. Which, of course, is how we met." Evie squeezed Cassie's hand. "I am still so grateful you were there with me that day, watching over me. Someone else would not have paid attention and I'd be gone."

"I doubt it," Cassie said. "I just happen to pay a lot of attention to detail."

"That's why you're a great author. Who would ever guess that not only would I meet my guardian angel that day, but one of my best friends and clients?"

Cassie smiled and let her mind drift as she gazed outside the limo window. Evie had survived the surgery and was very grateful for Cassie's personal care but had not mentioned Cassie's book again. Then one day, when Evie was transferred to a rehab facility, she asked if Cassie could come with her. When Cassie explained she wasn't employed there, Evie begged her to work as her personal nurse. Evie didn't trust the nursing home where she was scheduled to receive rehabilitation. Not completely sure why, Cassie agreed as she could use the extra money. As part of the deal, Evie insisted Cassie bring a copy of her manuscript to read while she was in rehab. Cassie was floored. During the three weeks stay, Evie not only read the manuscript but insisted Cassie make multiple changes. At night and on weekends, Evie would tell Cassie exactly what edits she wanted to see, and Cassie made them after she checked Evie's wounds and readied her for rehab or bed.

Once they were done, Evie never mentioned the book again, even after she was discharged and sent home. Cassie was grateful to have personal advice from a great agent and friend by that time and vowed she would use that education to write a better book next time. They met for lunch on occasion, always Evie's treat, and one day in the middle of lunch, Evie was thrilled to announce she had received a very lucrative offer from a large publisher for Cassie's debut novel. Cassie didn't believe her at first, but once the contract was signed and her first check was received, she never looked back.

"Penny for your thoughts?" Evie teased. "There's no need to be anxious about this. We have contacts on both sides of the pond, and I'll be going back and forth to our London office. Partly for business but to check on you as well. Your career will skyrocket."

Cassie looked at Evie and stammered. "I'm not sure I want that. I love to write, but you know how I feel about being in public."

Evie's laugh was throaty. "I wouldn't worry about that one bit. You'll be working most of the time, but who knows where this can go.

At any rate, you're writing a book set in England. What's the best way to get the right atmosphere in your book but to write in the actual setting?"

Cassie sighed as the limousine pulled up to the Waldorf Astoria. Her stomach clenched with dread as she realized there would be very little room to talk Evie out of this idea. She quietly drew deep breaths in through her nose as they were escorted to a table. They were told of the menu and asked for their drink of choice. Cassie also wondered how she was supposed to eat while having a panic attack. Her attention was drawn back when she heard Evie speak to the waiter.

"In addition to our drinks, we'd like champagne. We want a fresh bottle of sweet champagne and we'll both take the brunch buffet."

"Very good." The waiter looked at Cassie who merely nodded her agreement. When he walked away, Evie placed her hand over Cassie's. "So, tell me exactly what you're thinking and then let's brainstorm about what we have to do to make this happen as soon as possible."

Cassie shook her head. "I have no idea. I'm still trying to figure out what you're suggesting. You know me, Evie. I don't do well with a lot of change."

The waiter appeared at the table with their drinks. A dry martini for Evie and a cranberry tonic splash for Cassie. When he left, Evie sipped her drink, turned to Cassie, and said, "Let's review. You're a best-selling author who now has a contract to write a mystery set in England."

"Yes, that's right," Cassie said as she took a sip of her drink.

"You have the opportunity to write that book on location to make sure the true flavor of the setting and theme are perfect."

"So, you've said." Cassie's fingers trembled as she put the glass on the table. "And in return?"

"You would be obligated to submit research for a non-fiction book the publisher has contracted about the Wexley Police Department in England. In return, the publisher will pay for a place for you to live in the village for a year. They will offer a lucrative advance as well as guarantee marketing and promotion for both books. You would get editorial credits for the non-fiction as well as your usual best-seller package. The research will be easy as we already have contacts set up. We have already confirmed that you will receive help directly from the police department, specifically the officers, whether sergeants, inspectors, or constables. It's a given."

Cassie shook her head. "I don't know, Evie."

Evie downed the rest of her martini. "Cassie, what could possibly be holding you back?"

Cassie turned bright red as she set her jaw. "I don't know, everything, nothing, who knows?" She shrugged her shoulders. "Maybe, I don't want to uproot my life and move to England."

Evie stayed silent as the waiter brought champagne to the table and poured two glasses. She then asked for another martini. "What is the worst thing that could happen? I don't mean that sarcastically. I'm asking you to verbalize and mitigate your fears. What do you imagine as the worst thing that could happen to you?" Evie looked straight at Cassie as she plucked the olive from her martini and popped it into her mouth with her professionally manicured gel-laden fingernails.

A flood of emotions flowed through Cassandra. She felt her throat constrict. Her eyes moistened as her heart rate picked up and her face flushed. She waited two seconds to see if she would get dizzy. Deep breaths, in and out. Deep breaths.

Evie pushed. "Are you afraid of a medical event? A crime? What?"

Cassie shook her head as she looked up at the ceiling. "Evie, you don't understand people with anxiety or fear. It's not a specific event. It's whatever puts me out there where I'd be alone, without control. I'm afraid of being alone and frightened. I can't explain it to you any better than that." Cassie picked up her drink and took a big gulp before she continued. "I like routine. I try to always have a plan. I like to keep things on an even keel. Too much excitement about good things makes me nervous."

Evie nodded as she looked at her friend. "I always knew you were a quiet type, but I didn't realize why. It's funny, other people would perceive that as being standoffish. After all, you are the famous

Cassandra Ashcroft, bestselling author. Just out of curiosity, what would be different about moving to London then to another state in America?"

Cassie thought for a moment. "In all honesty, not much except the fact I'm in my own country for starters. I have no close family as you are aware, but, if necessary, I can make a phone call."

"Who would be able to get to you fast enough to avert your crisis?"

"I don't know, probably emergency services since there's no one else."

"Exactly, if you called me or another acquaintance, we would only call emergency services for you."

Cassie teared up. "That's sad, isn't it?"

"What's the expression? Freedom, growth, or everything you want is on the other side of fear?"

"I don't know," Cassie said as she wiped her face.

"As your friend, and I emphasize friend, I'm not backing down on this. As much as you'll hate me, you'll be stuck the rest of your life trying to avoid dying and crisis."

"Oh, Evie."

"I've been to the UK many times. They have phones which work as quickly as ours. They have emergency services, and we have friends, publishers, and contacts there. Some great restaurants and entertainment. They have a lot of fun and interesting things, too. Yes, it's a slightly different culture but Americans fit in well enough to work and live there on a regular basis. There are thousands of flights from New York to London each week. You're not getting dropped onto an island and fighting for survival, but I can tell that's your perception."

"Yes, that's exactly right," Cassie said. They quieted for a moment as the waiter placed a few dishes on the table and delivered instructions about their food. The room was becoming crowded, and the piano music seemed a bit too loud.

When he left, Evie turned to Cassie, her face pinched. "Summer is only six weeks away. Did you make any special plans to go anywhere this year?"

"Evie, you know I don't go on vacation by myself. I probably would have gone to the beach a time or two. I stare at the water and write in my head. It's very relaxing and helps to remove all the noise in my head, but I don't travel due to my anxiety."

Evie took another sip of her drink and tried again. "Do you have meditation exercises? An app to calm yourself when you're nervous. I'm sure you've developed your own routine by now."

"Yes, of course," Cassie said. "It includes walking, deep breathing, drinking water and meditations."

Evie nodded. "Okay, this is how we're going to do this. You're going to England. You'll have a beautiful little place in the village."

"Evie," Cassie started.

Evie held her hand up. "Wait until I'm finished."

"I have an intern that I want to orient to the London office. I'll send her with you. She can stay in your cottage for the first week, until you're settled, and then move on to a hotel or rental unit until I need her to return. I know you like your own space to work, and she can't stay more than a month, but that will give you enough time to see if you're comfortable. I want you to stick it out for four to eight weeks. If you hate it, or haven't slept the whole time, you can come back for a break or move back completely." Evie turned to Cassie and held her shoulders while she spoke. "I think this is important for you in so many ways. To grow, find yourself, and gain your confidence. Your books will always sell themselves, but you need this for you."

Cassie's mouth worked but nothing came out.

"Don't say anything now," Evie said as she picked up her champagne and handed Cassie a glass. "Let's make a toast to Cassie, then eat, relax, enjoy the hotel, and you can think about all this later today."

4

Cassie stared at the landscape as the runway closed in. The plane was minutes away from landing at Heathrow Airport. Cassie tried to distract herself during the flight by watching two movies and reading a novel of which she was not able to absorb a single word. She turned to her companion and smiled. "The flight wasn't bad, was it?"

"Not at all, this is so exciting! Imagine me, Laura Milton, flying to London with Cassandra Ashcroft, a bestselling author. I can't believe my dream of working in a literary agency is coming true."

"I'm glad for you," Cassie said as she returned the smile. Cassie turned back to the window, lost in thought. *Damn Evie.* She knew Cassie would be so caught up in helping this young intern, that it would take her mind off her own panic. *Well done, Evie. Well done.* Now they were in England, and she couldn't ask the pilot to take her home. There was no path except forward.

Cassie gripped the armrest as the plane touched down. The squeal of the tires on the tarmac, as well as a few bounces, had her stomach in knots. Laura was smiling next to her, staring out the window. She pointed out various buildings while the plane slowed to a stop at the proper terminal. They were instructed to stay in their seats before the plane fully stopped, but passengers were already on their feet, grabbing their belongings from overhead compartments and generally blocking the aisle for others. Cassie stayed in her seat, waiting for the aisle to open. She turned to Laura. "Give it a few minutes for the crowd to lighten up. It's not like anyone is going anywhere fast."

Laura nodded. "Have you been to England often?"

"This is my first time."

"Really? I would have thought a successful author like you has traveled the world," Laura said with a smile.

"There's a lot to say about traveling through the internet these days," Cassie said with a laugh. "But that's one of the reasons I'm here. I want to research the location of my next novel in the actual setting. The local flavor is always different than what you read or see online."

"I'm so excited that Evie sent me with you. Thank you for agreeing to be my travel companion. I was nervous, but I didn't want Evie to know. Once she told me I was going with you, I knew everything would be great and I was able to relax completely and enjoy the ride."

Cassie nodded as she squeezed Laura's hand. "I'm so glad to hear that. I hope this is a transformative trip for you."

"Evie sent a schedule for orientation in the London office. She's planning on being here at some point and I'll fly back to America with her."

"Excellent, we want you to stay safe." Cassie noticed the aisle was clearing so she stood, collected her belongings, and slid toward the aisle pulling Laura behind her. They exited the plane and after collecting their luggage, they cleared customs and made their way toward the exit.

"Hey look," Laura said excitedly as she tapped Cassie's arm.

Cassie looked up to see a gentleman in a suit holding a small sign that read *Cassandra Ashcroft*. The pair walked up to him and identified themselves. "Brilliant," he said. "I'm here to escort you to your hotel."

"Oh? Where are we going?" Cassie asked, always double-checking facts. As he answered and helped them toward the car, she texted Evie. *"Are we going to a hotel?"*

"Yes, the driver should be taking you to a luxury hotel in Central London. You'll love it! You need a few days to get used to London before your cottage is ready. Talk later!"

"My instructions are to take you both to the hotel," the driver said. "Your company has chosen well. Is this your first time to London?"

"Hell, yeah," Laura exclaimed with glee as she saw the car.

The driver laughed at her excitement. "I don't know how much time you have but while you're here you'll have to do the rounds. We have some great sites to visit."

"What do you suggest?" Laura asked with a smile.

"The usual rounds, miss. Big Ben, Buckingham Palace, and the Tower of London. The London Zoo and museums are great too," he said. "I have a feeling you'd have fun on the London Eye."

He opened the door so both Cassie and Laura could get into the back of the car. Laura leaned toward Cassie and grabbed her arm. "I love his accent."

Cassie couldn't help laughing at Laura's exuberance. "I'm glad to hear that as most of the natives have one. Although, there are a lot of visitors to London for business and pleasure, so you'll meet plenty of people without a British accent."

"This is so exciting," Laura said as the driver got into the right front side of the car. She looked at Cassie and raised her eyebrows as the car pulled out into the left side of the road. "I'm glad I'm not driving anything here. I'd probably wind up killing us both."

"Then you'd better not drive anywhere in the UK or Ireland," Cassie said as she winked. The pair watched the landscape roll by as they headed toward the hotel. Cassie had heard of the places the driver mentioned, but she was not the type to visit landmarks by herself. The thought that she was alone hit her hard and she felt her throat tighten. She would be happy to arrive at an isolated cottage and hide behind her laptop. Hopefully, she would lose herself in her writing and if it meant she could return to the States faster, she'd not only hit her deadlines, she would get ahead of them faster than any writer ever had.

The driver guided the car onto the highway and noted the traffic was relatively light. "Sit back and relax. It'll take about 45 minutes to reach Central London."

5

C assie tried to relax and watch the sites fly by as they drove. Laura chatted excitedly the whole time. She had researched several landmarks before she boarded the plane and was hoping for time to be able to visit them all.

"We're just about there," the driver said as he called back to them from the front seat.

"This is great," Laura said. "I thought we'd have to take the Tube although I wouldn't have a clue how to do that."

The driver laughed. "You'd have to take the Piccadilly line from Heathrow Airport to Central London. The Tube would be cheaper than the Rail, but it takes longer."

Laura shook her head. "I should have known the publishing company would send a car for a best-selling author. I don't know what I was thinking." Laura looked at Cassie. "You have no idea how nervous I would have been to travel to England by myself."

Cassie grinned. "Don't you worry. Evie manages to take care of everyone. She'll be an awesome boss as you journey through your career."

"I'm still in shock."

As Cassie glanced out the window, she said, "It's all about being in the right place at the right time. Then add a little pixie dust and hope for the best."

"Ladies, I hate to interrupt but we're approaching the hotel if you want to start gathering your things."

The two women only had a carry bag in the back seat with them. Their main luggage was in the trunk. They excitedly collected their things and watched the street as they arrived at a fancy hotel. Within seconds, the back door was approached by a man in uniform.

"That would be the porter. He'll guide you to the door and our service desk and then come back for your luggage. You'll register inside, and I hope you two ladies enjoy your very first trip to London."

"Thank you," Cassie said as the back door opened. She hesitated and turned back to the driver. "I'm sorry. I haven't had a chance to convert any money to tip you."

"No tip necessary," he said with a nod. "The pleasure of driving a famous author is all mine and I hope we meet again."

Cassie blushed as she smiled and nodded. "Thank you. You're very kind."

Laura bristled with excitement as she followed Cassie out of the car.

The women were escorted to the lobby and looked for the reception desk. Before they decided which way to go, a man approached them.

"Hello, my name is Simon Wolcott. I work for the London office. I believe you are Miss Cassandra Ashcroft and Laura Milton?"

"Hello, nice to meet you, Simon," Cassie said as she held her hand out. "I'm Cassie Ashcroft."

"An honor to meet you," Simon said as he shook her hand before turning his head. "And you must be Laura."

"Yes."

"I've already made arrangements with the service desk. We'll have your room keys shortly."

"Thank you, Simon," Cassie said with a smile. "You've made everything so much easier for us."

"My pleasure."

"Did Evie leave plans for the next couple of days?"

Simon shook his head. "No, nothing definitive. She wanted everyone to relax and have fun." He turned to Cassie. "Heather House, that's where you'll be staying, is being readied for your arrival and your visa has already been arranged."

"I didn't know we needed a visa," Laura said.

Simon turned to Laura. "Miss Ashcroft is the only person that needs one since she will be in England for a while. You don't need one for a short stay."

Cassie watched Laura's face fall.

"But we'll have a month to tour and explore and Evie said it's possible I may be able to go back to America with you to orient to New York."

Cassie smiled as she noticed the immediate chemistry between Simon and Laura. They appeared to be the same age, both must love to read and had endless energy.

"Excuse me." The group turned to see a young woman in a hotel branded business suit approach them. "Sorry to interrupt but I have your rooms ready." She turned to Cassie and said, "So nice to meet you Ms. Ashcroft. I've read all your books."

"Oh, thank you. I hope you liked them."

"Very much so and my mother adores you, too."

Cassie laughed. "I'm so happy to hear that. You'll have to send my regards."

The young woman beamed as she said, "You'll be in room 1804, one of our nicest guest suites on the VIP floor." She then turned to Laura. "We have a beautiful hotel room for you on the second floor – room 226. Your bags have been brought up by the staff so whenever you're ready."

"Thank you," Simon said. "I'll escort them upstairs."

The young woman nodded and went back to her office.

Simon looked at his two guests, "Shall we go?" He turned and looping his arms into those of the two women, they headed for the elevators.

6

When the elevator opened, Simon escorted the two women to a room down the hall. He pulled out the key card to Room 226 and opened the door. Stepping inside, he turned on the lights, opened the drapes and turned back to the women. "Laura, this is your room and here is your key card. You will use the same key card for the elevator. Your bags appear to be here but check through and make sure everything arrived."

"Thank you, Simon. This is so exciting."

Simon smiled. "I'm going to escort Ms. Ashcroft to her room and then I'll come back to check on you."

"I'll look forward to that." Laura walked them to the door.

"Make sure you lock the door and security latch. You can't be too secure in this crazy world."

"Will do," Laura said as she smiled and waved goodbye.

Simon and Cassie went back to the elevator. He pulled out another key card, but this one was gold. He swiped the card and hit floor 18. The elevator buttons for floors 16 – 20 were separated from the other floors and clearly not accessible unless you have a special access pass.

"Your room is one of the VIP suites. Evie didn't want you in a regular room."

Cassie smiled. "That's very sweet, but hardly necessary."

"She thought it would be a treat since you'll be here for a few days. I imagine she'll call and explain everything to you soon. I'll let her know you've arrived."

"You're very kind," Cassandra said with a nod.

Arriving at the upper floor, the pair walked down the hall to Room 1804. Simon used the gold key card to open the door and preceded Cassie into the room. Her bags were waiting in the living room area.

"This is lovely," Cassie said as she looked around. She walked to the large windows and pulled the drapes. "Quite an impressive view of London. I can see the Thames."

Simon stood next to her. "The building in the distance is St. Paul's Cathedral. If you turn to your right, you can see Buckingham palace."

Cassie did as she was told and said, "It's breathtaking."

"We could have a small geography lesson from this window, but I should let you get on with unpacking."

Cassie turned to face Simon. "Thank you for taking care of us."

Simon smiled and handed Cassie her key card. He made a slight bow. "My pleasure. I'll leave you to have some private time and go back to check on Laura. If you both feel up to it, the hotel has an excellent high tea starting at 4:30 p.m. and dinner later in the evening."

"Sounds lovely," Cassie said with a wide smile as she walked him to the door.

"We'll be in touch," Simon said with a slight nod as he waited for Cassie to close and lock her door.

7

Cassie flipped the latch then turned and leaned against the door. She blew out a small puff of air, looked around the living room and felt her heart racing. "What am I doing here?" Shaking her head, she walked into the living area of the VIP suite. She dropped onto the lush couch and remembered what her anxiety coach taught her. She tapped her forehead and neck several times and started making small circles on her chest with her closed fist while she took deep breaths. In through her nose for a count of four, out through pursed lips for a count of five. She kept her eyes closed as she let the adrenaline fade away. One day at a time, one hour at a time.

After ten minutes, she opened her eyes and looked around the suite. She took her time to acknowledge the furniture, the door to the rooms leading off the living area and the windows which held a gorgeous view. She knew that acknowledging concrete things around her would help her focus. She knew that pausing on the concrete things around her would ground her to the current situation and stop her mind from running away.

Cassie felt better after fifteen minutes. Standing up, she took a little tour of the hotel suite and had to appreciate the grandeur of the room. The bedroom was decorated in soft, quiet colors with duvet to match and could be kept dark when needed. The living room held a beautiful arrangement of chairs and sofas to accommodate company and business meetings, but what Cassie loved most was the desk.

A cherrywood desk was set up in the living area, near the windows, overlooking London and the Thames River. Cassie had always centered on the desk or writing table as the first piece of furniture to appreciate in any situation. As she stared at the view, she heard the suite telephone begin to ring.

"Hello?"

"Darling, you've arrived!"

"Evie, it's so good to hear your voice."

"And yours," Evie said with a laugh. "Don't sound so anxious."

Cassie paused for a moment. "You know me too well. I'm in a different country, with no idea what to do next. Of course, I'm anxious."

"I know. That's why I tried to put you up in a fabulous suite until your next stop."

Cassie looked around the room. "It is a lovely suite. But, what's the plan? Where am I going next and when? I've cooperated on all levels and it's time for some extra direction from you. I've put a lot of blind faith in you. That proves how much I trust you."

"And I appreciate that. That's why I champion you on all levels from the publishing houses to media and strange fans."

There was a small pause before Evie drew a deep breath. "Okay, sit for a moment and grab a pen and paper. I'm going to give you the details I'm aware of. I'm waiting for a few things to finalize but I'll keep you up to date on what I know."

"Excellent," Cassie said as she pulled out the desk chair and rummaged through the drawer for something to write with.

"Ready?"

"Absolutely. Go ahead."

"Here it is. I'm reading the memo I was just sent. You'll be going to Wexley which is west of London and south of Bristol. It's a lovely area."

"Is that the name of the town?" Cassie asked searching for any knowledge.

"Yes, it's a small village. It's in the county of Devon which is in Southwest England. Devon is where you'll find beaches, cliffs, moorland, and national parks. There are harbor towns and fishing villages. You can take day trips to see exciting places like Wales, Oxford, London, and Bristol.

"It sounds lovely," Cassie said.

"The south coast of Devon is also known as the English Riviera, so I think you'll love it there. I'll send you a map so you can spend plenty of time during the year exploring. The Bristol Channel is in the north and the English Channel is in the south. It's a beautiful area. As a matter of fact, I think I'm getting jealous."

Cassie couldn't help laughing. "Where am I staying?"

Evie paused for a moment. "The publishing company is in the middle of negotiations to rent a cottage at the end of the village."

Cassie sensed her hesitation. "Evie, out with it. What are you not telling me?"

Evie cleared her throat. "For complete transparency, the cottage and the land it's on, happen to be on the block but there's some legal complications so the estate is willing to lease the property for next to nothing for a year or however long it takes to unravel things."

"I don't think I like the sound of that." Cassie sighed as she imagined a rundown home.

"What I'm told is the house is quite lovely. The property is beautiful, and it should be a perfect place to write. The village is approximately two miles long, so you'll have an opportunity for a wonderful walk each day. You can visit the pub when you're done." Evie chuckled.

"Just me, sitting in a pub." Cassie rolled her eyes at the phone.

"The focus of your research for the publisher will be the local police, specifically Detective Chief Inspector, Alexander Knight."

"Let me write his name down." Cassie grabbed the pen and scrawled the name of the town as well as the DCI on the page. "Alexander Knight? "

"That's correct. He's known as Alex Knight. He is the DCI and apparently has a remarkable record and solve rate. The ghost writer will write the rest of the non-fiction book about police procedure in United Kingdom using Alex Knight as an example. Your research will be a large part of the book."

Cassie stopped writing. "Evie, by chance is this DCI aware that someone will be researching his record and history, most likely including personal details?"

"I believe so. From what I understand, the project was discussed with Joe Duffy, the Chief Constable overseeing Wexley. He gave final approval and of course, the police department will receive part of the royalties. Win-win situation."

"But has anyone told the DCI, Alex Knight?"

"I have no idea," Evie admitted. "You'll have to go in and test the waters. Perhaps smooth them if need be."

Cassie let out an audible groan. "I think I hate this assignment, already."

"According to the publisher, Joe Duffy agreed for you to have someone from the police department orient you and explain their procedure in detail. In addition, you'll have specific research to discuss with the detectives, especially the DCI. In your free time, you'll immerse yourself in the locale and culture to add realism to your fiction novel."

Cassie's heart rate quickened. "This can only end badly. It's one thing to stay in a cottage somewhere, keep to yourself and write. As a matter of fact, I love living in a fantasy world. Everyone is kind and I completely control those who are not. But the research horrible."

Evie's laugh was genuine as Cassie continued.

"What I don't do well is interact with others. You know that. If everything involves interviews and interpersonal meetings, there's going to be a problem. I don't want to go to the pub. I don't want to spend time with the DCI. He'll probably be difficult, especially if he's not on board with this project."

"Speaking of difficulty, you're going to have to set the tone for gathering information. Keep it impersonal. Have whatever representative they choose just give you the facts. No judgements or opinions. You're there to collect facts and then it will be up to the ghost writer, the publisher, and their contract to do the rest."

"Will my name be on this project? Because if it doesn't go well, it could tank my whole writing career."

"Believe me. I will not let that happen. If there's even a hint of dissatisfaction with this project, I'll scratch their eyes out before ink hits paper. I will protect you one way or the other and you can take that to the bank." Evie went through her desk as they spoke, and Cassie could hear the click of a lighter after Evie found a cigarette. Cassie envisioned Evie as she took her first drag and blew smoke out the side of her mouth. "By the way, how did it go when you told Ethan you were leaving?"

Cassie sighed. "He acted the part. He told me how wounded he felt, and the breakup came out of left field."

"What did you say?"

"I told him I would be in England for up to a year and I didn't want to hold him back since I wouldn't be able to go to public events with him. He agreed that made sense, but honestly, I think he wanted to save face, so I let him."

Evie laughed long and hard. "It's not you, it's me."

Cassie let out a small chuckle. "We shouldn't be laughing. But you know as well as I do there was no real relationship."

"Believe me, honey, most people know your purpose was only for display and to tie their law firm to the publisher. Bigger paycheck."

Cassie was quiet as she thought about how it felt to be used, but the sad reality was that she didn't have anyone else in her life. She lived, loved, and socialized through her writing.

"Hello? Are you there?"

Cassie's voice was thick. "Yes, I'm here. I was just thinking."

"Well stop that right now. I'm going to go, but I'll call as soon as I hear more about Heather House."

"What?"

"That's the name of your cottage. Heather House."

"Sounds pretty."

"If my information is correct, you'll be happy there. Now, I'm sending Simon back to you tonight. Make sure you have tea, or dinner or both. You've only been here for hours, and I can see he has his eyes on my new intern, Laura."

"She's so excited to be here and she seems like a lovely girl," Cassie said with a smile.

"Well, that's all fine and good, but you'll be going to Wexley, and she'll be here in London, learning the ropes, unless you need her to stay in the cottage with you for a week. If not, she'll be here with Simon." Evie sounded exasperated.

"Evie, let her stay here. I'm a big girl. Have a lovely evening and thank you for everything."

"But of course. Make sure you eat, enjoy your suite, and get some rest. Promise?"

"I promise. I'll talk to you soon." Cassie hung up and took a deep breath.

8

Three days later, Cassie and Laura were back in the car with Simon. After a few days of lavish meals and sightseeing, which Cassie skipped most of the time, they were on their way to Wexley. Simon and Laura were to accompany her to Heather House and make sure the cottage was clean, comfortable, and welcoming before they both returned to London.

Simon collected their travel bags and luggage and placed them in the car. Planning on staying in England for a year, Cassie and Evie had shopped and collected the most important things she would need. Evie had arranged for all to be shipped and held in storage until it was time to be delivered to the cottage, which had happened over the weekend.

Laura sat in the front with Simon while Cassie sat in the back seat and stared out the window. Laura had attempted to get into the back-seat, but it was obvious that Laura and Simon couldn't take their eyes off each other, and Cassie certainly didn't want to have to worry about being in the way. She preferred a quiet space to think during the ride.

The landscape was lovely, and Cassie watched as fields and meadows flew by. She had researched the low evergreen shrub called heather, while she was in London, and found that it was widespread in parts of Europe and Asia. The ripe seeds were the main food for many birds. The shrub grew up to three feet high and was the chief vegetation on many wastelands.

Cassie had stopped reading after that sentence. She wasn't sure what a wasteland would look like in Europe, but she got anxious about her agreement to live on the edge of a wasteland, in a rundown cottage, at the end of a village for a year. She could only imagine who would be visiting the property during the legal battle as well. The property was most likely unkempt as no one would have ultimate responsibility and she envisioned a parade of surveyors, buyers, and vandals. Cassie shivered as she imagined her future, but Evie had promised she could bail out in two months. She could easily lose herself with writing and researching during that time. She would disappear when she saw someone on the property and start reminding Evie of her promise as soon as possible. Evie laughed and told her she wasn't in prison.

"Heads up, we're about to arrive," Simon called out enthusiastically.

Cassie realized they had driven for several hours, and she missed most of the landscape, being lost in her thoughts. When Simon slowed down, she looked out her window and saw a beautiful hand-painted wooden sign hanging from a post with the name, Wexley.

Her stomach knotted as they entered the village. As they wound down the lane, which barely allowed two cars to pass side by side, Cassie watched as they passed several houses, a post office, community building, police station, pub, small store advertising specials and a beautiful, small church connected to a large village green. In the distance, Cassie could see other homes connected by roads and beautifully landscaped fields. Cows and sheep were in some of the fields while crops were visible in others.

Simon continued for another half mile, toward the other end of the village and pulled to a stop in front of a lovely home. "Here we are, Heather House," Simon said as he parked in a small drive, turned to her, and smiled.

Cassie looked at the home before her. There were two floors, and the exterior was stone. A low stone wall ran along the side of the road with a gate in front of a path to the front door. The lawn was neatly mowed and cultivated with gardens along the side, full of heather, roses, and other scented blossoms. Behind the house were large fields of heather. The air was fresh and fragrant.

Simon opened her door and helped her out of the car. "I hope you like it. Evie approved it from the photos and had strict instructions for decoration and comfort."

"It looks beautiful," Cassie stammered. "Not at all what I expected."

The trio walked up the path to the front door. Simon pulled a set of keys from his pocket and unlocked the front door. He pushed the door open but then stepped back to allow Cassie to enter first.

She stepped into the living room which was a pleasant neutral color with sunlight flowing in from large windows overlooking the fields. There was a lovely fireplace in the corner. As she continued, she walked through a large, bright kitchen with granite counters and into a dining room. Next to the living room sat a library which contained a wall of books as well as a desk which would be ideal for writing. Cassie longed to look at the titles of the books but was called by Simon to explore the upper part of the house. She noted three bedrooms with a large bath.

"This is the master bedroom. Evie had the room redone to how she thought you would like it but you're certainly free to redecorate or change anything you want. I can have people here to help move furniture if you'd like."

Cassie looked out the upper floor window across the field. "Is that water in the distance?"

Simon walked to the window. "Yes, I believe you have a small view of the English Channel, but it's still at a distance."

"What a beautiful view," Laura said as she peered out the companion window in the bedroom.

"It is, isn't it?" Cassie agreed as she looked across the field of heather.

"What do you think so far?" Simon raised his eyebrows to await her answer.

"It's so very charming. I was afraid," Cassie hesitated but then went on. "Oh, never mind what I expected. The cottage is lovely."

"Brilliant," Simon said with a large smile as he turned to Laura. "Let's go downstairs and get Cassie's bags."

As the pair flew down the stairs and out to the car, Cassie looked at the other two bedrooms and the bath. She then went downstairs. Turning about the rooms, she couldn't help but smile when she noted a pair of Wellingtons near the door. Returning to the kitchen, she opened a large modern refrigerator to find it stocked with all sorts of vegetables and heathy foods. There was a lovely brick arch which was retrofitted with new appliances. Pots were hung on pegs coming from the arch which managed a lovely quaint look. The cabinets held beautiful china that was decorated with a dainty pattern. The wooden floors were gleaming with scattered area rugs. Overstuffed couches and chairs sat in the living room and nearby study. The large empty desk was calling to her.

"Yes, Heather House will do quite nicely," Cassie said out loud as Simon and Laura returned with her luggage.

9

Cassie's luggage was brought upstairs and placed at the end of her bed. By the time Simon and Laura returned to the living room there was a loud knock on the door. Not expecting any visitors, Cassie looked up to see Simon answer the door and speak with someone there. Within minutes, he held the door open as two gentlemen carried in several trunks and large containers. They gave Simon something to sign and said their good-byes as they left the cottage.

"Here are more of your things," Simon said with a smile as he gestured toward the pile in the living room.

Cassie looked at the containers. "I packed extra clothes and a few things I might need but not all of this."

Simon laughed. "I'm sure Evie added an extra special touch for you."

"Let's open everything up," Laura said, hardly containing the excitement in her voice.

Laughing, Cassie shook her head and shrugged. "Why not?"

The trio spent the next four hours unpacking the containers. Cassie took extra time washing and storing items for the kitchen as well as taking stock of foods and spices to plan for meals she would cook. She could handle the research if she could hide in her cottage to cook and write.

Cassie was able to make a plate of sandwiches and fruit for the group as they sat around the dining room table. She found a coffee pot as well as grounds and fresh cream in the refrigerator. Cassie and Laura enjoyed the coffee while Simon preferred tea.

"Thank you so much for staying and helping me get settled," Cassie said as she smiled at the pair.

"You're most welcome." Simon took a sip of tea and laughed. "Evie would hunt me down if I didn't. Our job is to make sure you are completely comfortable before we leave this village."

"Well, I do appreciate all your hard work."

"I think it's so cool to be able to move to another country for a year to write," Laura said excitedly.

"You're young. Things become a bit more difficult as you become more settled."

"It's not like you're stuck here. You can go back and forth to America, right?"

"Very true," Cassie said as she thought about how much anxiety she would have with frequent air travel between countries.

"Is there anything else you'd like us to do?" Simon gestured around the home.

Cassie shook her head. "I don't think so, but please stay until I have my laptop set up and I am confident I have online access."

"No problem. Everything should be up and running and ready to go. Evie's orders."

"That would make things so much easier," Cassie nodded.

"Would you like to walk through the village and take a tour?"

Cassie laughed. "No need to do that. I want to keep a low profile if I can." Cassie watched Simon's face work through a series of expressions. "What are you thinking Simon?"

"Even though this is a small village, there are many people who've heard of Cassandra Ashcroft. Evie hired the local villagers to decorate, clean and stock the cottage and now your things have been delivered. News travels through these villages very quickly. Many celebrities come to the English countryside to have a place out of the limelight and this area is near the English Riviera. The one thing I will say is most people from the area will protect your privacy." Simon started to laugh. "The villagers are usually very sweet and helpful unless they're on the other side of being rude and deadly. "

Cassie raised her eyebrows. "That sounds like good research for my mystery novel."

"Are you sure you don't want to take a walk through the village with us? You could get all the initial staring out of the way. Maybe we could get a pint and throw some darts at the pub."

"No thank you. That's not on my to do list for today."

"Do you feel comfortable being here? Would you want Laura and I to stay the night with you?"

Although Cassie's immediate thought was yes, she remembered they had planned to visit a nightclub later in the evening. Cassie reached out and covered Laura's hand with her own. "I think you two have done enough babysitting for the week. I'm in my early thirties and I enjoy being alone. I'm hardheaded and can handle myself just fine. Evie is trying to pamper me because she knows she railroaded me into this position. I think it's time for you two to return to London and do something fun before Evie gets hold of you for the work week."

"Are you sure?" Laura asked. "It might be fun to go to the pub."

"You and Simon are free to do whatever you'd like. If you want to stay, you're welcome to sleep here. I want to set up my laptop and make sure the internet is working. I want to take a long bath and hang up my clothes. I'll get to the village soon enough. Keep in mind, you are welcome to visit as often as you'd like. I'm sure Evie will have you checking on me anyway."

The pair laughed as they knew that to be true. Simon smiled at Laura. "Why don't we head back to London once Cassie's writing area is settled. There's a good band playing in town. We can come back on the weekend."

"Sounds like a plan," Cassie said as Laura nodded.

10

They spent the next hour arranging Cassie's desk. She set up her laptop and Simon took time to make sure all was connected to the internet. Cassie entered her passwords and finally had access to her email, work in progress, financial records and more.

"Make sure you open one of your emails and try to respond," Simon encouraged. "I know what it feels like to be in a foreign country without my email. Then, go to one of your favorite shopping sites and make sure you can load items into your cart."

Laughing, Cassie reviewed her email which she hadn't read since they left London. There were several from Evie, all asking her to respond to confirm she was set up.

Cassie wrote back and happily advised she was up and running. She then went to the online site for her favorite bookstore and placed several books she wanted in her cart but didn't purchase.

"Don't forget, some of your shopping sites have dedicated UK websites. You could have things shipped from America, but it may cost much more and get hung up in customs. Try to use the UK websites if you can."

"I'll have to get used to that. I would guess it's not an issue for digital items," Cassie mused as she fussed over the computer.

"No, but the prices may be different so make sure you check."

"I promise I will. I'm up and running and I sent an email to Evie so you two had better be off. Once it gets dark, I won't be able to tell if I'm in England or America."

"I don't know about that, but we should leave if we're going to make it back to London tonight," Simon said as he looked at Laura.

Laura ran over and gave Cassie a big hug. "I hope you love it here. Thank you for letting me share your journey. I'm so inspired, I can't wait to go home and start writing."

Cassie hugged her and smiled. "Thank you for helping me get settled. The process was completely smooth. The best thing you can do if you want to start writing is keep a journal of your trip. You could fill three journals with everything we've already done."

"I will, I promise," Laura said as she teared up. "We'll come back this weekend and you have my cell phone if you want to talk. You can call me anytime."

"Thank you, I'll remember that. You never know, I may ask you to pick up a few things before you come out. I'll look forward to seeing you both."

Simon leaned in and hugged Cassie before he and Laura left the cottage. Cassie stood at the door and watched their car as they drove down the lane. She stood there a moment longer, looking at the beautiful view but hearing nothing but quiet. The lack of sound was quite peaceful but unnerving at the same time. Glancing at her watch, she stepped back inside and closed the front door. Leaning forward, she fiddled with the locks to make sure they were properly engaged. Thankfully, Simon had checked the rest of the doors and windows to make sure all was locked before he left.

Not knowing what to do next, Cassie sat at her desk. Taking a deep breath, she closed her eyes and cleared her mind. Her brain was screaming, she was all alone in another country with no idea of her whereabouts in the village. Now that it was dark, she wished she had taken a short walk with Simon and Laura, but the truth was she wasn't ready to meet or greet strangers.

To distract herself, she connected to the internet and decided to do some research and touch base with her favorite websites. Startled, she jumped a short time later when her phone rang.

"Hello?"

"Well, what do you think?" Evie paused as she waited for Cassie to respond.

"Evie?"

"Of course, dear. I promised not to leave you hanging. Were you expecting someone else?"

"No, of course not. You know I don't talk to many people."

"Yes, and one day I will break you out of that shell. Don't get me wrong, I know you love your characters, but you need to socialize with real people too. As a matter of fact, you can come up with more ideas that way."

"Evie," Cassie warned. "You know it's not easy for me with the anxiety."

"How do you like the cottage?"

"It's lovely. You outdid yourself and I am so grateful. I don't know what I expected, but the cottage is light and lovely. Thank you for all the extra deliveries."

"You're welcome. Truthfully, I had a wee bit of guilt that I uprooted you and sent you to another country. I imagine that would be nerve-wracking, but it will benefit your career and the publisher will be ever grateful they didn't lose all the money they've invested in this book about the Wexley Police Department. Who knew the ghost writer would up and have a heart attack?"

"I feel bad for him," Cassie replied.

"We all do," Evie said. "He was one of those writers who didn't leave his desk to exercise much. Speaking of which, have you seen the village yet?"

"No," Cassie admitted. "Simon wanted to walk with me, but I wasn't ready to meet villagers yet. I need a week to settle in."

"About that," Evie started.

Cassie frowned as she looked at the phone. "I hate when you start a sentence that way."

"I know but please hear me out." Evie moved papers around her desk before she started speaking again. "You have tomorrow to relax, settle in and explore the village if you're ready. Day after tomorrow, you'll be going to an event to meet the department members of the Wexley Constabulary or police department if you will."

Cassie's face turned red, and she felt her stomach clutch. "Do I have to address the group?"

"No, nothing like that. This event had been planned long ago as the annual party at the Chief Constable's estate. His name is Joe Duffy." Evie continued to read through the notes sent to her by the London office. "He sounds like a decent guy. Everyone associated with the police force is invited to attend which means almost all members of the CID will be there."

"CID meaning Criminal Investigation Department?" Cassie asked.

"Yes, that's correct. That's the branch that most plainclothes detectives belong to in the United Kingdom."

"Got it," Cassie scribbled on the yellow legal pad. "And I assume the DCI will be there for the CID?"

Evie laughed when she heard the question. "Yes, the Detective Chief Inspector should be at the party for the Criminal Investigation Department."

Cassie shook her head as she took notes. "I did a little research about this. I read that the CID deals with more serious crimes. They run the investigations and then sometimes assist uniformed officers with less serious crimes."

"I believe so. I think they have similar rank structure and there are a bunch of branches, but I'll leave that to your research. That's why the publisher sent you there."

"Okay, I'm on it," Cassie said as she put down her pen.

"The gathering is an experiment in immersion for you. Go to the party and take it all in. You'll slowly be able to organize it as time goes on."

"How does this work? Do I need to report to someone or send my notes to you?"

"We'll see. I want to make sure you have an assistant of sorts, even if only virtual. Also, I'll give you the name of a contact in the police department that can help answer questions. You'll speak to them for general information and then the officers or investigators for more specific information. Once the publishing company has the facts, they'll have their ghost writer concentrate on the actual book while you use the immersion into the area to concentrate on your fiction novel."

Cassie sighed. "I feel overworked already and I haven't started yet."

"That's because you're not organized yet. You know you're a maniac once you set a plot in your head, so I'm not worried a bit."

"That makes one of us," Cassie said with a frown.

"You're something. You've only just arrived and you're understandably anxious. Take a week, get your bearings, and start to plot. You already have an outline of a story in your head. I know you. Your presence there will add flavor and depth to your fiction novel."

Cassie shook her head, held out the phone and frowned.

"Cassie, are you there?"

"Yes, I'm here, Evie." Cassie put the receiver back to her ear.

"Good, I arranged for a car to drive you to the event. Someone will pick you up at 6:00 p.m. and make sure you get back home. You need to dress business chic. Apparently, the guests will either be in their uniforms or formal."

"I haven't unpacked everything yet," Cassie said as she looked about the room.

"You have all day tomorrow to work on that. Okay, I must dash. Please try to sleep tonight. I know how nervous you get in the middle of the night."

Cassie chuckled. "We'll see, it depends on how many things go bump in the night."

Cassie never realized how real her concern would be.

11

Hours later, Cassie found herself upstairs after checking the locks several times. To be sure, she placed a chair in front of the doors. The house was very quiet, and she was trying to orient herself with the location of working lamps and lighting. Thankfully, she needn't worry about heat as they were approaching the end of the spring.

She found her nightclothes, chose something soft and comfortable and changed. She realized wearing pajamas made her feel more vulnerable and she would continue to feel that way until she was used to the house and the village. Cassie realized it would take time to orient herself. A new village, a new country, a new chapter in her life.

Running out of steam, she pulled back the covers and got into bed. She and Laura had made sure the sheets and blankets were clean. They hadn't had time to put away all the clothes, but Cassie was determined to start that chore immediately tomorrow morning.

She turned on a lamp that sat on a beautiful Victorian side table and slipped under the covers. Knowing she was nervous, she was grateful she could distract herself with her phone. She watched several reels from her favorite social media sites and then read a novel she had downloaded earlier in the day.

She rested her head against the pillow but didn't want to turn the light off. She couldn't fight the exhaustion she felt after a long day of travelling from London and moving in. It was hard to believe that earlier that morning she was in a hotel in London. She had only been there for a couple of days but already felt nostalgic.

Cassie had been asleep for several hours when a loud crash woke her. She jumped up in bed and looked around. She turned and checked the time on her cell phone. Something had crashed and broke downstairs and now she was paralyzed. Cassie waited a few minutes and listened but didn't hear any further noises. Looking at her phone she tried to recall what Simon had told her about calling 911 in the UK. He had said it would automatically transfer to the UK number, which was 999 or 112 but it would be better to call direct. She took a deep breath and held her phone. There was no other noise.

Getting out of bed, she crept to the doorway and listened. After five minutes, she didn't hear anything. Cassie was thankful she left the light on in the hallway as well as her room. She was also grateful for the sharp fireplace poker that was placed near the fireplace hearth in her bedroom.

Slowly, she stepped to the top of the stairs. The squeak clearly announced her location but after several minutes she realized she was still alive. No one had raced up to kill her. Taking a deep breath, she walked down the stairs and turned on the lights.

A broken plate sat on the floor. The remainder of the plates were stacked near the end of the counter. She looked through the rest of the rooms and noted the chairs had not been moved. The doors and windows were locked. Cassie couldn't imagine how a plate would tumble off the counter in the middle of the night, but she couldn't find any other way to explain the crash. She grabbed a broom and a dustpan and swept up the mess before she returned to her bedroom. She was used to sleeping in a Manhattan apartment alone for years, so she was used to strange noises.

Tucked back in bed, she read for a while and after closing her eyes at dawn, she slept for several hours.

12

C assie looked at her watch to check the time. Waiting for her ride, she turned to the mirror and smoothed the front of her Persian Blue dress. She'd been told many times she was attractive with her chestnut hair and bright blue eyes. Her facial structure was exquisite according to the last make-up artist from a national interview. She had lost a little weight since then and had to admit the dress looked good on her with matching heels. She took extra time with her hair and makeup and was happy with the result despite dreading the thought of attending a party.

After getting out of bed the day before, she spent time putting her clothes away. It took her 30 minutes to decide what to wear for the event, but she liked the dress. When she felt anxious, she would escape to her computer or phone to distract her from her thoughts. She spent time organizing her kitchen and examined the pots. They were beautiful except for one that stuck out too far due to a misaligned brick. After lunch, she took in the back garden and spent the day getting used to the cottage. She didn't notice anything else out of order and had no problems sleeping the second night.

She heard a car pull up to the front of the cottage and Cassie opened the door. A kindly gentleman got out of the right side of the car and waved. He took his hat off his head and held it in his hands. "I'm looking for Miss Cassie Ashcroft. Would that be you?"

Cassie nodded. "Yes, that's me." Cassie had a little trouble understanding him as his accent was thick.

"I'm here to drive you to the Chief Constable's house. Would you be ready to go, ma'am?" He smiled and blushed as he looked at her.

"Of course, right on time," Cassie said as she grabbed her purse. She closed her door and locked it and then walked to the passenger side of the car. She still wasn't used to the opposite seating.

"My name is James. I live here in the village, and I'll be happy to help you get around or answer any questions you have while you're settling in."

"Thank you, James. I appreciate it. It's going to take time to get use to England and the village."

"Have you seen any of it, yet?"

"I took a small walk yesterday but mostly into the gardens and field behind the cottage."

"It's a lovely cottage," said James. "I'm glad someone is living here again, even if for a while. Mr. Blake spent the last five years getting it all redone." James pointed to the right as they slowly drove down the narrow lane. "See the woman in front of the church? That's Mrs. Witherspoon. She's the vicar's wife. Very nice lady, she is. I'm sure she'll be around to welcome you soon."

"Oh, yes, I see her. Thank you, James."

"And that woman over there is Mrs. Peabody."

Cassie nodded as she watched the woman look at her as they rode by.

"Just so you know, Mrs. Peabody spreads our gossip and town news faster than the guests at the pub." James started laughing. "You'll be careful to watch what you say to the likes of her."

"Oh?" Cassie didn't know how to respond. "How far away is the Chief Constable's house?"

"It's several miles via the lane, less if you cut through the fields, but we need to travel slowly as there may be some people walking in the lane. Especially if they plan to drink. The Chief Constable throws a spring party each year for the police force, but townspeople are welcome too. It's only a few hours with a bit of food and drink but around here it's something to look forward to."

"Sounds lovely," Cassie said with a smile.

"Here we are now," James said as he rounded a corner and entered the large driveway. Cassie was surprised at the size of the large, brick mansion. "It's a nice estate. I'll drop you off at the front door."

"Thank you, James." Cassie said as she watched a handful of officers walking up to the door.

"You're most welcome. You look beautiful in those fancy shoes. I'm not being rude, but you may want to get yourself a good pair of Wellingtons if you plan to walk around these parts a lot. A good pair of walking shoes, too."

Cassie smiled as she opened her purse. "I'll remember that advice." She started to pull out the money she had asked Simon to change for her in London. "I'm not sure what to pay you."

"Oh no, ma'am. I've already been paid. You put your money away. Once the villagers get to know you, you'll find we do for each other without money. That's our way."

"Are you sure?"

"Absolutely. It was nice meeting you and I look forward to helping you again."

Cassie didn't have a chance to respond before James parked the car and jumped out to open her door. He helped her out and walked her to the bottom of the stairs. "I'll be back for you in a couple of hours. If you have any trouble, you can call my number. I'll be home helping my wife make our dinner. Her arthritis is getting on, so I do the heavy pot and pans."

James handed her a piece of paper with numbers written on it. Thankfully, Simon had shown her how to dial the US exit code and use the UK country code since she would continue using her cell phone for now.

Cassie smiled. "I appreciate all your help, James. By the way, please stop calling me ma'am. My name is Cassie."

"No problem, ma'am. I mean Cassie. You'd better go in now so you can get to know everyone. Remember, the Chief Constable is Joe Duffy. He's a right nice man."

James got back into the car and waited for her to start up the stairs. As she went through the front door, sandwiched between several officers, he started the car and pulled away.

13

Cassie pulled to the side as she entered the foyer. She spied a marble floor, antique wooden foyer table, ornate paintings, and decorations on the wall as well as uniformed staff walking throughout the rooms with serving trays laden with drinks and food. Inside what would be the living room she saw guests with plates and drinks in their hands. The guests wore uniforms, suits and ties, while others were dressed in plain clothes.

Some of the guests nodded in her direction as they entered the front door and turned toward the main party. Cassie stood frozen and smiled at them. She watched as they mingled, laughed, and ate but Cassie didn't move. She felt awkward not having a companion, so she stood and watched. After a little while, she felt a bit dizzy and nervous. Pursing her lips, she blew out a few breaths.

"Excuse me. Are you feeling well?"

Cassie turned her head to her right and noticed a tall, handsome man in his 40's, dressed in a beautiful silk suit, smiling at her. "Excuse me?"

"Are you feeling all right? Do you need help, Mrs. ...?

"Miss. It's Miss." Cassie fumbled her words. "Excuse me. I was feeling dizzy for a moment."

"Have you eaten? It is a bit hot in here."

"No, I haven't eaten anything, but it looked busy inside to be honest."

The man turned and signaled a server who approached with an empty tray. "Would you be so kind to bring some tea and sandwiches?

"Of course, sir," the server said with a slight nod. She turned and left for the kitchen.

"Here, come to this side table," the man said as he guided her by the arm. "I wouldn't want you to fall on my watch."

Cassie did as she was told. He helped her into a comfortable Victorian chair and then turned to answer a question from a woman in uniform. Cassie took the moment to appreciate her rescuer. Tall, broad shouldered, handsome, polite, authoritative, and confident. He wore a beautiful suit with a crisp white shirt and elegant tie. Light brown hair, easy smile, and piercing blue eyes.

"Now, where were we?" He said as he turned back to Cassie.

Cassie's focus snapped back to attention as the sandwiches and tea arrived.

"Aw, here we are." The gentleman waited until the server had placed the tray on the table and distributed small plates with sandwiches as well as a pot of tea. "How do you like your tea?"

"Milk and a little sugar, please?"

"Here you go," he said as he placed the tea in front of her. "Miss...?" He raised his eyebrow expecting an answer.

"Cassandra, Cassandra Ashcroft but my friends call me Cassie."

"That's a lovely name," he said as he leaned toward her and extended his hand. "My name is Alex. Alexander Knight."

Cassie smiled but was dying on the inside as she realized what Alex Knight's first impression of her would be. "Of course, you are."

He cocked his head, "Excuse me?"

Cassie cleared her throat. "Thank you for the sandwiches and tea. I'm feeling better now. I arrived but didn't quite get the chance to mingle before I started feeling dizzy." Cassie realized her dizziness was more to do with social anxiety disorder but didn't want to admit that to this attractive man.

"I've heard that name," Alex said with a smile. "Are you the writer from America?"

Cassie nodded her acknowledgment. "Yes, that's correct. I've just arrived in England two days ago so I'm trying to settle in."

A group of townspeople walked by, laughing and slightly inebriated as they bumped into her chair.

Alex extended his hand to steady her. "How about we take a little walk through the garden? I'm sure it will be quieter than here."

As Cassie stood up, he extended his elbow. Cassie took a second before she put her arm through his. He guided her toward the back door and into the formal gardens of the estate. She enjoyed his British accent as they started their walk.

"I've heard your name mentioned at the station but I'm afraid I don't remember the details," Alex said as he smiled at her.

Cassie relaxed as she smiled in return. "It's a bit of a long story, so first I want to thank you for helping me. I was feeling overwhelmed. Sometimes, it takes me a while to ease into a situation especially when I don't know anyone or anything about where I am."

"Yes, that's very understandable," he said. "You're very welcome."

Cassie noticed he had small crinkles around his eyes when he smiled which only made him look more attractive.

"Let's start over. My name is Cassie Ashcroft. I'm a writer from America with two projects to complete while in England."

"Go on," he encouraged her as they continued to walk.

Cassie took a deep breath as she admired the beautiful array of flowers and cultured lawn surrounding the estate.

"I have several books already published and I'm currently writing another set in England. My agent thought I would be able to describe the region more accurately if I visited."

"That makes complete sense." Alex nodded.

"I'm also here doing research for the publisher for a non-fiction book contracted with your department."

Alex pursed his lips before he spoke. "I've heard them talk about that project, but I thought a gentleman was going to write it."

"Yes, however the gentleman recently died of a heart attack so the publisher thought it would kill two birds with one stone and sent me. Oh, I shouldn't have said it like that."

"I see," Alex said with a hint of a smile. "The Chief Constable knows about all of this?"

"From what I understand, he's the one who contracted the book. The book will be about the Wexley Police Department. It will showcase the constabulary as an example and I believe part of it centers around you, Mr. Knight. You are the DCI, Alexander Knight?"

Alex looked at her, his face unreadable for a moment. "Yes, yes I am," he said quietly.

Cassie's stomach flipped. She knew a man with his reputation would not want his work showcased or presented to the world. She sincerely hoped he didn't believe she fabricated her anxiety just to meet him. He had approached her, not the other way around.

"I believe the Chief Constable mentioned something about that, but we'll have to gather more information. If I remember correctly, there's to be a meeting on Monday at the station for all officers."

"Oh?" Cassie said, surprise showing in her face.

"Yes, very well then. How are you feeling? Are you ready to go inside?"

Face flaming, Cassie wanted to admit she was ready to crawl under a rock. "Yes, I feel better now, and sincerely thank you once again."

"Of course," Alex said as he guided her to the rear of the estate.

As they approached the French doors, the Chief Constable, Joe Duffy, was standing there. "Alex, you've already met our writer although I haven't met her myself."

"Yes, this is Cassandra Ashcroft," Alex said by way of introduction. "She will be doing research for two projects."

Joe Duffy leaned forward and shook her hand. "That's wonderful. I hear you're staying at Heather House in the village."

"Yes, that's right. The publisher decided to rent the cottage while I'm here. I'm only settling in, but it seems lovely."

"I'm glad you're staying there. It is a fantastic estate; however, the owner died intestate. We're not sure if there are biological children, stepchildren, or any descendants at all. It's good that the property is not in a state of abandon until the issue is settled."

"What happens if no one is found," Cassie asked, unfamiliar with the laws of intestacy in the UK.

"Eventually, it would go to the Crown. In the UK, if an heir criminally caused the death of the decedent, they are barred from inheriting as well."

Cassie's eyebrows raised. "Was the owner murdered?"

Alex shook his head. "Quite the opposite. The owner was a bit full of himself. Always offering an opinion on things. He was at the pub, having won game night and drinking the winner's pints when he had a heart attack in front of most of the village. There was no thought of poison or wrongdoing. They tried to save him but unfortunately, they were unsuccessful."

The Chief continued the story. "His property is a large estate on the edge of town. Beautifully laid out and nearest to the water. There are calls coming in from many people claiming to be a relative so it will take a while to sort out."

"I see," Cassie said. "I believe the publisher has currently negotiated for a full year depending on what happens."

"Brilliant," the Chief said as he rubbed his hands together. "You living there will keep all sorts of dodgy people away. In the meantime, we have a meeting on Monday for the constabulary. I'd love for you to be there if you can. It would give me an excellent opportunity to introduce you to everyone, discuss the project, and define your purpose. We want everything to be accurate and above board."

"Thank you," Cassie said hesitantly. "I'll make every effort to be there."

"Wonderful. I must attend to my guests now but in the meantime please help yourself to food and drink."

As they entered the foyer, Cassie saw James standing near the front door holding his hat in his hands. She smiled and waved to acknowledge him, hoping her relief of being rescued was not evident on her face. He waved back to show he saw her.

Cassie turned to Alex. "My ride is here. Thank you for helping me tonight. It would have been very awkward to faint at a party where no one knows your identity."

"My pleasure, entirely," Alex said as he took her hand and bowed his head ever so slightly toward her.

He was close enough for her to notice his exquisite cologne. As she walked toward James and her escape, she mentally kicked herself for having such an awkward first meet with the handsome man she was sent there to do research on.

She chided herself again when she was inside the car. At that point, she couldn't resist mentally telling herself, *Home James, and step on it.*

14

_____

"Evie, I made a fool of myself," Cassie said as she clutched the phone in her hand.

"I'm sure it's not as bad as you think."

"I doubt it. I almost had a nuclear panic attack and then I'm rescued by the one person I didn't want to alienate," Cassie rushed on. "By the way, do you know anything about a meeting at the station next Monday? The Chief Constable asked me to attend."

"No, I don't know anything about a meeting, but that's an excellent development. Once you're introduced to the department the schedule is up to you and them. The publisher will only want the research. You know they're not going to be involved in the day-to-day happenings."

"Fine, I'll go but I'm not hoping for much."

"All positive thoughts, Cassie. Now tell me about the man, the myth, and this hunk you're supposed to do research on."

Cassie laughed. "What?"

"Part of this book will deal specifically with Alexander Knight. He has an excellent solve rate and although he's technically an eligible bachelor, he's impenetrable by coquettish females."

Cassie's laugh increased. "What are you talking about? I'm here to research policing in England. I'm not providing fodder for a gossip magazine."

"Yes, but apparently they'll be using his reputation as the hook for sales."

Cassie was silent as she counted under her breath. "How long did you say I have to stay here?"

"Until the work is done. C'mon Cassie, give me your first impression."

Cassie scowled into the phone. "The man is very polite, he smells great, and he doesn't seem to have any problem invading someone else's personal space with an authoritative air. He is very handsome. Now that you mention it, I can see impressionable women swooning in his presence. If they're the sort looking for a husband or wanting to please."

"Interesting," Evie said as she listened.

"Let's be clear, Evie, I'm here to collect data and that is all. I just ended my relationship with Ethan."

"And you still owe me for that."

Cassie shook her head. "Evie, I need to go calm down."

"Of course, I understand. Simon and Laura will pop up this weekend to see you. Spend the next couple of days orienting yourself and learning about the village. Monday we're off to the races. Think about how you want to organize your questions and research and then ask the Chief Constable how that could be accomplished on their end. I can assure you the publisher wants the department to be portrayed in a positive light, so you'll receive whatever support you need to collect your data. Perhaps it will help with your fiction novel as well."

"Yes, I'll do that," Cassie replied as she took a deep breath.

"If there's any problem or concern, I'm only a phone call away. We have plenty of time to do this so let's calm down and have fun, okay?"

Cassie chuckled. "Of course, Evie. I'll talk to you soon."

"Bye, Darling. Stay well."

"You, too, Evie. I know you mean well."

15

Cassie spent the next couple of days trying to relax and get used to her new living arrangements. She continued to stock closets and explore the cottage. She took copious notes of items she needed including proper shoes.

Purposely spending extra time at her desk, she started files for her new fiction novel as well as her research for the publisher.

Next, she planned to explore the fields and woods immediately surrounding Heather House. Her goal was to make a comprehensive list of the things she needed so she could accept Simon and Laura's offer to take her shopping and orient her to the village when she saw them over the weekend.

Looking through her closet, Cassie couldn't find a sturdy pair of walking shoes or sneakers. She decided to try the Wellingtons that were left in the house. She had to add two extra pairs of socks to fill the boot as the previous owner had larger feet than hers.

It was a beautiful Friday afternoon, the sun was warm, and Cassie felt her spirits lift as she looked forward to visiting with Simon and Laura. Boldly she walked out the back door and through the garden. She admired the flowers. It was early in the season, and she decided she would weed the areas within twenty feet of the house. The garden was small in comparison to the one she walked through at the Chief Constable's estate, but it would be a refreshing area to visit after writing a good part of the day. Cassie envisioned a cold pitcher of iced tea on the garden table as she watched the sunset.

Coming to the end of the garden, she followed a path through the field. Cresting a small hill, she saw sheep to her left and woods to her right. Continuing to explore, she walked toward the wood to see if there were any obvious paths or hiking trails. As the summer approached, she'd love to see more of the countryside and cliffs. London was beautiful but she wanted to learn more about rural England.

Deep in thought, Cassie looked up and realized she was in the middle of the woods. She turned back but had trouble finding her way. The sun must have set as it was darker than she realized although daylight was dampened inside the woods. She pulled her phone out of her back pocket and was dismayed to find there was little to no reception.

Jamming the phone back into her pocket, she found a path and walked in the direction she believed would lead back to a road. She walked for twenty minutes before she admitted she was fully lost. She stopped to listen for sounds. The village was only two miles long and she was sure she was somewhere behind the structures of the village, but she didn't hear any music or people talking or cars along the road. Cassie knew it had to be near dinner time since the sun was setting. Perhaps, everyone was indoors with their meal.

Looking toward her right, she noticed the sky appeared lighter through the trees. She turned and followed that direction hoping she would reach the end of the woods. She would prefer walking on a road knowing it would lead somewhere although there were plenty of miles between villages in this area. Once she was home, the first thing she would buy was a current map of the village and woods.

She stumbled and fell several times as she tried to walk through the woods with the large Wellingtons on her feet. Nearing the edge of the trees, she finally emerged and saw a road. She hurried through the waist high scrub but didn't notice the gully lining the edge.

Cassie slipped and landed on her back, staring up at the night sky which wasn't as dark as it had appeared from the woods. Pulling her phone from her back pocket she realized it was only 8:45 p.m. despite feeling like midnight. Still no service.

Hungry and shaking, Cassie stood up. Her right foot was cold, and she realized she had lost one of the Wellingtons. She tried a small search in the scrub but couldn't see anything without a flashlight. She wiped her hands on her pants and finally managed to reach the road. Small stones cut into her foot, as she hobbled to the center of the road. Seeing lights to her right, she half limped, half stumbled in that direction. She had traveled a small way when a car approached from behind and caught her lumbering gait in the headlights.

Cassie was thrilled. She turned to appeal to the driver, not realizing her face was bloody, her hair was astray, and her clothes were full of dirt. The officer driving the compact police vehicle immediately turned on the strobe and stopped the car.

16

An hour later, Cassie sat in a chair at the police station. She was still a mess and had not been allowed to clean up. The constables asked for her identification, which she didn't have with her. Cassie left her purse at the cottage as she didn't expect to be out long.

She was limping, bleeding, dirty with no identification and trying to explain that she lived at Heather House.

"I'm sorry, miss, but no one has lived at Heather House since the owner died."

"That's not true," Cassie pleaded. "The publishing company took out a lease for a year. I've been living there for a week. Please check. Call the number I gave you."

The constables had tried calling Evie, but she didn't answer her phone. They tried calling the publishing company, but it was a Friday night so of course no one was available and there was not an answering service.

"Let's go to the cottage and get my identification." Cassie was upset, embarrassed and angry that she couldn't get through to the two constables that had brought her to the police station.

"We've called the Head Constable. We must wait for further

direction, but the cottage is locked up tight as far as we know. We can't leave the station until we have more information."

"Then send the constable on patrol to the cottage. You'll see, I'm living there."

"Are you supposed to be living there, miss? Do you have a rental agreement or anything to show?"

"Oh, for crying out loud," Cassie said as she crossed her arms. From the corner of her eye, she saw Alex enter the police station. It was now 10:00 p.m. and she had no idea why he was still working. He was dressed in another tailored suit, despite the hour, with a crisp white shirt and tie. She had already embarrassed herself with him and he looked like he was going to climb a staircase to the second floor. Without realizing what she was planning to do, she jumped up out of her seat and yelled across the room. "Alex, Alex Knight."

The entire room froze. The room was silent except for a ringing telephone and the constable saying, "That's the DCI."

In what seemed like slow motion, Alex turned his head toward the area where Cassie was standing. He witnessed a constable jump up and grab her arms to restrain her although they knew she had no weapon or possessions when she was brought into the station.

When it became obvious there was no physical threat of violence, most of the officers relaxed back down into their desk chairs. The station was busy for a Friday night. Alex saw Cassie struggle with the constable and immediately walked to the desk.

"What in the devil is going on here?" Alex demanded to know.

"We're sorry, sir. We found this woman hobbling on the road. We brought her to the station as she has no identification and she's making a few strange claims."

"Alex, please help me." Cassie pleaded, her hands now zip-tied behind her back but her face full of fear.

"Cassie, what's going on?" Alex asked as he looked her over. "Are you all right?"

"You know her, sir?"

"Yes, yes, I do. We met at Chief Constable's house. As a matter of fact, she is a guest of this police station, invited by the Chief

Constable himself. If she hasn't committed a crime, I'd suggest you release her immediately."

The constable nodded and did as he was told.

Alex drew Cassie into one of the wooden chairs and sat beside her. "Cassie, what's happened? I don't understand."

Cassie looked at Alex, tears flowing down her cheeks. She swallowed and then repeated her story that she had gone for a walk in the wood and got lost as the daylight faded away. She found her way out of the wood and fell into the gulley where she lost her borrowed Wellington. As she hobbled onto the road to find her way, the constables had pulled up behind her and the rest was history.

Alex felt sorry for her. He clenched his jaw tightly to suppress any expression.

"Oh dear, that sounds like a dreadful experience. This has been a bad start for you, hasn't it?"

The constable broke in. "She said that she's staying at Heather House, sir."

Alex turned to him and nodded. "That's correct. She moved in about a week ago. The Chief Constable had a talk with Cassie and I about it the other day."

"Oh, we didn't know anyone was staying there due to the legal trouble."

Alex showed his displeasure. "I'm sure you'll be hearing more about it very soon."

The constable reddened and said to Cassie. "I'm sorry, miss. I wasn't aware."

"Please escort Miss Ashcroft to the bathroom and let her clean up," Alex said to the constable.

"Ashcroft?" The constable asked with eyebrows raised. "We didn't believe her."

"As in Cassandra Ashcroft, the famous best-selling writer from New York. She's here to gather information on the Wexley Police Department for publication and this has not been a good start." Alex put his hand on Cassie's shoulder as he smiled kindly at her. "I have to go upstairs to get some paperwork, but I'll pack it right up and then be back to take you home."

Cassie voice was low as she was still choked up, but she mouthed, "Thank you," as she swallowed.

Alex looked at the constable and nodded to Cassie. "Please, let her clean up and I'd suggest you toss any paperwork you have in this matter. Also, you'd better make sure none of this makes it to the press or we'll have plenty to answer to."

"Yes, sir. Of course, sir." The constable nodded to Alex and then turned to escort Cassie to the bathroom while Alex ran upstairs.

17

Ten minutes later, Cassie emerged from the bathroom in better spirits. Her face was clean. Her hair was wet, and finger combed but without leaves or debris. She had removed the remaining Wellington and walked in her socks across the floor to the bottom of the staircase.

After waiting a few minutes, she was rewarded when Alex descended the stairway with his briefcase in hand. He smiled when he saw her. "You look more relaxed now."

Cassie looked down at the floor and then back at Alex. "Thank you for helping me. I'm not sure what would have happened if you didn't come along."

Alex reached the bottom of the staircase and smiled. "I'm sure they would have heard it from someone when the dust settled. Come, let's go to my car."

Together they walked through the first floor and out the front door to the parking lot.

"Thankfully it's warm or those socks would be a problem. I'd offer you my shoes, but I don't think they'd fit."

"I think I've had enough with borrowed shoes, thank you." Cassie shook her head as Alex opened the passenger door of a BMW for her. "Your work car?"

"Not at all," Alex said. "They want me to use one of the compact cars, but I need to be comfortable if I'm driving all day or going on a stake out."

"Is that why you're working so late on a Friday?"

Alex nodded while tilting his head in thought. "When you're a Chief Detective Inspector, you're always on call for investigations. You must be available when the evidence comes to light."

"That will be the first line of my research," Cassie said as she nodded. She tried to imagine Alex on a stake out. His tall, broad-shouldered frame sitting in a car watching his target. She imagined there would be other detectives. "Do you always wear a suit and cologne on a stake out?"

Alex laughed. "I do when the person I'm watching happens to be in a nice restaurant. You need to dress the part, you know."

"And the exquisite cologne?"

"Ah, that's Creed Green Irish Tweed Cologne, a favorite of mine and very helpful when you can't take a fresh shower every twelve hours."

"Thank you for that, I think," Cassie said with raised eyebrows.

"I understand you want all the facts," Alex teased. "The job is certainly not as fun as it looks."

Cassie watched him for a moment before she responded. "It doesn't sound fun at all, but the cologne is wonderful."

"Glad to please," Alex said almost sarcastically. "Ah, here we are now, Heather House."

They pulled up to the front door of the dark house. Cassie hadn't left any lights on as she never expected to be out past dark. Alex opened his door and went around to open her door and help her out of the BMW. "Do you mind if I come inside with you? I want to make sure you're settled, and all the doors are locked." Alex laughed. "I'm starting to feel very protective of you."

Cassie paused for a moment, before handing him her key. They approached the front door. Alex unlocked the door, went inside, and turned-on multiple lights.

"You seem to be familiar with the house," Cassie noted as she walked inside.

Alex handed her the key. "Yes, I've been called here multiple times, so I do have some familiarity with the house and it's foibles."

"Oh?"

"Don't worry, but I'd like to check a few things if I may while I'm here."

Cassie shrugged. "Help yourself."

"Have you had any problems since you've moved here?" Alex hesitated for a moment. "See or hear anything strange?"

Cassie shook her head and then hesitated. "Well, the first night I was here, I had made myself comfortable in bed when I heard a crash."

"Really? What happened?"

"I grabbed my fireplace poker and came downstairs. I didn't see anyone or anything strange except that one of the dishes I had placed on the counter was broken on the floor. I'm pretty sure it wasn't near the edge, but it was the first night at the house and I was very nervous."

"Has anything happened since?"

"I don't think so, but I'm trying very hard to get used to the cottage and my new situation. I don't think it's gone smoothly, yet."

Alex looked down at her squeaky-clean face and smiled. Without makeup, and her hair completely natural, she looked young and vulnerable. "Would you mind giving me your cell phone number, please?"

Cassie stammered before reciting the number. Alex placed the number in his phone, adding what he needed to call her directly. Within a minute, she heard her cell phone ringing. "Oh, my phone."

"Don't worry, it's me. You should have my number in your caller ID now. Mind you, very few people have that number, so I'll hold you to keep it private. But if anything strange happens, anything at all, please call or text me and I'll be here to help you or make sure someone is."

Cassie pulled her phone out to confirm the number. She looked up into his eyes. "Thank you, I appreciate it. I know you don't know me, but I'm not like this. Hopefully, I'll get everything together soon."

"I have no doubt that will happen," Alex said as he put his phone in his suit jacket. "On that note, I'll leave now. You've had an eventful day and must be exhausted."

Cassie walked him to the front door. "Thank you, once again for your help."

"You are very welcome. I'll stand outside until I make sure I hear that front door lock," he said with a pointed look.

Cassie nodded as she closed the door. She made sure she locked the door immediately and then watched Alex get into his car and leave. Taking a deep breath, she gathered herself to go upstairs and shower. It had been a strange day, but she felt better now that she had a local connection she could call on, despite appearing helpless. Hopefully, she wouldn't need to.

18

Cassie was toweling off after a long hot shower when she heard her cell ring. She ran from the bathroom and answered. "Hello?"

"Cassie, it's Evie. Are you all right?"

Cassie sighed and sat on the edge of the bed. "Yes, I'm okay but I embarrassed myself tonight."

"I was worried about you. I received several calls from the Wexley Police Department, which is fine considering our project, but I didn't expect it would be on a Friday night. When I called them, they said you'd already gone."

Cassie chuckled. "You're never going to believe it. I went for a walk through a field and the woods. I got lost for several hours. Then I tumbled into a gully and lost one of my shoes. I made it out to a village lane where two constables picked me up as a vagrant." Cassie waited in silence. When Evie didn't immediately respond, she continued. "I was then brought to the police station, without identification. I looked like a mess. They wouldn't believe anyone had been living in Heather House for the past week, so I was trying to establish my identity by asking them to call you."

"I am so sorry," Evie said. "I didn't hear my phone."

"I don't expect you to be at my beck and call twenty-four hours a day. Anyway, I wanted them to call the Chief Constable and they thought I was being a difficult American."

"So, what happened?"

"I turned and saw Alex Knight walking into the building and as desperate as I was, I shouted out to him."

"I'm sorry. Are you saying that you, Cassandra Ashcroft, made a scene?"

Cassie chuckled until tears formed in her eyes again. "Yes, I did. What I didn't expect was for the officers to restrain me when they saw a raging woman in the office."

"That's not funny."

"No, it was not."

"Alex Knight helped you?"

"True to his name, he rescued me and admonished the constables to erase all records so the media wouldn't get hold of this tidbit." Cassie paused for a breath. "Yes, he had them take me to the bathroom to clean up and then he personally drove me home and checked my house as if I was a pathetic damsel in distress."

"For once in my life, I think I'm speechless."

"Well, I'm mad. At myself, mostly. I'll admit I have some anxiety, as anyone moving to a new country by themselves would, but I certainly didn't want to come here giving the impression I'm an idiot."

"I'm sure they don't think that," Evie said as she tried to console her.

"I'm going to that meeting on Monday, and I intend to let them know I am a serious writer."

"Good, that's the determination I'm used to hearing from you. I'm sure you'll do well. In the meantime, Simon and Laura will be there by 9:00 a.m. tomorrow. Make sure you have them take you where you need to go for shopping or otherwise."

"I will and I'm looking forward to seeing them."

"I'll call you before the weekend is out to make sure you're completely prepared for Monday."

"Thank you, Evie. I would appreciate that support."

"Of course. Don't make me feel guilty that I talked you into this arrangement and make sure you stay safe. I'll be in London soon. We'll get together then."

"Great. I can't wait to see you."

19

Cassie took another look in the mirror to smooth her jacket. She was dressed in a dark blue Polo Ralph Lauren executive business suit with a beautiful ice blue silk shirt. Her hair was nicely coiffed, and she silently blessed Simon and Laura as she slipped on a pair of medium heels.

They had a fun weekend. Simon and Laura arrived early Saturday morning and brought breakfast with them. Cassie made coffee and they sat at the wooden kitchen table and shared stories from their first full week abroad.

Cassie retold the story that led to her visit to the police station but the chuckles and giggles from her young visitors made it seem more like an adventure.

Checking off items on Cassie's list, the trio spent the day shopping. Cassie was thrilled as she now owned multiple pairs of new shoes. She bought properly fitted Wellingtons, hiking shoes, sneakers, and several pairs of adorable heels although she didn't know where she would wear them but couldn't pass them by.

They went sightseeing near the Bristol Channel and then back to Wexley. This time, Cassie agreed to go for a walk through the village with Simon and Laura although she didn't want to enter any of the buildings. They walked past the church, quaint cottages, fields, a small store, the post office, and the town pub. There were villagers out and about and several stopped to stare as they went past. Cassie made it a point to wave to those that looked at her and they smiled and returned the gesture. The pub must have been brimming with gossip over their little group. Cassie refused to go in as she had had enough interaction with the village until Monday.

Giving her mirror a final glance, she was ready to go to the station. At 4:00 p.m. a car drove up to the front door. The path from the house to the drive was lined with beautiful rose bushes. Off to the side, heather filled the fields around the cottage. James popped out of the car and waved to Cassie. "I was sent to pick you up for a drive to the police station. Official business I'm told."

Cassie smiled at James, a friendly face amongst the villagers. "Yes, I've got a meeting at the police station. It's part of my research for the publisher." She settled herself in the car and put her belt on.

"I'm glad it's business. I heard about your visit there Friday night."

Cassie inwardly groaned. "I see news travels fast in the village. I got lost."

James chuckled and nodded. "Oh yes, you'll find everyone knows everything about everyone in the village at some point. Don't believe everything you hear as tongues tend to wag and make up stories, especially in the pub."

Within twenty minutes they were at Wexley Police Station. Cassie thanked James, who assured her she didn't owe him any money. She turned and walked through the front glass door and into the small lobby. The building was a three-story square brick structure. The rooms off to the sides could only be described by Cassie as separate squad rooms and possibly one for records. There was a front desk at which a visitor had to state her business before she could get into any of the rooms. An officer would come to the lobby and escort the visitor to the section needed. Cassie didn't recognize this area. Perhaps because she had been there on a dark Friday night, or she was distraught, or they may have used another door.

"Can I help you?" An unsmiling uniformed female constable sat at the desk.

"Yes, I'm here to meet the Chief Constable, Joe Duffy," Cassie said with a smile.

"Oh, you must be the American writer," the constable said with a nod.

"Yes, that's correct."

The woman pointed to a chair on the side of the door. "Please have a seat. I'll let him know you're here."

Cassie did as she was told and within minutes, Joe Duffy walked into the lobby. Cassie held out her hand which he clasped in both of his. "It's so good to see you again. Thank you for agreeing to this introductory meeting. I know it's late but it's the best way to catch two shifts. The night shift will have to follow along."

He led her past the desk and into a larger room. There were rows of folding chairs set up as well as a podium with a microphone and a large screen on the wall for display. Once again, Cassie imagined it was like the police roll call room at the start of shift in Manhattan.

When they reached the corner, Joe Duffy turned to her. "Before anyone else arrives, I wanted to discuss some things with you."

Cassie's stomach clutched for unknown reasons. "Yes?"

"First, I'd like to apologize for last Friday night. We do aim to keep the community safe so the constables were doing their job, but it should not have been that hard to confirm your identity. Your photo is all over the internet and on the back of your books."

"I understand completely," Cassie said. "And clearly, I should not have shouted across the station, but I wanted to get Alex Knight's attention and I wasn't sure they would call him over."

Joe nodded as he spoke. "That brings me to my second point. I know you're collecting research on the department. Homicide is blessed with Alex Knight. He has a fantastic solve rate. However, he's very direct, and can be tenacious in his work. I told him he must work with you, and he will be polite, but I don't want to put you off."

"I understand," Cassie said. "Quite frankly, he has been nothing but kind to me so far and has helped me through two awkward episodes. I can see you're concerned. Please let me assure you that I am not or never will be associated with gossip or sensationalism. From my understanding, this book is to be an educational piece, something to be proud of. If there is any negative information, I will surely discuss it with you first."

Joe Duffy smiled. "Thank you. I'm not asking to hide anything but we both know there's always different perceptions of situations."

"Of course," Cassie said, thinking about how Simon and Laura were so amused by her Friday night adventure compared to her own humiliation. "The publisher may not use half of what I give them anyway. I will deliver raw notes and what is chosen is at their discretion, but I'll make sure there is nothing that is misrepresented."

"Brilliant," Joe beamed.

"Hello again." Cassie and Joe Duffy both turned when they heard Alex Knight walk into the room. He had another man next to him.

"Hello," Cassie said as she waved.

"I'd like you to meet my Detective Sergeant, John Miles. We call him Miles for short."

"Pleased to meet you," Cassie said as she reached out and shook hands with Miles.

"Same," Miles said with a grin. He was a young man, in his late 20's, with a boyish face and dark hair.

"Well, I'd better go grab a chair," Miles said as he moved away from the group.

As they watched him walk away, Cassie turned to Alex, her face slightly red. "Thank you for helping me Friday night. I'm not always that obnoxious or delinquent."

"You are most welcome," Alex said as he leaned forward and whispered. "You look lovely today so I don't believe anyone will think of you as a vagrant."

Cassie's smile widened with the compliment. She had wanted to look fully in control today.

The room filled with officers and clerks who sat in the chairs and stood around the periphery of the room. Not everyone was wearing smiles. Some had their arms crossed in front of them and leaned back on the wall. Cassie had no idea what they expected but she was only a guest.

After a few minutes, the Chief Constable cleared his throat so all would quiet down. "Okay, settle down, settle down." He waited another minute, then gave a pointed look to someone who was still talking. When all was quiet, he began. "Thank you all for coming, although it was mandatory." Several people started snickering. "I want to go over a few changes that are being made as well as some policy updates. The usual shift will start after this meeting is complete."

Joe Duffy then went through his prepared statements and took questions from the audience. Once the questions quieted, he started to speak again. "Many of you have heard rumors and chitchat about a guest to Wexley. I would like to introduce Ms. Cassandra Ashcroft to all of you." He pointed to Cassie who waved to the crowd. There was some applause, a few whistles and spontaneous chatter. "Quiet please." He waved his hands in front of him. "As the mystery readers in our group know, especially my sister, Miss Ashcroft is a best-selling mystery writer from New York. She is here to do research for her publisher about the Wexley police force as well as research for her current fiction novel." Heads turned toward Cassie to watch her reaction.

Cassie waved and said, "Please call me Cassie."

Joe Duffy continued. "We have agreed to have an educational novel written about the United Kingdom police and specifically Wexley in exchange for part of the royalties. Some of you will be speaking to Miss Ashcroft about generalities in our department. We will not be giving out specific case studies or information and Miss Ashcroft will not be asking for such. You are not to talk about any fellow department members by name. Do I make myself clear? If asked to meet with Ms. Ashcroft about structure or such, I ask you to be accommodating and polite.

"We will have a separate chapter on the CID – Criminal Investiga-tion Department and the detectives will take turns working with Ms. Ashcroft on technique and skills. I expect the department will be equally accommodating and you will receive a schedule. Any questions?"

Several members of the crowd asked questions about publication and welcomed Cassie to the department. Once again, Joe raised his hands. "That's all we have time for now. I don't want to delay the next shift. If there are any burning questions, you can call my office."

The group then dispersed with several people coming to the front of the room. Cassie was introduced to all. She had a good memory but also took quick notes for her journal when she got home. Joe Duffy and Alex Knight escorted her to a smaller office and once again welcomed her to Wexley while offering to help in any way possible. They agreed to have someone from the CID contact her within a day or two to give her a list of names so she could hear different perspectives.

Cassie then thanked them and made her exit from the police station to find James leaning against the car. He smiled when he saw her and waved. She waved back and blew out a deep breath. Seated in the car, she was once again more than happy to silently say, *Home James and step on it.*

20

Once Cassie left the building, Alex Knight loosened the knot of his tie. Joe Duffy closed the door of his office and sat behind his scarred wooden desk. He immediately pulled two old glasses from the bottom drawer and poured two fingers of single malt whiskey in each. Handing one to Alex, he asked, "What do you think?"

"I'm sorry, sir. I still don't understand what this is all about. She looks like a lovely woman but why are we doing this?"

"Why else? We need the money." Joe took a large gulp of his drink. "As the world becomes a smaller place, we were offered a nice deal to allow someone to research the police structure and rankings in the UK. Obviously, we don't want to get too specific due to security concerns so it's general information only. Alex, you well know that police stations have been closing due to lack of funding. We can't allow Wexley or this region to be in that category, so we agreed. Of course, the agreement was presented to me by higher ups to begin with, so I had no choice."

"Will someone read what's to be published before the book is released?"

"I wasn't the one to sign the contract, so I don't know the final arrangement, but I want kit gloves with this assignment." Joe stopped talking and looked directly at Alex.

Alex took a sip of his whiskey and then stopped. "What?"

"I want you specifically, old chap."

Alex frowned to show his irritation. "Why me? I don't have time to babysit. I'm the Chief Detective Inspector and must oversee many things."

Joe laughed at his response. "I want you for many reasons. First, you've been a detective for a while and therefore more settled than our younger ambitious detectives."

"You make me sound like I'm ancient. I'm 42 years old."

"Yes, which is why you're experienced enough to handle this perfectly. You have patience, you're polite, even with criminals, and you have the most integrity of anyone on this police force, so I trust you to do what's right, not what's easy. Also, I expect you to keep on topic which could be difficult with a woman of her looks. She is very beautiful and composed."

Alex laughed. "I haven't seen a lot of the composure yet, but I understand what you're saying."

"C'mon man, you're almost already set in your ways. You're mature, so you'll be respectable."

"So far, I haven't enjoyed this meeting," Alex said as he finished his drink. "May I remind you, I'm not a babysitter."

"I'm not asking you to take over the whole project. I want you to start the ball rolling, establish a schedule for whatever she needs and be there if there are problems. As the CDI, you will step in if anyone steps out of line."

"Oh, this is nonsense."

"But you'll do this for me, Alex. I trust no one better than you."

"Do I have a choice, sir?"

"No, so make sure you contact her within a couple of days. Besides, you've wanted to get into Heather House for a while now to work on your unsolved case. This is a perfect way to spend some time there without suspicion."

"That's true," Alex agreed.

"Turn a negative into a positive. Just don't let her think we're using her for that purpose."

"Easy for you to say, sir. I'll have to work with it, somehow."

"Right-o."

Shaking his head, Alex placed his glass on the Chief Constable's desk and walked out of the police station.

21

C assie arrived home and immediately threw off her shoes and changed into comfortable clothes. She was proud of herself. She remained calm, composed, and intelligently articulate throughout the meeting. Finally, her anxiety was calming, and she could get down to the business at hand.

Sitting at her writing desk, she opened a file for her work notes. Once she had everything she needed, she would organize the information and send it to the publisher minus names and other sensitive information.

Working Notes

1. *Joe Duffy – Chief Constable*
2. *Alex Knight – Chief Detective Inspector*
3. *John Miles – Detective Sergeant – partner to Alex Knight*
4. *Olivia Lambert – Detective Sergeant – works with Alex Knight*
5. *Bryce Graham – Detective Inspector*
6. *Arlene Green– Records clerk at Wexley Police Station*

PAUSING TO REVIEW HER THOUGHTS, she lifted her head and sniffed the air. When she arrived home, she noticed a peculiar smell, like hay, but she thought it was something she picked up on her clothes from her meeting. However, she noticed it again in the library and the smell seemed stronger than before. She had changed her clothes and shoes, so it was from another source.

The windows were all closed. Cassie opened one hoping she could air out the library. The night air was warm and fresh and didn't smell like hay. Once again, Cassie searched the trash, the kitchen and her clothing but found no source of the smell.

She went back to her computer and spent time answering emails, checking social media, and finally working on her fiction novel. Yawning, she stretched and decided to call it a night. She wanted to relax in bed and start a book she brought with her from Manhattan.

As she drifted off to sleep, she made a list of the questions she wanted to ask of the Wexley Police Department when the proper time arrived.

22

The next day arrived with sunshine and fluffy clouds. After stretching, Cassie jumped out of bed, ready to face the day. For the first time, she felt settled into a routine. She made her breakfast and planned to tour the garden before going back to writing. Her best ideas happened while she was away from her computer. She often thought her process of writing was typing what she created in her mind earlier in the day.

After doing the dishes, she finalized the arrangement of her dishes in the cupboards and her food staples in the pantry. The pots were all clean and hung nicely except for the one that stuck out due to the mislaid brick. She made a small list of the meals she planned to make this week. Maybe she would take Simon and Laura to the pub for a hamburger when they returned but she didn't want to go there alone.

As she finished stocking a shelf hanging on the back wall of the pantry, she heard the doorbell ring. Opening the door to the cottage, she saw James with two ladies.

He pulled the hat from his head and smiled. "Morning, Miss Cassie. I hope we're not interrupting you."

Cassie opened the door wider. "Of course not, James. Welcome to Heather House."

The three visitors moved inside the cottage. One of the women smiled and held out a basket. "I've baked some welcome treats for you. Sponge Cake with cream and raspberries, chocolate chip cookies and blueberry muffins. I wasn't sure how much of a sweet tooth you had."

"Thank you very much," Cassie said as she took the basket. "That is kind of you."

James held his hand out toward the woman and said, "Miss Cassie, I'd like you to meet Mrs. Emma Witherspoon. She's the vicar's wife and they live next to the church."

"So nice to meet you."

"And this is Mrs. Thelma Peabody. She lives on the green."

Cassie held out her free hand. "So nice to meet you as well."

Mrs. Peabody nodded without smiling.

"Would you all like to come in for tea?"

James started to say something about not bothering her, while Mrs. Peabody walked straight into the living room to look around.

James raised his eyebrows at Mrs. Witherspoon. "Are you sure you have the time, Miss Cassie?"

Cassie smiled at him. "Of course, let me put the kettle on. Please, come sit down."

The cottage had an open design where Cassie could speak with her guests while she stood behind her granite counter and made the tea. James and Emma Witherspoon sat on the couch with an awkward smile while Mrs. Peabody toured the living room with her hands behind her back. She examined almost every object in the area.

"Are you familiar with Heather House?" Cassie asked as she placed teacups, saucers, sugar, and milk on a tray to bring to the living room. She placed several treats from the basket onto a plate and added it to the tray.

"Not so much the house as the rumors," Mrs. Peabody said.

"Oh? What rumors would that be?" Cassie asked as she placed the tray on a small table in front of the couch.

Emma Witherspoon bit her lip and looked at James.

"Heather House is haunted," Mrs. Peabody says. "Evil things go on here."

"Oh," Cassie said as she looked up with raised eyebrows.

"We don't know that to be true. Please, excuse us," Emma Witherspoon said with a nervous smile. "We came to welcome you to the village and let you know we're here if you have any questions or needs."

"Yes, anything at all," James chirped after her.

"Thank you, I appreciate that," Cassie said with a smile.

"Have you heard or seen anything strange?" Mrs. Peabody returned to her line of questioning.

Cassie stuttered for a few moments. "I'm still trying to adjust to living in a new country. There have been many new things but nothing I can honestly say was a ghost."

"Perhaps you're not paying attention," Mrs. Peabody said.

"Thelma!" Mrs. Witherspoon turned to James. "Perhaps we should be going."

"Yes, I believe you're quite right," James said as he stood and held his hat.

Cassie walked to the couch. "Are you sure? The tea is ready."

"I think it would be better," Mrs. Witherspoon said as she nodded toward Thelma Peabody. "However, I would love to chat some other time with you. I'd like to welcome you to the vicarage."

"That would be lovely," Cassie said with a smile. She then leaned in toward James and Mrs. Witherspoon and whispered. "Is there anything I need to know about this house?"

"Don't worry about it, dear."

James leaned close and whispered. "And don't pay her any mind. They don't call her nosy body Peabody for nothing."

Cassie had to cover her mouth to stop a laugh from erupting.

"Come Thelma. We're leaving now."

Mrs. Peabody turned from her study of the house and was about to walk into the library when Emma Witherspoon called. Cassie felt relieved as her writing desk was there and she was very sensitive about anyone looking over her writing or research before it was ready for public view.

James and Emma smiled and shook Cassie's hand. Thelma Peabody nodded on her way out, but Cassie caught the scowl on her face after she had passed by. Cassie watched them walk down the road and saw James turn and wave at her again. After waving back, she closed the door of the cottage and made sure the door was double locked.

23

Cassie spent the rest of the day exploring the property. The day was warm. She made sure to wear the proper shoes to hike the property and chose the garden path instead of nearing the woods. In the field toward the back property, she crested a small hill and was thrilled to see a fantastic view of the English Channel in the distance. The water was blue, with white clouds in the sky.

Cassie loved being near the water. It didn't matter if it was the ocean, or river or lake. Water had always made her concerns and anxieties feel small in comparison. She always felt better by the sea.

Cassie stayed in the lane, close to her property. On her travels she crossed a stone bridge. There was a small river with a steady stream of water. Looking down, she saw the area under the bridge was dark and muddy, but she steered clear of that area, especially as she was alone. She turned at the corner of the property that marked Heather House and headed back to the hill to look at the English Channel. Coming in from the back, she noticed a large yew tree off to the right. She had read about yew trees being some of the oldest trees in southern England. Looking off to the side she spied a red fox with her litter of babies, so she steered clear of that area.

As she reached the tree, she realized it marked a small cemetery. Cassie walked over to examine the gravestones. The headstones were in obvious disrepair, tilted in various positions and she was not able to read inscriptions due to years of rain and exposure. She walked through and saw a recent grave with a headstone that read, "William Blake." There was no other sentiment and no recorded dates of birth or death. She had heard that name somewhere before and realized it was the grave of the recent owner of Heather House. She immediately added William Blake and Heather House to her research list. As she walked back to the house, she wondered if the village had a library. Realizing not everything is found on the internet, she wondered if Emma Witherspoon could answer some questions about village life and particularly Heather House for her.

24

"Hello?" Cassie pushed the speaker on her phone while she dried her hands.

"Cassie? It's Evie. What are you doing?"

"I'm making dinner." Cassie finished with the dish towel and laid it on the counter.

"It's only noon."

"I'm making an old-fashioned pot of chili. I put it on to cook through the day while I'm writing."

"Excellent. I'm glad to hear you're writing. How are things? I wanted to catch up on the police station meeting."

Cassie shrugged though Evie couldn't see her. "I think it went as well as expected. I believe everyone was there including the Chief Constable and our Detective Chief Inspector. I met most of the department as well as the constables that tried to arrest me."

"Now Cassie," Evie blew out a cloud of cigarette smoke.

"I wish you wouldn't smoke when you call me. You know how I feel about that."

"I know, I know." Evie ground the cigarette out in an ashtray on her desk. "Okay, it's out."

"Good. We've already had a scare with you. Please stop smoking."

"As long as I don't have to stop drinking as well." Evie laughed. "You got the liquor I sent with Simon?"

"Yes, I did although I don't know how much I'll be drinking. Are you preparing me for something?"

"Not at all. However, you'll probably have some guests and I have it on good authority you should have some available when the need arises." Evie rushed on before Cassie could comment. "So where do we stand with our research? You've been there about two weeks. Can you believe it?"

"No, I can't, but I'm getting settled."

"Good to hear," Evie said with genuine concern. "The research?"

"Ah, yes. I met a lot of people including most of the detective sergeants that work with the department and especially Alex Knight. They seem very nice. I met some of the clerical staff who may not be as nice. From what I understand, two things will be happening this week. I'll be given a list of names so I can make up a schedule to meet with officers to help me understand their process. I believe they want to start with Knight and then they'll rotate. Also, I'll be meeting with general staff to learn about the police ranking system in the UK. So far, I've learned that detectives wear suits or plain clothes and constables wear a uniform."

"Same as America?"

"As far as I know," Cassie said.

"Well, it's a start. How is your fiction novel coming along?"

"So far, I'm doing well. I'm trying to keep to 1000 words a day. I have the plot in my head, but I'll need to do some traveling to get to know the area better. I'll need to see some of the famous landmarks as well."

"I'm sure it will all fall in place," Evie said. "By the way, I was in the elevator today when Ethan hopped in."

"Oh?" Cassie gripped the phone.

"He asked about you."

"Really? What did he want to know?"

"He asked how you were. Maybe he misses you?" Evie pushed harder.

"Obviously, the breakup went well if you want to think of it that way. He hasn't called my cell phone and it doesn't sound as if he had any burning questions for you."

Evie paused before she answered. "Actually, he was holding hands with a blonde bimbo."

Cassie laughed. "I'm sure he's moved on. Like five seconds after I told him I was leaving. Maybe before."

"He was no good for you. I'm glad he's with someone else and neither of you are bothered. That's one thing I don't have to worry about anymore."

"I'm happy to make your day," Cassie said sarcastically. "Listen, I've got to go work on my word count. I'll let you know when I hear from someone from the police station."

"Excellent and call me if there's any trouble. Technically, you're an employee of and representing the publisher so we can help you."

"I appreciate that, Evie. I'll call if I need to."

"Good. I'll wait to hear from you then. Have a good day, Cassie."

"You too, Evie, and thank you."

"For what?"

"I know you've gone out of your way to make things comfortable for me and I do appreciate it."

"I know you do, Cassie. You're that type of person. Keep well, dear. I'll be in touch." Cassie heard the soft click of the phone and for a few minutes felt nostalgic for New York and her apartment in Manhattan.

25

Cassie spent the next five hours writing. She made good progress on her novel and continued to surf the net looking for information on the Wexley Police Department. She made a list of questions she wanted to ask.

Finally, she closed her laptop, rubbed her eyes, and stretched. She had taken a walk around the garden to stretch her legs but returned quickly when it started to rain. This was her first day with rain since she moved to England. Not sure if it was Evie's phone call or the cottage temperature, but she felt cold and melancholy this evening. Moving to the fireplace, she laid a nice fire to dispel the raw, gloomy feeling.

Cassie went into the kitchen, set a place for one at the dining room table and fixed a salad. She stirred and added a bit more chili powder before she turned off her crock pot. She had pulled a bowl of cheddar cheese from the refrigerator when she heard a knock at the door.

She opened the door to find Alex Knight standing in the rain.

"Come in, you're soaking wet." Cassie stood back from the door.

Alex smiled, looking his debonair self in a three-piece suit, silk shirt and expensive tie. Cassie wondered what the salary was for a

DCI in Wexley, but Alex always had expensive suits, nice cologne, and a nice car. She glanced in the mirror next to the door and frowned when she saw her visage in yoga pants and casual shirt, stained with food.

Alex crossed the threshold and immediately wiped his feet on the entry rug. "I hope I'm not interrupting you. I was on my way home and thought this might be a good time to touch base. I would have been here earlier, but it's been a day." Alex looked into the cottage and saw the table setting. "Oh, I'm sorry. I didn't mean to disrupt your dinner."

"Don't be ridiculous. Come stand in front of the fire and dry off."

Alex followed her to the hearth. Cassie couldn't stop herself from rambling, but it was that type of day when she didn't want to be alone. "Have you eaten dinner yet? Would you like to join me? It's old-fashioned chili."

"Chili? I've not had that before."

"Well, it's big in America. Do you like spice?"

"Yes, I do," Alex nodded and smiled.

Cassie was sure she had never met anyone more polite.

"I don't want to appear forward, but I'd suggest you take your jacket off. That's a beautiful suit, but your jacket's wet and you don't want to spill chili on it."

"Are you sure?" Alex asked. "I know you wanted to talk about the book."

"Of course, I'm sure. You're the first human face I've seen today. We can talk about the research over dinner." Cassie walked to the cabinets and grabbed an additional bowl, plate and set of utensils. "I hope I don't insult you if you have a trained palate. Chili is good comfort food for a rainy day."

"No, not at all. I see way too much of Shepherd's pie and fish and chips."

Cassie laughed as she bustled about, plating salad, chili, and fresh, piping hot, bread with butter.

Alex took his jacket off and moved around the cottage. He glanced at the library, noting the large windows and Cassie's writing desk, set up with a computer and laptop. There was a flat screen on one wall with comfy couches and chairs scattered about the room.

"I see you've made a few changes since you've moved in."

"Evie, that's my agent as you know, had the place fixed up before I got here. I'm sure she hired some of the villagers to do the work. Are you familiar with how it looked before?"

Alex looked at the titles of the books on the shelves. "I am. I was called here quite often before Mr. Blake died."

"Oh?"

"Yes, I didn't have a chance to look around when I brought you home last Friday night, but I can see there have been a lot of changes. I can't say that's a bad thing."

"The food is ready if you'd like to sit down." Cassie made a mental note to bring Heather House and William Blake up in conversation.

Alex waited for Cassie to sit before he took his chair. "Do you enjoy cooking?"

Cassie nodded. "Yes, it relaxes me, especially after I've been writing. Sometimes, the best writing comes into my head when I'm doing other things like cooking, walking, or doing dishes."

Alex watched Cassie before he tried his own food. After a few bites, he put his utensils down to take a bite of bread. "I must say, the meal is marvelous," Alex said as he went back to his meal.

"Thank you, I'm glad you're enjoying it." Cassie blushed as she continued eating and offered more.

"No, thank you. I'm quite full. I often work through dinner, so I'm not used to a full meal during the week."

Cassie nodded as she put her fork down.

"Not because I'm not hungry. I don't have time to go to the pub and I don't have time to cook."

"That makes sense, but it may not be healthy," Cassie said as she stood and started to clear the table.

"Here, please let me do that," Alex said as he collected his things. "You've cooked."

"And I'm going to wash," Cassie said as she tossed a dish towel. "It's only a few dishes but you can dry if you like." They made quick work of the dishes and then stepped into the living room. "Would you like a drink?" You can pick what you'd like."

Alex walked to the fireplace, restoked the fire and turned to the liquor cabinet. "You've got some excellent single malt here. Do you like scotch?"

"Oh no, I don't drink except for a bit of brandy or whiskey in my tea on occasion. Or a good bottle of wine with dinner. I generally don't like to drink if I'm alone, but please help yourself."

Alex opened a bottle of single malt, grabbed a whiskey glass, and poured himself two fingers.

"Would you like some water?" Cassie asked as she watched.

"No, thank you. I'll drink it neat."

They sat across from each other on the couches. Alex took a sip of his whiskey and then set the glass on a coaster on the coffee table. "I'm here at the request of Joe Duffy to begin the process of helping you with your research. I must admit I don't understand what you need to know."

Cassie paused for a moment before she answered. "As I understand the project, the publisher entered into an agreement with someone to write about the police force in the UK. Positive things, of course. This book would be for education or interest. I'm not here from a gossip magazine and I'm not interested in specific cases. It's my understanding that it may be a comparison of training, procedure, and forensics with other countries."

"How does the CID fit in?" Alex watched her with keen interest as he continued to sip his scotch.

"From what I understand, the CID or Criminal Investigation Department in the UK may be different from the U.S. department. In America, the CID is commonly associated with the army or FBI. But also, it may be a civilian police department. It depends on who committed the crime and where it happened." Alex didn't answer right away, which she was sure was one of his best techniques to make witnesses talk as she continued to babble. "Let's think of it this way. I am a friend who wants to join the police force in the UK, and I want to make sure I climb the ranks one day. So, I'll ask you to teach me everything you know about police work. How do I start? What do I need to do? How did you get started? I'm sure each detective has a different story, so that's why they've asked me to get different perspectives, but I do understand they want to have a special nod to you due to your impressive solve rate and tenacious skills."

Alex nodded with a grin. "That's nice to hear, but I've learned the best way to be successful is to stay out of the public eye."

"I understand completely. I've retreated since I've become more popular with readers."

Alex was quiet for a moment as he finished his drink. "I believe I have some items that will help you understand the force. I can bring them by for you to borrow and then we can discuss any concepts you'd like to clarify."

"Thank you, that would be a good start. I'll want some perspective though. I want to know what you're thinking and feeling when you start an investigation."

"How do you feel when you start to write a new book?" He placed his glass on the table.

"I don't know how to answer that," Cassie said. "Many emotions, unanswered questions. There's a sea of research to do before the writing itself."

"And what happens when you're writing?"

"The story evolves with each new fact, or concept." Cassie frowned as she thought about the process of writing. "I never finish in the place I thought I would when I started."

"You've now answered the question you asked of me." Alex said with a smile. "You start with everything, begin to whittle away and go where the journey takes you." Alex stood up and put his dry jacket on. "Thank you for a most pleasant evening and saving me from some leftover Shepherd's Pie."

Cassie jumped up after him. "You're welcome. To be honest, I enjoyed the company. I enjoy bouncing ideas off someone I trust."

Alex tilted his head and smiled as he opened the door. "That's one of the first steps of the investigation. Get the witnesses to trust and talk to you like a friend. They'll tell you most everything. Good-night, Cassie. I'll wait outside until I hear the door lock."

"When will we meet again?"

"As soon as I can free up time from the day. I'll try to assign a little more to Miles and Olivia."

"I hope you trust them," Cassie said awkwardly.

"Please go inside and lock the door."

Cassie did as she was told but stood at the window, frowning as she watched Alex get into his car and drive down the lane.

When he was gone, Cassie returned to her computer files and opened her notes. She spent the next sixty minutes trying to jot down the salient points Alex had made after dinner. She was pleased to have broken the ice but continued to push back the feeling that she had been outwitted.

26

Alex walked into the station early the next morning. He had not slept well, thinking about the evening before. Interestingly, it was a very relaxed evening. Cassie was a marvelous cook and Alex enjoyed being with someone who spoke with intelligence. It was a wonderful time. However, he was annoyed that he had broken one of his cardinal rules and enjoyed it.

From the minute he laid eyes on that woman, before he knew who she was, he felt protective. She had been standing there, all alone, at the Chief's party looking like a lost soul on the verge of a panic attack. Tall, lean, beautiful, with chestnut hair and electric blue eyes.

Alex was normally ready to take charge, which is one of the reasons he was fast-tracked to Chief Detective Inspector, but even if she hadn't been distressed, he wanted to approach her the minute he saw her.

He had sworn years ago, after all the anguish of his girlfriend being threatened as revenge for his work, that he would never allow himself to be close to anyone that could suffer because of him.

Damn the Chief and the book. He wanted to walk off and not be bothered.

Alex spent the next twenty minutes going through calls and email that had arrived yesterday afternoon. He had several open homicides now and was looking to his detectives for progress. It was at this point that he usually went back to the scene of the crime and started over again. He would try to visualize the murder in his head and make sure they had considered all leads, possibilities, and details. He was very detail oriented.

Breaking for fifteen minutes, he pulled a banker's box onto his desk and rifled through his lower desk drawer to pull out orientation materials for new detectives. He filled the box halfway and let it sit there.

"Knight."

Alex looked up when he heard his name. Joe Duffy was standing across the room beckoning to him. Frowning, Alex stood and walked into the Chief's office.

"Knight, how are you?"

"Little busy right now, sir. I've got three open homicides on my desk. I'm sifting through reports and then need to make field visits today."

"Are you making progress with any of them. Could they be related?"

"Two of them are clearly not related, but one could be. I need to get to the scene with Miles today and get more information. There's a witness I want to talk to about his statement as well."

The Chief Constable nodded. "You'll figure it out. You always do. You have the nose of a blood hound."

Alex stood straight up. "Thank you, sir."

"Which is why you're the person I chose as our spotlight for the book."

Alex frowned and pulled his suit jacket closed. "I wanted to talk to you about that."

"Have you made contact with Miss Ashcroft yet?"

Alex paused for a moment. "Yes, I did. I met with her last night for the first time, and she had some interesting points to make."

"And?"

"She gave me some idea of what she was looking for. She wants us to meet again, but honestly, can someone else do this?"

"Do you think the detective sergeants have enough experience to answer all her questions?"

Alex answered haltingly. "No, not really, sir."

"Then who would you have me send? Bryce? He's the only other person I can send to answer questions about the CID. Do you want that?"

Alex was surprised to find the thought of Bryce Graham sitting at Cassie's dining room table aggravated him. He knew he felt protective but had no right to feel proprietary. Alex took a deep breath in through his nose before he answered. "No, sir. I'll do it, but I need to spend today looking over the casebooks. I gathered material for her. Maybe we can get the research done fast enough for her to leave sooner than she planned."

"Good. You're the only inspector I trust to work with her for obvious reasons. Have Miles drop it off and you can go another day after she's had time to review it."

Alex nodded. "Yes, very good sir."

As the door slammed, Joe was glad Alex didn't see him sit back in his chair and chuckle.

27

C assie jumped when she heard the doorbell. She walked to the front door as she continued to fret about her novel. She had written several chapters and made good progress with word count during the day but knew the depth of the novel would be improved if she could visit more of the setting in person. She was about to research information on William Blake and Heather House when the bell rang.

Opening the front door a few inches, she was surprised to see John Miles and Olivia Lambert standing there holding a box.

"Good afternoon, Miss Ashcroft," Miles said.

"Hello, how are you?" Cassie stepped back and opened the door wide. "Would you like to come in?"

The pair stepped inside and looked around. "The cottage looks great," Olivia said admiring the new furniture and curtains.

"Thanks so much, but I didn't do the decorating. It was done for me before I arrived." Cassie smiled and offered a quick shrug. "Were you here often?"

"Oh, no," Olivia said. "I was only here when Mr. Blake died. We had to check his home for papers and anything unusual even though he died in the pub."

Cassie nodded. "I'm hearing that same thing from a lot of people in the village." She turned to Miles. "Do you want to put that box down? Is that for me?"

"Oh, yes," Miles said. "It's from Detective Chief Inspector Knight. He asked us to drop this off to you today."

Cassie pointed to the coffee table. "Why don't you put it down there. What's in it?"

"I believe it's copies of the orientation manuals we must read when we start at the department. He asked if you could look through to see if any of this information would help you."

Cassie sifted through a few of the papers on top of the box. "I'll certainly go through and see what information I can use. Thank you for bringing it by. I guess you're having a busy day."

"Yes, ma'am," Olivia replied with a nod. "We have several open homicides and appointments set up for today."

"I see," Cassie said. "I appreciate you taking the time to drop this off. When you have time, I'd like to get your personal perspective of working for the police force. I don't want to talk about any specific cases and I'm not asking about your co-workers, but I'd like to hear what drew you to the police force. What your opinion of the training and job is. How you enjoy working for Alex Knight and what he's taught you. Things like that."

Miles looked at Olivia with eyebrows raised. "That sounds lovely. We're busy today and we would have to check our schedule with the DCI, but if he gives us clearance, we'll be here."

"Thanks so much," Cassie said. "It's always good to have different perspectives and I would especially like to hear a woman's point of view on this subject as well." Cassie smiled at Olivia.

"We'd better go, now," Miles said as he touched Olivia's arm, and they turned toward the door. "Have a good day, Miss Ashcroft."

"Same to you and please call me Cassie."

The pair walked out the door and to a small police car waiting on the edge of the lane. As Cassie watched them go, she wondered about their relationship with Alex Knight. He seemed to be a tough boss but probably watched out for them.

Cassie made herself a cup of tea and sat down in the living room. She pulled the box close and unpacked a large amount of training manuals. She found policies, procedures, proficiency testing and other documents. The details would satisfy the factual requirements of the book but not approach the human story and experience. That was the piece that Cassie wanted to catch from interviews with members of the department. How were they affected by crime, violence, homicides, and family grief? How did they balance that part of the job?

For now, she would read manuals and by the amount of them on her coffee table, she had a lot of dry reading to attend to.

28

Friday morning, Cassie woke up and decided to go for a walk. She wanted to stretch after working at her desk the day before. She was determined to walk more of the property and look for clues about William Blake and Heather House. She also had an appointment to go to the police station and pick up additional materials regarding police matters in England.

Pulling on her hiking boots, Cassie dressed in jeans and a warm sweater, so her clothes were appropriate for the distance and weather.

She pulled the door closed after her and set out in the opposite direction from where she had already gone. Walking down the lane, she passed the beautiful landscape. She took photos of green fields dotted with sheep and crops. As she crested a hill, she paused on top and was awe-struck as she realized she was seeing the English Channel in the distance. The water was a gorgeous blue and the landscape was beautiful. She wanted to get to the water's edge one day and see the actual coastline. Perhaps she could ask James to take her there. Nodding, she determined to ask Mrs. Witherspoon about the best place to visit.

After taking a few seconds to breathe, Cassie turned and headed toward the police station. Using her phone, she continued taking photos to refer to when she described the landscape in her novel. The station was miles by car but less when walking through the fields.

Nearing the police station, she stopped and looked at the building. This would be her third visit to the building since coming to England. It was an ordinary, administrative, brick building. Nothing fancy or unique. Most likely, the larger issues were dealt with in the larger cities, with more appropriate courts and jails.

Climbing the few steps, Cassie went inside and met the constable at the front desk. "Can I help you?"

"Yes, hi, I'm Cassandra Ashcroft. I'm here to meet one of your clerks, Arlene Green. I'm picking up some material."

"Please take a seat. I'll call her."

As Cassie stood in the lobby, the door opened, and two men walked through.

"Miss Ashcroft, how nice to see you." The man extended his hand as well as his smile as he veered over to her.

"Thank you," Cassie said as she took his hand. "I'm sorry, but I haven't memorized everyone's name yet."

"Of course," he said before proudly announcing himself. "I'm Inspector Bryce Graham."

The other man jumped out from behind him. "I'm Detective Sergeant Dennis Osborne. It's so nice to meet you and I look forward to our interview."

For a moment, Cassie froze as she thought he was going to bend forward and kiss her hand.

"Thank you. I appreciate your help with these interviews."

"Our pleasure, we are happy to help."

Inspector Bryce appeared to bristle as he cut off his sergeant. "Yes, but right now, DS Osborne and I have a case to investigate." He took her hand once again in both of his. "I'll look forward to when the two of us can meet again."

Cassie smiled and nodded as they left. She couldn't help wiping her hand on her pants as she took deep breaths.

Five minutes later, Arlene Green opened the door and waved Cassie over.

"Hi, come into the office," Arlene said as she led Cassie to a record room. There were piles of paper and files stacked throughout the room. She sat at a desk and encouraged Cassie to sit. Folding her hands in front of her, Arlene took a deep breath and said, "So, how do you like England?"

Cassie smiled to be kind. "It's lovely, but I'm still learning."

"What does your husband think about all this?" Arlene bent forward, eager to hear the answer.

"Oh, I'm not married." Cassie could feel herself shutting down. She felt as if she were being interviewed for a local gossip show. "I came to pick up the paperwork for this week's research section."

"I know," Arlene said with a smile. "We hardly got a chance to talk to you the other night. Everyone would love to know more about you."

Alarm bells went off in Cassie's head. She offered a slow smile as she remembered her training for public interviews. "My name is Cassandra Ashcroft. I'm an author." Cassie tapped her lip with her finger. "I have several bestsellers to my name and now I'm in England writing and researching two books."

Arlene nodded. "That's exciting. I think everyone would love to write a book. It's hard finding the time to sit down and do it. There are so many other things you must do to work and keep your house clean."

Cassie maintained her smile as she felt herself become prickly inside. "Well, I don't want to keep you from that. Do you happen to have a packet for me today?"

"It's exciting that you're researching the police structure. I bet you love a man in uniform."

Cassie didn't respond as she was speechless for a moment.

Arlene continued. "Most of us love a man in uniform. As a matter of fact, most of the constables and detectives here are married or taken, if you know what I mean."

"I'm not here to find a man in uniform or otherwise," Cassie said as her smile faded.

"Oh, do you identify in a certain way?"

"No," Cassie said as she stood. "I'm here to write a book. Would you be so kind to give me the material I requested?"

"Of course," Arlene said with a smile. She appeared happy that Cassie was rattled. "I didn't mean to pry. I wanted you to know that there aren't many dating opportunities around here. You know, we girls must stick together." Arlene softly poked her with her elbow as she handed over the packet.

"Of course," Cassie said. "Although, the last thing I'm interested in is starting a relationship with anyone."

Satisfied with Cassie's answer, Arlene smiled her best Cheshire grin.

As Cassie left the police station, she shook her head and made a face that couldn't be seen by anyone behind her. Obviously, Arleen's love life felt threatened. *Why did this have to be so hard?*

29

Cassie arrived at the cottage and placed the packet on her desk. She'd get to it eventually but wanted to start dinner. She placed a lasagna she had made earlier in the week into the oven. She enjoyed cooking and did some of her best writing while cooking or doing dishes. Back in America, she used to feed Mrs. Roberts in the apartment next door. Thinking about her, Cassie felt nostalgic and missed being home. Although she had met a few friends, the move to Wexley had not been an easy one. If things continued this way, she would take Evie up on her offer of moving back as quickly as possible.

Cassie sat at her desk and opened the envelope when her cell phone chimed.

Hello, it's Alex. Okay if I stop by later today?

CASSIE LOOKED at the sender's name and decided to be bold.

Of course. I hope you like lasagna. Bring wine.

CASSIE PUT her phone on the desk and picked up the paperwork for the third time. An hour later, the lasagna was ready, the table was set, and Cassie had freshened up to salve her pride.

She opened the door when she heard a knock and beckoned Alex inside. He smiled and held up a bottle of red wine.

"My, don't you look nice today," Cassie said as she noticed another silk suit and the wine. She silently inhaled the scent of his Creed Green Irish Tweed cologne as he walked past.

Alex gave a shy smile, took off his jacket and hung it up near the door. "I got your message. It was a very long day. Had to be in court all morning, followed by the autopsy suite and witness interviews. Not my idea of a fun day, but necessary."

"I hope you didn't wear that suit into the autopsy suite."

"No, they gave me a special set of scrubs to wear."

"Are you sure you're up to discussing the research? Maybe you'd like to go home and rest?"

Alex looked at her with an unreadable expression. He took a breath and said, "What I'd like to do is start with a glass of your single malt, if you don't mind."

"Of course not," Cassie said as she pointed toward the dinner table. "I already have it out for you."

Alex smiled and walked to the table where he poured himself a generous two fingers of malt. He savored the first two sips and turned toward her, smiling. "Thank you. That was very considerate, having a drink ready. To answer your question, discussing the research is perfect. If I go back to an empty home or office after that type of day, I'd obsess for hours."

"Well, then happy to oblige," Cassie said as she turned and headed toward the kitchen. "I hope you like lasagna. I had already put it in the oven when you texted."

"I haven't had it in a long while but I'm sure I'll enjoy it. You seem a marvelous cook."

"I enjoy cooking. It relaxes me." Cassie shrugged. "I guess it's a form of therapy. The problem is I don't want to eat all the food I make so I'm twice as happy to share with someone who enjoys a home cooked meal."

"I appreciate that, but I want to make sure you know that I would never expect you to cook for me."

Cassie laughed. "As long as you realize, that as a born and bred Jersey girl from America, I never would if I didn't want to."

"Brilliant," Alex said as he toasted her with his glass. "Shall I open the wine?"

"Please," Cassie replied as she carried the lasagna, fresh salad, and bread over to the table.

The pair sat down. Cassie handed the food to Alex so he could serve himself and pass it back. "Dinner looks delicious. How are you getting on with groceries and all that?"

"It's fine. I think Evie planned to have a local farmer send vegetables weekly. They've been showing up on my doorstep. She knows I like to cook to keep myself busy."

"Please check with her to be sure. You never know who has ulterior motives around here."

Cassie stopped and looked at her food. "Should we throw it away?"

Alex laughed. "No, no. I'm sure the food is good either way. I don't want someone thinking you owe them after the fact."

"Okay, I'll trust you on that." Cassie loaded her plate and the two enjoyed a delicious dinner while chatting about their day and the police department.

"I normally wouldn't bore you with some of these details, but I assume these are the things you are looking for?"

"Exactly," Cassie replied. "I walked to the station to pick up a packet of public relations material. I had the oddest exchange with Arlene Green."

"A perfect example. That proves my point. She would be a good person to avoid. What was she going on about?"

"She wanted up close and personal details about my love life and my intentions, I think."

Alex sighed and put his fork down. "I am so sorry. I should have warned you about her and her little group of friends. I hope you didn't give her the satisfaction."

"I didn't, but she realized I was getting agitated, and I think that pleased her."

"You would do well to avoid her as much as possible while you're here. She'll not only ask for your personal details, but she'll feel free to give her opinion about them to anyone she encounters."

Cassie smiled as she looked at Alex. "You sound like you've had some experience there."

Alex frowned and took a sip of wine.

"We do have a little problem in that area," Cassie said as she looked down at her plate.

"Oh?"

"As you should know by now from your Chief Constable, part of the book is to deal with you. They are planning on having a section dedicated to you. Your impressive solve rate and such. But the human-interest side will dictate asking questions about your personal life."

"Such as?"

"Such as whether you're married, have children and such."

Alex stopped eating and put down his fork. "I won't answer any personal questions. It's a safety issue."

"I understand," Cassie said as she nodded. "And, by the way, I agree."

Alex looked at her for a moment and nodded. "I think you would be one of the only people who would. You're in the public eye. How do you handle interviews and personal information?"

Cassie chuckled. "It's funny that you say that. I was made to go through training for interviews and public details. I thought of that training the minute Arlene started grilling me today."

Done with their food, Cassie collected the dishes and brought them to the sink. Alex carried the rest of the dishes to the counter. "Why don't you let me wash the few dishes so you can put the food away and we can get on to the material?"

"Are you sure?" Cassie asked. "I can get back to all this later."

"I'm absolutely sure." Alex unbuttoned his cuffs and rolled up the sleeves of his crisp clean shirt. "I'm not here to be served and the sooner we get to it, the better."

"Fine with me," Cassie said as she stored the left-over food in the refrigerator. Once she was done, she dried the dishes and put them away, while Alex poured another glass of single malt.

The pair settled in the living room. Alex with whiskey and Cassie with a cup of rich coffee.

Alex looked through some of the materials that Miles and Olivia had dropped off. He then looked at Cassie and said, "Now, where were we?"

Cassie settled back into the couch. "I've read over the materials I was given, so I see the dry facts about orientation and the police department protocols. I'd like to hear from you what the differences are between a Chief Detective Inspector, an Inspector, Sergeant and so on. There are times that what you do does not match the description, so I'd like to know the differences in a realistic situation."

Alex nodded. "Okay, we can go over that material. What else?"

Cassie took a deep breath. "Since you asked, I'd like to know more about William Blake and Heather House. I've walked most of the property and I saw the graveyard on the hill by the tree. I want to go back and look for other family members. I'm not sure if Wexley has a history section in the local library, but I can't seem to find the library. You had mentioned you were here several times. Would you be able to tell me anything about those visits?"

"Why do you want to know this?" Alex tilted his head as she waited for the answer.

Cassie stared back at him, almost mesmerized by those blazing blue eyes. Maybe Arlene had a point but that was not why she was in England. She swallowed before she answered. "The history interests me for a couple of reasons. Everyone keeps making vague references to this house, but also having a better understanding of a typical estate would help me create a fictional one for my novel."

"So, you wouldn't be printing specific facts or material?"

"Of course not," Cassie said as she frowned. "It's important to research a lot of background about normal lifestyles, scenery, economy and more when you're writing a novel. As a matter of fact, I'm thinking of asking James to take me around to get a wider view of the area."

"That makes sense. What areas do you want to see?"

Cassie hoped she didn't sound silly as she answered. "Anything and everything from natural landscape to bigger villages. I'd like to learn more about the culture and general lifestyle of England. From the rural areas to cities like London. I want to see where people shop. How they interact. What town activities are like. The only thing is I need to stay as invisible as possible, if you know what I mean. I want to observe and make my own conclusions. If any activity involves me, then it's not what would happen naturally. Does that make sense?"

Alex smiled. She couldn't help noticing his eyes were set off by his tan. "That makes perfect sense. In a way, that's exactly what I do. I go to a crime scene or meet a suspect and watch and observe, at first. Once I come to a few conclusions, I can dig deeper for specific information."

"Can I use that line for the research book?"

Alex laughed. "I suppose." He sipped his whiskey and appeared to be lost in thought. "How about this? I'll be more open to giving you material and information if you let me see what you plan to submit when you're done. I've known you long enough that I feel I can trust you. I usually read people well."

Cassie blushed. She hoped he couldn't read her thoughts about his eyes. "That sounds fair," she said as she nodded. "What exactly are you referring to?"

Alex sat forward and placed his empty whiskey glass on the coffee table. "A couple of things. First, I'll answer your questions about the difference in rank although we're all out there investigating."

"Fair enough," Cassie nodded with a smile. She handed the bottle of single malt to Alex. "In case, you'd like a bit more after a bad day."

"Thank you," Alex said. "Just a smidge. You mentioned they were interested in my solve rate, which may not reflect my conviction rate."

Cassie nodded her understanding as Alex continued.

"One of the biggest cases that has remained unsolved, and which bothers me quite a bit, is that of William Blake."

"Really?" Cassie's face showed her surprise.

"Yes," Alex said as he nodded. "Since you want to see how a case progresses for your research and since you've promised not to use names or factual material, and you're interested in Heather House and Mr. Blake, I will go over that case file with you to show you how we do an investigation."

Cassie bounced forward with a large smile. "That would be phenomenal."

"But you must keep your promise. I am trusting you." Alex cautioned as he looked at her with that intense gaze. She could understand how a suspect would crack with questioning if he looked at them the same way. She was ready to confess to something and she hadn't committed a crime.

"I promise," she said. "But that would be a great compromise and I would appreciate it so much."

"And I appreciate your kindness this week with dinner," Alex said with a small smile. He silently kicked himself. For some reason, Cassie was one of the only women who was able to get him to drop his guard and quite easily at that. He was breaking his own cardinal rules and that angered him. "By the way, the lasagna was excellent. I don't normally eat a lot of Italian food."

30

L ater that night, Cassie reviewed the evening as she went upstairs to bed. They had spent another hour discussing some of the details Cassie had asked for. During the evening, Alex stepped outside to make a phone call and then again when he received a reply. Cassie didn't think it was a fresh homicide as he seemed very pleased with the information.

They finished their session about rank. Cassie had taken copious notes and asked intelligent questions. Once they were done, Alex helped bring all the glasses to the kitchen and put away the whiskey. He turned to her before he put his jacket on.

"I know this is sudden and tomorrow is Saturday, but would you be free to go out?"

"Out?" Cassie questioned.

Alex nodded. "Yes, out of town. I want to thank you for your kindness this week. I'd like to return the favor and I know an excellent place to start with the culture of England." He then smiled and said, "I've just found out there will be tickets waiting for us. I don't want to ruin the surprise, but I think you'll absolutely love it."

Cassie stammered for a second before she smiled. "It sounds great. How should I dress?

"Glad you asked. You don't need a gown, but perhaps a business dress? Dress as if you were going to a fancy hotel for lunch."

"Sounds like a nice day," Cassie said nervously, feeling as if she were in unchartered territory.

"I believe you'll enjoy this event," Alex said. "I hope this helps with the research you need for your novel."

"Thank you."

"I'll be by at half-past eleven to pick you up. It will be a bit of a drive."

"I'll be ready."

Nodding his head and with a polite smile, Alex left the cottage. He waited until he heard the lock engaged and then hopped into his car and drove away.

Cassie made sure all the dishes were put away, turned off her laptop and lights and went up to bed. As tired and nervous as she had been, she was now lying in bed rethinking everything that had happened that day. She realized it was one of the worst things to do but either she continued to rethink her conversation or suffer anxiety about Saturday.

Every trip and function Cassie had attended since she arrived in England had been arranged by Evie. This would be the first trip she arranged independently. She trusted Alex and for whatever reason, he had been her protector up to this point. His help certainly wasn't expected, but Cassie was grateful and flattered by it. Especially, knowing he had a reputation for keeping his emotions as well as his distance in check. That was okay. Cassie was not in England for a relationship, but she certainly appreciated having someone she could trust and rely on if she needed him to help her.

Closing her eyes, she took deep breaths in the darkened room, willing herself to fall asleep. She started to doze, but jumped when she heard a crash downstairs. Heart thudding, she sat upright for a minute to listen for more noise but heard none. Questioning whether she had dreamed the noise, Cassie decided to get out of bed and check.

She grabbed the heavy metal fireplace poker and slowly

descended the stairs. She crept slowly, listening at each level to see if she heard anything further. To comfort herself, she tapped the pocket of her robe to make sure she had her cell phone ready.

When she reached the bottom of the stairs she stopped as she was assailed by the smell of hay and cigarette smoke as well as the tendrils of an oncoming panic attack. Her breathing heavy, she dashed across the foyer and snapped all the lights on in the area. She stopped and listened and heard nothing. No one ran toward her or out the front door. Step by step she crept into the living area and looked toward the kitchen.

She felt her throat constrict when she spied the bottle of single malt sitting in the middle of the counter and a broken glass on the floor. She could smell the aroma of freshly poured whiskey. Cassie was sure everything had been put away before she went to bed. She continued to walk around the house, flipping lights on as she went. Before long, the house was blazing with light, yet there was no activity or persons to be seen except for the broken glass, bottle of whiskey and smell of cigarettes and hay.

It had now been 30 minutes since Cassie had come downstairs. She put the fireplace poker on the counter and retrieved a broom and dustpan from the pantry. She swept the floor several times to clean the glass and turned back to use the garbage in the pantry. She chided herself that she should start calling it the bin but wasn't in the mood to concentrate on linguistics.

As she approached the pail, she looked down and stopped short when she noticed a small clump of muddy hay on the floor between the pantry and the kitchen. The smell of cigarettes was stronger in the area as well. She didn't touch the hay as she knew it was not there when Alex left. She needed to talk to someone but couldn't quite remember whether she should dial 999 or 101 for help. She had Alex's phone number but didn't want to text or call him in the middle of the night. She didn't want to give him the wrong idea.

Knowing it was only 9:00 p.m. in Manhattan, Cassie pulled out her cell and dialed Evie.

31

"What happened?" Evie asked as she blew cigarette smoke from the side of her mouth and snubbed out her cigarette in an ashtray.

Cassie answered in a rapid, shaky voice. "I was trying to fall asleep, and I heard a noise. I came downstairs with my fireplace poker and found someone had taken out the bottle of single malt, filled a glass and for some reason, dropped it on the floor. There was broken glass and whiskey on the floor. I also smelled hay and cigarettes and when I went to throw out the glass, I found a clump of hay in the kitchen. And now, I'm having a panic attack."

"Okay, calm down and breathe. Let's do that together. In through the nose and out through the mouth. Are you sure no one is there?"

"It's been an hour now and I don't see or hear anyone. I guess I'm getting myself worked up."

"Are you sure the kitchen was perfectly clean?"

"Absolutely," Cassie said.

"Does anyone else have a key?"

"I don't think so. Did you have the locks changed when you got the house ready?"

"Absolutely, but don't forget I hired people from the area, so it's possible someone has a copy."

"Fantastic," Cassie said.

"Did you call the police?"

"No, I couldn't remember what number to call."

"Oh, darling. It's 999 for an emergency and 112 if you're using a mobile phone."

"Besides, Alex Knight had just left here at 11:00 p.m. and I didn't want to aggravate the man any further."

"Has there been problems?" Evie asked concerned. "I was under the impression all was moving along."

"No, not problems," Cassie said. "It's probably just me being socially awkward. I'm doing my best to work on this project but if you told me the publisher changed their mind, I'd be at Heathrow in a couple of hours."

Evie held her glass up to the waiter for another drink as she continued to speak to Cassie. She was grateful her companion for the evening remained quiet and respectful of her conversation with Cassie. He knew it was early evening. Despite disrupting their dinner, Evie immediately took the call when she saw Cassie's name as she realized it was late in England. Despite his silence, Cassie could hear tinkling in the background.

"You're out to dinner," Cassie said with a sigh. "I'm sorry. I know dinner runs late in Manhattan."

"No problem. I've told you several times. If you need me, call me day or night. If necessary, I'll yank you out of there and fly you home immediately. There is no contract or book that is more important to me than you. Do you hear me?"

Cassie smiled to herself. "Thank you for saying that. It's been hours and there's nothing going on here so I'm going back to bed. I want to let you know that Alex Knight is taking me on a road trip tomorrow. He's helping me see the area so I can create a bit more realism in my novel."

"Oh? From what I've heard, that's unusual for him, isn't it?"

"I don't know, Evie. Frankly, he's been my protector since I've arrived. He's already helped me out of several scrapes. I don't know where we're going but if I don't make it back, you'll know where to start."

Evie started laughing. "I don't think that will be a problem. Keep your cell phone on and text me the minute you get back or if there's any problem. And remember, the emergency number is 999 in England."

"Got it," Cassie said. "Now go back to your dinner and company. Sorry to disrupt you but I appreciate you picking up the line."

"Anytime. I mean that," Evie said as she hung up the phone.

Cassie sighed and went back to bed. She left the muddy hay near the pantry. Climbing the stairs, she looked down several times but didn't see anything. It would have been easy as every light in the house was still glowing.

32

The next morning, Cassie rolled over and moaned. Sunshine was pouring in the window, and she could feel the day warming already. She kept herself awake for a while the night before but must have fallen asleep at some point. She glanced at the bedroom door. It was still closed and the dresser she pushed in front of it hadn't moved.

Cassie got out of bed, used the bathroom, and took a hot shower. Toweling her hair, she felt better as she looked in the mirror. She thought back to the night before, gauging her anxiety and tried to figure out how much was proper reaction and how much was pure panic attack. Evie was used to her panic attacks. Thank goodness she had picked up her call.

Cassie jumped when she realized it was already late morning. She only had thirty minutes to check downstairs and get fully dressed before Alex arrived. Unlocking the door, she stepped out into the hall and stood listening for a full minute. Embracing silence, she slowly crept down the stairs. Nothing had changed and the clump of muddy hay was where she left it last evening.

Satisfied, she turned and ran up the stairs and into her bedroom. She opened the closet and quickly picked a pastel dress that would look nice with her chestnut hair. It took another fifteen minutes to fully dress, pick out the proper shoes and do her hair and makeup. Not knowing where they were going made the process harder, but she doubted they would be hiking. Looking in the mirror, she fretted over the shoes. The heels made her legs look nicer, but it would be hard to walk far. She couldn't wear hiking boots with her dress.

Her plan was to run back downstairs and have a quick cup of coffee, but she barely got to the bottom of the stairs before the doorbell rang. Taking a deep breath and one last look in the hall mirror, she opened the door with a quick smile for Alex.

"Good morning, Cassie," he said with his usual charm. He was dressed to kill. "You look absolutely lovely." If nothing else, the man was always polite.

"Good morning. Would you like to come in?" Cassie wasn't sure what she should do and felt very awkward.

"To be honest, we don't have enough time. We've got a bit of a ride and I don't think you'll want to be late for this event."

"Okay," Cassie said as she swallowed. "Does this look appropriate? How about the shoes? I hope there's not a lot of walking."

"You're perfect," Alex said as he smiled and waited on the doorstep.

"Great." Cassie reached to the side and grabbed her purse. She took a deep breath, stepped outside, locked the door, and walked toward the car with Alex. For a moment, she went to get into the wrong side of the car. "Sorry. I'm still not used to the driver sitting on the right."

Alex opened the passenger door and waited until she was belted in before getting into the driver's seat.

"How long will it take for us to get there?" Cassie asked.

"It should take about an hour," Alex said as he continued to stare at the road. "Hopefully, we won't get stuck behind any tractors or wagons today."

"Wagons?"

"Sometimes the farmers use the main roads to scuttle about,"

Alex said. He looked at Cassie and saw that her jaw was set as she stared straight ahead. "I'm sorry. I wasn't thinking straight."

She turned to him. "What?"

"I'm realizing that this mystery approach is probably not the best idea with your anxiety. I wanted to surprise you. I think you'll be royally pleased."

"Is that a hint?"

"What?"

"Royally pleased?"

"Oh, oh no. I didn't mean to mislead you."

Cassie shook her head and chuckled. "No, I'm sorry. It's me. I didn't sleep very well last night."

"No? Is everything all right? I hope I didn't upset you." Alex was trying to watch her as she answered but he continued to drive as well.

"I'm fine, really. Please watch the road." Cassie looked out her passenger side window as the view flew by. "I'm happy to take a lovely ride through the area. This is the first time I've been able to do that."

Alex nodded and went back to driving. Another ten minutes went by as he drove. They passed fields, countryside, and larger towns. Cassie saw modern business buildings and stores.

"This is wonderful. I was in London for a couple of days when I arrived and then only the village since then." Cassie realized they were closer to water. "Is that the English Channel in the distance?"

"Why, yes, it is," Alex said with a small smile. "I thought you'd like to see the coastline on our trip."

"Thank you, it's beautiful." Cassie quieted and continued to watch the view. "Can I ask you a strange question?"

"Will I have to start an investigation?" Alex laughed as he snuck a glance at her.

"I hope not." Cassie relaxed and laughed as well.

"Go ahead and ask."

"Would you happen to know if William Blake was a smoker?"

The question caused Alex to pause for a moment. He tilted his head and frowned. "I don't believe he was. I haven't reviewed the case file recently, but I think I would remember that."

"Why do you ask?"

"Did he have a cat or a pet?"

He turned to her with a strange look. "No, I don't believe he did. Where are all these questions coming from? You're upset today. Did something happen last night?"

Cassie frowned and looked out the window.

"Cassie, you must tell me. I can stop the car if you want to." Alex started to pull to the side of the road.

"No, keep going. I'll tell you. It's probably just me anyway."

Alex looked at her with brows raised, waiting for her to continue.

"After you left, I made sure everything was clean and I went upstairs to bed. I had trouble falling asleep. I was lying in bed when I heard a crash downstairs."

"Another crash?" Alex turned his head toward her. "Like a window?"

"It was glass, but when I checked downstairs, it turned out to be a whiskey glass. As a matter of fact, it was the exact tumbler you used last night."

"What?"

"And the whiskey bottle was in the middle of the kitchen counter."

"Impossible. I put the single malt away in the cabinet myself."

"I'm sure you did," Cassie said with a small smile.

"Anything else?" Alex asked as he turned a corner.

"There was that odor of hay and cigarette smoke again. I thought maybe there was a pet door that an animal was using."

Alex tilted his head and pinched his lips. "I know a lot of people who have pets that use their own doors, but I've yet to meet a pet that smokes and drinks whiskey."

Cassie nodded and started to chuckle. "I knew it sounded crazy."

"No, I think we need to talk about this." Alex crested a hill which brought the English Channel into full view. The water was a dark blue and the view was stunning.

"Where are we?" Cassie asked as she leaned forward. "It's breath-taking." She pointed out a Ferris wheel and other parts of the town.

"We're approaching Plymouth. This is the city from which the Mayflower finally set sail in 1620."

"This is so exciting."

"Plymouth is an interesting city," Alex said as he passed cobblestone roads. "There's a lot of shipping here as well as a great Aquarium and other things to do."

"It's wonderful," Cassie said as she twisted her head side to side.

"And they have plenty of bookshops," Alex said with a satisfied smile.

Cassie turned to him. "Wait a minute. You're taking me to a bookshop on the coast of England?"

"Yes, I am," Alex said with a big grin. "There's an event there today and, to be honest, the only reason I was able to get tickets is that my cousin owns the shop."

"Your family owns a bookshop along the coastline of the English Channel?"

"Bloody hell," Alex yelled as a woman stepped into the street. "People need to be more careful walking around here." He was able to find a parking space and checked his watch. "Come, we must hurry."

They got out of the car. Alex came around and grabbed her hand. They quickly walked toward a crowd forming ahead. "I want to get you inside before anyone else gets in."

Cassie was dying to ask what was happening but didn't want to disrupt their progress. As they approached, Alex waved to a man standing on the side of the building and he beckoned for them to come toward him. When they approached, he quickly opened the side door. "Good day, guv'nor." He nodded toward Cassie and directed them to a small kitchen inside the back of the store.

Alex turned to her and whispered, "Now would be the time to use the facilities or grab a drink if you need one."

"I'd love a cup of coffee. I didn't have time for breakfast this morning."

Alex grimaced. "Off you go to the powder room. Come right back. I'll arrange a drink."

Moments later, Cassie returned, and Alex directed her toward the main shop. Placing his hand at her back, he escorted her to a group of chairs and had her take a seat in the front. To her left was a small table. Cassie sat and moved over for Alex, but he declined. "I'll be on the side in case I get a phone call. Sit here, near the table, and I'll bring you something to eat."

Cassie turned toward the front and saw a large poster board advertising the event. There was a photo of the famous but reclusive author, Sir Charles Effingham. Cassie's jaw dropped as she grabbed Alex's arm. "Is Sir Charles Effingham going to be here?"

"Yes! That's my surprise and thank you for being so kind this week," Alex whispered into her ear. "Besides, you haven't had a proper introduction to England."

"No one gets an audience with Sir Effingham. He's famous."

"From what I understand, you're famous as well," Alex laughed.

"But nowhere near his level," Cassie said in awe. She turned and noted the room was beginning to fill.

"Well, he's here to talk about a new book and meet a very select group of people. By the way, my cousin was very excited to get the chance to meet you and would like to spend some time speaking to us when this event has ended."

"I'd love nothing better," Cassie said excitedly. "Thank you for this."

"You're most welcome," Alex said as the room started to hush. He slipped away and within a few moments, a woman stood at the front of the room. She made a short speech and then introduced the famous English author, Sir Charles Effingham. The crowd stood and applauded as the elderly writer silently appeared from behind a screen with a mischievous grin. He then stepped onto a small dais and sat in a blue, velvet covered, Crown Tiffany throne chair. Cassie joined the thunderous applause as Charles looked around the room.

Cassie turned when she felt someone at her side. Alex was there and whispered that he had placed coffee and a plate of scones on the table next to her. He wanted her to have something to drink and eat while Charles spoke. His look was stern as if he knew she would feel it was disrespectful. He nodded toward the plate and cup of coffee and held up his phone. Once everyone was quiet and seated, Cassie took the coffee and sipped as surreptitiously as she could. Realizing how hungry she was, she pulled small pieces off a delicious scone and ate while she listened.

Sir Charles Effingham spoke for a full hour about his lifelong career as a writer. He recounted the myriad of menial jobs he had as a youth and then, despite being tired, he would read and write at night. He usually hid his work in his bed or under his pillow. As he grew older, he was able to obtain some basic education and land a job with a magazine. His writing journey continued when he met a publisher while researching one of his articles. The publisher agreed to read his work and after many long years, he was a traditionally published novelist. His career continued to soar. He was honored with the title of Sir by the Queen of England for his creativity.

When he was done answering questions about his new book, he signed many copies. At last, Charles stood up, wished the crowd a good day and said he must rest. He was escorted off the dais and behind the screen.

Within seconds, Cassie felt Alex at her side. "Did you enjoy that?"

"Yes, so very much," Cassie said. "Now I feel inspired to go back to the cottage and write for a week."

Alex laughed. "I'm glad, but it's not over yet. Once the crowd clears out, you'll meet him face to face."

Cassie turned to Alex with a gleam in her eye. She didn't have time to respond when Sir Charles and his publicist came out from behind the screen. Sir Charles walked up to Cassie and Alex and extended his hand.

"Cassandra Ashcroft, I am honored to have you attend my talk today." Charles made a small bow and kissed her hand.

"Sir Charles, it is I who is greatly honored." Cassie stammered as she spoke.

Charles turned to Alex. "So, this is the famous, Alex Knight I keep hearing about." He chuckled and said, "Mostly from your cousin, I dare say."

Alex blushed with a flattered expression. "I'm sure that's the case, Sir Charles."

"No, really. I've heard great things about your career and I'm sure the Queen and I thank you."

Alex gave a slight bow of the head as Sir Charles turned to Cassie. "What brings you to England, my dear?"

Cassie felt her stomach tighten. "I'm here writing a novel, but also doing research for my publisher for a non-fiction book on the Wexley Police Department."

Sir Charles raised his eyebrows. "Well done. That sounds like a bit of a task. How are you getting on?"

"I've been here almost a month. It's been difficult for me to acclimatize but Alex has been a wonderful help with that."

"I'm sure he has," Charles said. "I've read some of your work and love it."

"Really?" Cassie asked with eyebrows raised.

"Yes, dear, I have." Sir Charles called his publicist over. "I'd like you to give Ms. Ashcroft your number, please."

"Of course, sir."

"And then, I would be most pleased if you would take a couple of photos of our group together."

Sir Charles turned to Cassie. "I hope you don't mind?"

"I would love it," Cassie said excitedly.

"Is it okay if they make the London papers? The press is very tenacious you know."

"Yes, that would be fine." Cassie's hands started to shake. Alex realized what was happening, grabbed her hand and squeezed it while they were positioned for the photos. He let go when they were each positioned on opposite sides of Sir Charles.

The publicist then took photos of Sir Charles and Cassie. When she was done, Sir Charles stepped back and once again bowed and kissed her hand. "I hope to have an advanced copy of your next novel, if you'd be so willing to indulge me."

"Of course," Cassie said with the largest smile she could muster.

"You can contact my publicist for an address and such."

"It would be an honor, sir."

"I must go, now. At my age, you can't get too excited."

They watched as Sir Charles took the hand of his publicist and left the room.

Cassie was so excited she turned toward Alex. They instinctively embraced, but then broke apart quickly when they saw someone watching them.

A man approached, who looked like Alex. "Cassie, this is my cousin, Thomas Knight. Owner of the Books by the Sea Bookshop."

"It's a pleasure to meet you, Ms. Ashcroft," Thomas said as he took her hand and covered it with his own.

"Thank you for allowing us to be here today," Cassie said. "I am beyond thrilled to meet you and see your shop."

"Once again, the honor is all mine," Thomas said with a smile. "I'm not so innocent, you know. I'm hoping you'll agree to a book signing before you return to America."

"I would love to do that," Cassie said. "It would be my absolute pleasure."

"Excellent," Thomas said. "I love it when we all work together."

Alex thrust his hand out. "Thanks again, Thomas. I think I need to take Cassie for a proper bite before she becomes peckish."

"You're welcome," Thomas said as he raised his eyebrows and slapped Alex on the side of the arm.

33

A lex took Cassie's hand and led her from the shop. "I'm a bit hungry myself."

"That was phenomenal," Cassie said effusively. "I wanted to see the culture and the coastline, but never in a million years did I expect to meet Sir Charles Effingham. And to have him say he wants my next book? I'll send him whatever he wants."

The pair continued down the street and passed the car. "Where are we going?" Cassie asked as she looked around.

"I'm taking you to one of the most popular pubs on the coast."

"Like Wexley?"

"Oh no," Alex laughed. "It's larger, more modern and has a dance floor and live music."

"Sounds lovely," Cassie said. She continued to hold Alex's hand and was amazed she felt so comfortable and safe being with him.

Alex looked at his watch. "It's already late afternoon on a Saturday. I hope there are open tables. It's quite a popular place."

Cassie nodded and took it all in. She would have loved to take photos with her cell phone, but she didn't dare impede their progress toward an early dinner.

"There is it," Alex said. Within minutes, they were standing in front of the Sea Treasure Pub. They waited behind a party of four and then were seated to the left in the main room. Cassie was amazed that a live band was setting up to play for the dinner crowd.

A young woman, dressed in a maritime uniform visited the table and asked if they were ready to order. Alex turned to Cassie. "Would you like something to drink?"

"Perhaps a glass of wine. I'm not a big drinker."

Alex turned back to the waitress. "Can you give us a moment. We'll order a bottle of wine with our dinner."

"Of course," she said as she gave him an appreciative smile and walked off.

Cassie looked down at her setting so he wouldn't see her grin.

"What would you like for dinner? Please order something you wouldn't normally have at the cottage. It is a day out after all. Once we know what we want, we can order the appropriate wine."

"Do you have any suggestions?" Cassie asked.

"Yes, there are many delicious items on the menu. Do you like seafood? How about steak?"

"Yes, to both," Cassie said with a shrug.

"Excellent. Do you mind if I order?"

"Not at all," Cassie said. "I would appreciate it."

When the waitress returned, Alex ordered fillet steak with garlic prawns and Caesar salad for both. He then picked out an appropriate wine.

"Excellent choice, sir," she said as she walked away with a trailing smile.

Cassie laughed when he turned to her. He genuinely didn't seem to notice the flirtatious efforts of the waitress. "What? Did I get it wrong?"

"No, not at all. The waitress seemed very happy to take your order."

"She's a young girl," he said, getting flustered.

"Old enough to work and old enough to flirt," Cassie said.

"Well, I don't need that type of bother, do I?" Alex asked pointedly.

After a slight pause, Cassie spoke. "Can I ask a candid question? Totally between you and me. Your answer has nothing to do with the research novel."

"I suppose, but I'll refuse to answer if I feel it's appropriate."

"Fair enough. You and your cousin are both good looking men, with some means and a bookshop in the family. I can't imagine you wouldn't be overwhelmed with attention from women. Why are either of you not married?"

"Perhaps I have frequent offers," Alex said with eyebrows raised.

"I am sure you do," Cassie said as she laughed. "With all due respect and honesty, I'm wondering why you aren't in a relationship."

"I'll answer your question truthfully if you answer mine."

Cassie turned red. "That's fair, but you answer first."

"I decided not to be in a relationship for a couple of reasons. One thing you may discover with your research is that it's difficult to maintain a relationship when you're on duty most of the time. There are many missed events and functions which creates dissatisfaction with a mate. The other reason is that having a relationship makes your loved one a target."

"Excuse me? Please explain," Cassie asked.

"Being in the police force does not make many friends when you make arrests for homicide. Occasionally, someone tries to get revenge. When I was a sergeant, I had a girlfriend and we planned to marry one day. I was working with my chief at the time, and we charged someone. To this day, I still believe he was guilty, but he wasn't convicted due to lack of evidence. He showed up at a fete that the police were attending with our families. He threatened myself and my chief, but he did it by grabbing my girlfriend and saying I would find her in pieces one day. That relationship didn't last. She took off. It's okay if they go after me, but I would never want a criminal to go after a loved one. I don't know if I could handle it if someone were hurt because of me. Since then, I purposely haven't been in a serious relationship for those reasons."

"But if that's the case, they could go after your cousin, or other family if you have any."

Cassie sat back when their salads arrived. They waited for the waitress to leave, picked up their forks and tasted the food.

"This is delicious," Cassie said. "I haven't had a Caesar salad like this in a long time."

"Yes, it is good, isn't it?"

"About your cousin?" Cassie a few minutes later.

Alex chuckled. "Are you interested?"

Cassie scowled and said, "Please go back to our discussion."

"I'm not worried about my cousin. You see, we were raised in such a way we can defend ourselves. Plus, there's a reason his shop sees a lot of dignitaries, so he has certain privileges as well, but that's another story completely."

They finished their salads, and their plates were retrieved. Meanwhile, they each received a fresh glass of wine.

"Okay, now you," Alex said with that intense interrogation whispered voice. "Why would an extremely attractive, best-selling, famous author not be married or in a relationship? Please tell me what I'm missing here."

Cassie looked at the table and then up at Alex with a shrug.

He peered at her. "Or are you married and not telling me or anyone else. Perhaps you're on a break or something?"

Cassie sipped her wine. "I have trust issues."

"Please explain," Alex said as he gestured for her to continue.

Cassie swallowed and nodded her head. "Before I was a full-time writer, I worked in medicine, in a hospital. That's where I met Evie, my literary agent. Anyway, I was engaged to one of the residents. We also had a very hectic, barely see you, type of schedule so I can certainly understand what you mean there." She paused and sipped her wine. "We celebrated when we could. We loved to dance and hike. When you're in a profession that constantly sees life slip away, you celebrate things like that whenever you can." Another sip of wine. "Our wedding weekend arrived, and we had bartered to have the whole week off. For at least one week, we would be completely together. Nothing was going to get in our way." Cassie paused and picked up her wineglass again. The band played slow jazz as the dinner guests placed their orders.

"Except?" Alex prompted her but felt bad when he saw how emotional she got.

"He was killed by a drunk driver on his way to our wedding rehearsal. It's funny really, except it's not. I was at the rehearsal hall with a roomful of doctors waiting for him. He didn't show up and we didn't find out what had happened until it was too late. He was gone."

Alex immediately reached out and placed his hand over hers. "I am truly sorry."

"Thanks, I'm okay. It's been years. Anyway, Evie was starting to place my books and I threw myself into my writing. As I did, I became more popular and prosperous. The problem was that most of the men who wanted to befriend me were looking for something I wouldn't provide. I like to stay under the radar, and I am not one to flaunt money or fame. I don't like to be shown off to friends or treated like arm candy. I am suspicious of most relationships, so I have trust issues with most people I meet."

Alex nodded. "I understand that and how it feels when someone befriends you to buy favor."

"You understand why I didn't explain all this to Arlene when I was accosted in the police station." Cassie laughed. "I tried to tell her that I was not in England to meet someone or start a relationship. I simply want to write my book. I don't think she believed me."

Alex took a sip of wine. "Duly noted. No relationships. And I agree that Arlene is rather a pain and an intrusive person." Alex turned when the waitstaff showed up at the table carrying dishes. "Our dinner is here."

"It smells divine," Cassie said as she leaned back so she could be served. The pair listened to the music as they ate their dinner. Cassie realized this was the first time she had talked about her feelings so openly to a relative stranger. He must be excellent at interrogation.

The dinner was delightful, and they both finished their plates. "I haven't had a meal like that in ages," Cassie said. "The food was delicious."

"I'm glad you're pleased," Alex said with genuine feeling.

They listened to pleasant melodies from oldies to beach tunes. "This band is good," Cassie said as she finished her wine.

Alex turned to her. "This may sound unexpected, but would you dance with me?"

"What? I haven't danced in years."

"Is that what your fiancé would have wanted?"

Cassie didn't answer as she looked at Alex, so he continued. "I haven't danced in quite a long time myself. You can't ask a woman to go dancing and tell her you're not interested in a relationship, but since we've covered that already, would you dance with me? Just two friends blowing off steam."

He offered his hand to her and stood up. Cassie took his hand and stood as well.

Alex led her to the dance floor. The band was playing a few slow songs so the dinner guests could ease into working off their food. After a few moments of flitting into the proper position, they began to move to the music. It took the entire first song for Cassie to relax and become one with Alex as a partner.

During the second song, he said, "You dance very well."

"And you." She had to admit to herself that they moved as if they had been dancing together for years. She thought she would never dance again much less be in the arms of an attractive man. What was she thinking?

The next song started. It was a popular tune by Kenny Chesney about a specific place in the British Virgin Islands. The pair had danced quietly for the first two tunes as they each gathered their thoughts. Halfway through the song, Alex leaned his head back and whispered, "Have you ever been there?"

Cassie looked up at him. "Where?"

His face was mere inches from hers. "Jost Van Dyke. The island in the song. I thought you might have visited that part of the Caribbean since it's near the Florida Keys."

Cassie stared at his eyes and quietly answered, "No, I haven't traveled anywhere in a very long time."

She placed her head back on his shoulder and heard his whisper, "Neither have I."

Cassie tried to stay in the moment, concentrating only on what was happening around her. She didn't know if it was the wine, or their emotional chat but she was acutely aware of Alex's broad shoulders, his strong arms around her waist and her back, the clean scent of his Creed Green Irish Tweed Cologne, his warmth through his suit, and their bodies swaying together. His very being encompassed her entire sense of self and she felt swept away. Her heart rate increased, and her breath became ragged. She desperately tried to distract herself by focusing on her breathing, counting the breaths as she held tight.

After what seemed like an eternity, the song ended, and the band announced it would be on break. He hugged her a bit tighter and whispered into her hair, "Thank you."

34

Fifteen minutes later, the bill had been paid and they were in the car on their way back to Wexley. They were quiet in the car for the initial part of the ride, neither willing to break the small moment of escapism they had shared. Halfway home, Alex cleared his throat. "I hate to bring this up, but I was wondering if you could go over what happened last night with me before we get to the cottage?"

Cassie's phone chirped. She looked down at the text to see a message from Evie.

Everything okay? Do I need to call the police?

Cassie quickly texted back.

All good. Need to talk later. A lot has happened. Still with AK.

Evie answered her right away.

I'll be waiting!

Cassie looked at Alex. "I'm sorry. That was Evie checking in on me. She wants to touch base when I'm free. I called her after I went downstairs last night."

"I wish you had called me, but I'm glad you got in touch with someone. I'd like to go over it again before we get to the cottage if you please?"

"All right, I went downstairs last night and cleaned the broken glass and whiskey. As I said, everything was perfectly washed and put away before I went up to bed. I was trying to fall asleep when I heard a crash, and it sounded like glass. I was worried someone broke a window and got into the cottage."

"What did you do?" Alex asked with eyebrows raised.

"I waited and listened for a while, then grabbed my heavy fireplace poker and crept downstairs. I turned on every light I could find. The doors and windows were secure, but on the floor, near the kitchen counter, was a broken whiskey tumbler and the bottle of single malt was on the counter.

"I put that bottle in the cabinet myself before I left last night."

"I know," Cassie said. "I checked to make sure everything was cleaned up."

"You said something about cigarettes?"

"Yes, the last two times this has happened," Cassie was unable to finish her sentence.

"The last two times? How often does this go on?"

"It's happened several times since I've arrived. The first time there was a distinct smell of wet hay. I think I told you about it. Anyway, the last two times there was the smell of cigarette smoke and hay. But last night, I found a clump of muddy hay in the kitchen near the pantry. I swept up the glass but didn't touch the hay. I thought I would show you or take a photo of it or something."

"Next time, if there is one, can you promise to call me? Day or night, just call, please."

"Yes, I will," Cassie said and then started to laugh.

"What's so funny?"

"I asked you about William Blake. I wanted to know whether he smoked in case it was his ghost coming back. I asked about the pet door thinking there may have been a pet that's still alive and looking for its master."

"I can see a cat knocking a glass off a counter but not pulling the blasted whiskey bottle out of the cabinet."

"That would be some cat."

"No, something else is odd about this house. There always has been but I've not been able to figure it out. I'll be bringing the case file to you this week so we can discuss it as long as none of this information winds up in any book."

"I promised, didn't I?"

"Yes, you did, and I trust you on that."

Cassie continued to watch the scenery go by. Although it was early evening, the sun wouldn't set until later. As they approached the village, Alex slowed down to go through the lane. In addition to having a great day with Cassie, he realized he hadn't taken any time for himself in quite a while.

He pulled into the drive near the cottage, turned off the ignition and turned to Cassie. "Would you mind very much if I went into the cottage first?"

"No, of course not. Do you think there's any danger?"

"I doubt it but let me check. Please stay at the door until I have a look around."

"Okay," Cassie said as she handed her keys to Alex.

They got out of the car and walked to the front door. Alex looked through the windows and when he didn't see anything out of the ordinary, he unlocked the door and crossed the threshold. Cassie stayed back at the front door but was able to watch Alex walk through the rooms of the cottage on the first floor. Alex checked each room as well as the liquor cabinet. He then walked around the kitchen counter and squatted next to the muddy hay. He stood, found a piece of blank paper in the library where Cassie worked and went back to the hay and scooped it onto the paper.

Cassie gingerly walked into the front parlor and watched Alex. He turned to her. "Everything seems to be in order. I found your muddy hay and I'll have it analyzed to see if there's anything distinctive, we can identify."

"Great."

Alex went back to the liquor cabinet and pulled out the single malt between his thumb and forefinger.

"Would you like a drink?" Cassie asked. "I don't think that's a good idea."

"No, but I'd like to take this bottle with me if that's okay." He held up the bottle. "This is the one that was on the counter?"

"Sure, help yourself," Cassie asked with a grin. "You're not going to drink and drive, are you?"

"Actually, I was going to check for fingerprints to see if there are any other than yours and mine on the bottle."

"Great idea," Cassie said. "I'm glad you're taking the bottle. I was going to dump it out in case someone put poison in there."

"Such a waste of good whiskey."

Cassie took a paper bag out of a drawer and brought it to Alex. "Here, you can place it in here. Just don't let an officer catch you with an open bottle of whiskey in your car," Cassie laughed.

"Good advice," he said with a nod as he brought the bag to the front door and placed it on the entryway table. He turned back to her with a smile. "Cassie, will you take me to your bedroom?"

Cassie whirled toward him. "Excuse me?"

He laughed. "Don't look so anxious. I'd like to see what locks you have on your door."

Cassie turned red and laughed nervously. "Oh, sure. Of course.

Follow me." She rushed by him and hurried upstairs, feeling very embarrassed.

He followed her up the stairs and turned at the newel post. There were several bedrooms on the upstairs floor. Cassie walked a few feet down the hall and stopped at one of the bedroom doors.

"I don't know which one Mr. Blake slept in, but this is the bedroom I am currently using."

Alex took a moment to look at the door of her bedroom as well as the others. He came back to her and checked the door frame as well. "The doors are old, and the frame is brittle. As far as I'm concerned, the lock is non-existent. What did you do last night?"

"I closed the door and pushed a piece of furniture in front of it."

"That was good thinking," Alex said as he continued to examine the door. "Is there a bathroom in your room?"

"Yes, this way." She led him into the room, silently cheering that the room was clean and presentable. No wash on the floor, everything in its place. The bathroom was orderly as well.

Alex took a few minutes to examine the bathroom door as well as the window. "The window is okay, but we're on the second floor."

"Do you mind if I ask what we're looking for?"

Alex nodded. "Of course. Why don't we go back downstairs and talk about it?"

They went back to the kitchen and took a seat at the dining room table. "Alex, would you like some tea?"

"That would be lovely. Yes, I would."

Cassie took a few minutes to make tea. She placed cups, milk, sugar, dessert plates and cake on the table.

"This looks delicious," Alex said.

"Thank you. I made the cake myself. I hope you like it." Cassie said with a shrug. She brought the teapot to the table, poured two cups of tea, and sat down. "Okay, so what are your thoughts."

"I'm not happy with what I'm seeing, but I can't identify a threat as of this moment. My mother had anxiety like yours. You're a rock in the moment but get nervous before or after the fact."

"Thank you, I think."

"Would you ever consider moving to another location?"

Cassie was silent at first but then shook her head. "Not if there wasn't a direct threat."

"That's what I thought you would say, so then the next step is to help ensure your safety. The locks on the doors upstairs are atrocious and if you wouldn't mind, I'd like to come back tomorrow and install new locks on your bedroom and bathroom door. If someone did break in, you can buy some time by locking the bedroom door, blocking it with furniture, then going into the bathroom. Lock that door and if you must leave the house, use the window. Although we need to put something soft outside the window for you to land on."

"Do you think all that's necessary?"

"It could be. I don't know. Please call or text me as soon as you hear anything strange next time. I can come by immediately. You stay locked in your bedroom until I check things out. In the meantime, I'm going to have the hay and bottle analyzed for anything we can use. Waste of good whiskey."

Cassie laughed. "I'll try to restock something for you, don't worry."

"May I come over tomorrow? I know it's Sunday. I'm not sure if you have any special plans."

"I need to catch up on my writing so nothing special. New locks would be fine if you think I'd be safer. I have an extra key to the front door I can give you. I'm trusting that you're not a crazy person."

Alex leaned toward her. "You never know, do you?"

"Perhaps I should rethink that key."

Alex placed his hand over hers. "I'm only kidding. But I would feel better if you were safe or had a place you could hide in an emergency."

"Okay then tomorrow it is. Are you sure that's convenient for you?"

"Tomorrow would be the best day for me," Alex said. "Monday's schedule is busy already."

"Tomorrow it is then."

"Great, I'll come around noon. You said you didn't sleep last night, and it's been a busy but fun day. I'm glad we got to go out and let off some steam."

"So am I," Cassie said. "Thank you for bringing me to the coast. It was exactly what I was looking for and I'm glad we were able to go together. I can't say enough about meeting Sir Charles. That was exciting."

"I'm glad," Alex said as he finished his tea and stood. "Let me help you with the dishes."

"I've got this. Please don't worry yourself." Cassie waved him off.

"Are you sure?"

"Absolutely. I'll see you tomorrow."

They walked to the door together. "I'm not leaving until I hear the door lock. Please keep it locked and call me if there's any trouble. Any at all," Alex emphasized as he looked at her with that intense gaze.

"I will," Cassie said as she stood with him at the open door.

There was an awkward moment when Alex turned to leave. He gave her a quick hug and stood outside pointing at the door.

Cassie nodded, "Goodnight Alex." She closed the door and locked it.

She watched through the window until Alex got in his car and drove away.

Cassie went back to the table and started clearing their cups and dishes when her phone rang. She reached over and picked it up. "Hello?"

"Is everything all right?"

"Evie, I was going to call you. Alex just left."

"Oh? Something you want to tell me?"

"Yes, I had an exciting day, but it's not what you're thinking."

"Okay then, let me get my drink and sit down. I was getting ready to call the police."

"Thanks for checking on me," Cassie said as she placed the dishes in the sink then sat and waited for Evie. After some background noise, Evie came back on the line.

"Okay, so spill. What happened today?"

"You'll never believe who I met today?"

"The Royal Family?"

Cassie laughed. "I wish, but no."

"Just tell me, already," Evie said as she sipped her drink.

"Alex took me to a private event at a bookshop by the sea, the English Channel to be exact."

"Really? And you haven't married him yet?"

"Stop, Evie. No relationships. We discussed that today."

"One day, Cassie. One day. Anyway, who was there?"

"Are you ready? Sir Charles Effingham spoke about his new book."

Evie sat up straight, spilling some of her drink on her chest. "What?"

"You heard me. I was in shock."

"Start from the beginning. Tell me all about this."

"Alex said he wanted to surprise me and thank me for dinner this week, so he got tickets to this event."

"Wait, back up. You had dinner this week?"

"No, we didn't go out to dinner."

"You're losing me," Evie said as she shook her head.

"Alex came by the cottage several times this week to discuss the research. He sent paperwork which we discussed in detail so I can decide what to include for the publisher. Anyway, he couldn't get here until after work and I was sitting to eat so I fed him as well. It was relaxed, friendly and very casual. He's a nice man, Evie."

"Oh, really? How nice?"

"He's very polite and very respectful. I've heard he's polite to the suspects he interrogates, but everyone loves him. I can't explain it, but when he enters a room, there's a sense that a pleasant but very strong authority has arrived. From what I'm told, even some of the suspects come to attention. He's electric and fills the room as soon as he arrives."

"This is all very interesting. I wonder what his background is," Evie said musing to herself. "I'll have to investigate that myself. Anyway, go on."

Cassie rolled her eyes. "Evie, listen to me. He trusts me. Do you hear me? Because I promised not to reveal certain things, he trusts me to go over the process but not specific info. Please don't do anything to compromise that for the sake of the publishing company."

"Oh, you're defending him too?"

"Evie! He's been my nicest friend since I've arrived."

Evie nodded her head, glad that Cassie couldn't see her. "Okay, so go on with the rest of the day. What happened?"

"He didn't tell me where we were going until we got there but he brought me to Plymouth, UK. The bookshop there, Books by the Sea, is owned by his cousin."

"Interesting," Evie said as she listened. Cassie could hear her taking notes in her head.

"They snuck me into the shop through a side door, sat me down right in front, and out walked Sir Charles Effingham. His talk was amazing, but the best part is afterward I had a private meet and greet. He wanted to meet me. Did you hear that? He wanted to meet me. He said he was aware of my books. I'm dying!"

"Are you serious?" Evie said loudly.

"Yes, and he had his publicist take photos of us together."

"Oh my, do you know what this could mean for your career? Did you tell them to take one on your phone?"

"No, honestly, I was afraid it would be intrusive, but I have the publicist's phone number. Sir Charles said I was to call her with my next book, and he wanted me to have a copy of his book. He also offered to help with anything while I'm in England."

"My mouth is hanging open right now and, honey, that does not happen often."

"I know, right?"

"And Alex Knight arranged all this?"

"Yes, and then we enjoyed dinner and dancing nearby."

"Is this Cassandra Ashcroft I'm speaking to?"

"Yes, Evie, it's me."

"I swore you just said, dancing?" Evie asked as she tipped her head.

"Yes, he asked if I would dance with him. Let me tell you, he's a good dancer. We had a conversation about why neither of us were in a relationship. We agreed that there was no relationship date pressure and had a great time."

"I am absolutely intrigued. What kind of music? Is he a *Tea for Two* type of guy?"

Cassie laughed at her suggestion. "I know from everything you hear; you would think that. The music was a wonderful mix of favorites. We did a couple of slow dances."

"And how did that feel? You haven't danced since you lost your fiancé."

Cassie paused for a long moment. "You know, Evie, it felt very nice. Like I'm opening a bit. I had some anxiety, but I feel completely safe with Alex. I know my old therapist said I must feel comfortable with life and not individuals but it's a start. I'm trying Evie."

"I couldn't be any happier for you, darling. Seriously."

"He's had experience with someone because he can tell when I'm starting to spiral. The night I met him at the Chief Constable's event, I was having a panic attack in the hall, and he was the one who rescued me then. I don't know how to explain it. He understands so I feel safe with him, and it doesn't happen as often. He did mention his mother having anxiety. I guess he thinks I'm like his mother. Just my luck," Cassandra laughed.

"Speaking of safe, what were his thoughts about the whole business last night?"

"He examined the doors, the windows and took the whiskey bottle as well as the muddy hay in for analysis. By the way, I need more single malt."

"I will have that sent out tomorrow. I'll send several bottles and a variety as a way of showing my gratitude for his care."

"Thank you, Evie. Anyway, he's putting new locks on my doors tomorrow. He said he'll let me know if they find fingerprints but honestly, I get the feeling he won't tell me until he's had a chance to track down and interrogate someone. He acts like my protector at times. I also got some great ideas for my novel today. A winner of a day. The best since I've come to England."

"I am no less than thrilled that this is working out so well." Evie frowned to herself about the fact that Cassie felt she needed someone to protect her. She had been assured that cottage was safe, remote, and quiet.

"I'm sure I won't see him as much, once the research is done, but it was a nice day and one I'll always remember."

"That's great, honey." Evie's ice cubes clinked as she finished her drink. "You must be tired, so I'll let you go. Are you sure you feel safe right now?"

"Yes, I do and I'm sure I'll sleep tonight."

"Great, if anything happens you call me instantly. If you don't mind, I think I'm going to check in a bit more often. It seems there's more going on than simple writing."

"I would like that, Evie."

"I'm coming to London in a couple of weeks, so I'll be seeing you in person soon."

"That would be great."

"Sleep tight, Cassie. Be safe."

"I will. Goodnight Evie, and thank you."

"Love you," Evie said as she disconnected the call. She got up from her chair and poured herself another drink. She wondered if she should call someone about Cassie. She hadn't worried up until now. Evie never expressed her feelings, but Cassie had always felt like the daughter she never had. Ever since Cassie nursed her back to health from her near-death experience, Evie had sworn to stay by her side when needed. Later, when Cassie's fiancé died and her world crashed, Evie's only way of keeping Cassie from going mad was to encourage her writing and promoting it the best she could. Cassie had really done all the work, but Evie had been able to protect her from getting hurt up to now. She didn't want to see everything come crashing down.

35

Cassie checked to make sure everything was put away and went upstairs. She couldn't bring herself to turn the lights off. Maybe tomorrow when the new locks were added. After she changed into her night clothes, she slid furniture in front of the door and went to bed. At first, she listened for sounds and foreign noises but eventually drifted off into a peaceful night of sleep.

The next morning, she awoke feeling calm and rested. She showered and dressed for the day, taking extra care as she knew Alex was coming over. As she sipped her morning coffee, she took a moment to review her writing goals as well as what she planned to cook.

Cassie started in the kitchen and decided to cook roast beef and soup for the day. She spent the first hour pulling out ingredients, chopping, blending, and putting her soup on to cook.

She opened her laptop to write several pages when she looked out the window and saw Alex's car pulling up to the cottage. She left her writing desk and opened the front door.

Alex parked the car and stepped out. He was dressed in crisp button-down shirt and slacks. It was the first time she saw him without a proper jacket and tie, yet he still seemed impeccably dressed and smelled great.

"Good morning," Alex said with a smile as he went around and opened the trunk of his car. He removed a few tools and bags and walked toward the cottage. He lifted his hands. "I've got everything we need right here."

"Great," Cassie said as she backed away so he could get inside the cottage. "I feel bad taking up your Sunday."

"Not at all. I'm having a great weekend. It's good to do something different occasionally."

"Is there anything you need, or can I do anything to help? Would you like a cup of tea or coffee? Don't mind me. I'm babbling."

Alex laughed. "A good strong cuppa would be great. I'd like to go straight to work so I can finish quickly."

"Okay, I'll start there. Let me know if you need me to help you with anything."

"I'll be fine," Alex called back as he started up the stairs.

Cassie checked her soup and put on the roast. She congratulated herself for making sure her room and bathroom were spotless before she went downstairs that morning. Ten minutes later, she climbed the stairs with a tray laden with tea, milk, sugar, spoons, and a small plate of cookies.

"How's it going?" Cassie put the tray on a nearby table. "I'm not sure what you've planned but I've brought your tea if you'd like to take a small break."

Alex stood and turned to her with a smile. "I'm trying to put a new lock on your door which was accomplished but the frame is weak so I'm having trouble with the deadbolt and the strike plate. You don't normally have a dead bolt on an inside door, but it will provide a little extra protection for you if someone comes into the house." Alex picked up his tea, took a sip and examined the door frame again.

"Oh," Cassie said, not sure if she felt well protected or if she was crazy for not running out of the cottage for good. She also picked up her tea.

"This is very good, very good indeed," Alex said as he sipped the tea. "You're getting used to preparing tea, British style."

Cassie laughed. "I learn something every day."

"How did you sleep last night? Any noises or problems."

"No, I didn't hear anything. I may have been a bit nervous at first, but I put the furniture in front of my door again. To be honest, I was a bit exhausted from the long day, so I feel asleep quickly."

"Good, I'm glad although I'll feel better once we put all this business to rest."

"Me too," Cassie said as she finished the last of the tea.

"I didn't realize you had such a lovely view from this window. You can see the English Channel in the distance, right there." He pointed as he looked outside.

"Yes, it is lovely, isn't it?" Cassie stood beside him at the window and although they weren't touching, she could feel a current of electricity between them. She took a deep breath, broke away and collected the cups.

"I'll bring these to the kitchen. Is there anything I can do to help?"

"No, I need a different tool. I'll have to go to my car." Alex reached over and took the tray from her hands. "Please, let me take that downstairs for you."

Cassie nodded and started down the staircase before him. They walked into the kitchen where Alex placed the tray on the counter.

"Thank you," she said as she pulled the cups off the tray and placed them in the sink.

"No bother at all. It was very good," Alex said as he turned and headed for the front door. "I'll be back in a moment."

Alex went to his car, opened the trunk, and rummaged in a neat box of tools. He heard a car and looked up to see a sedan pulling to the side of the drive. Alex watched the driver's side window open and saw Miles and Olivia looking out at him.

"Is everything all right, sir?" Miles asked with genuine concern.

"Yes, I'm trying to add extra security on Cassie's door upstairs. I'm certain she had an intruder in the house the night before last, while she was there, but I don't want to alarm her. What are you two up to? Any problems today?"

"No sir. We're following some thoughts with the current investigations, but it's been quiet," Miles said with a smile.

"Then how about you come in and give me a hand with this upstairs door? You have time?"

Miles looked at Olivia and raised his eyebrows before he turned back to Alex. "Yes, of course, sir."

He turned off the car and Miles and Olivia stepped out as Cassie popped out the front door. "I thought I heard voices. I wasn't sure what happened."

"Look who I found outside," Alex said. "Miles is going to give me a hand upstairs, okay?"

"Sure," Cassie said with an awkward shrug. She smiled at Olivia. "How are you?"

"Very well, ma'am."

"Please call me Cassie. I don't think I'm that old, yet." She laughed as Olivia kept a straight face. The group moved into the cottage.

"We'll be down in a bit," Alex said as he grabbed Miles and pulled him toward the stairs. When they were out of sight, Alex whispered in Miles's ear. "After we're done, take a quick look around and see if you find any back passageways or anything strange."

"Will do, sir," Miles said with a nod.

Cassie and Olivia watched until they were out of sight from the foyer. Cassie felt tongue-tied and awkward with Olivia. She breathed a sigh of relief when Olivia's cell phone rang.

"Excuse me, I need to take this," Olivia said as she held up her phone.

"Of course." Cassie went back to the kitchen counter. Her soup was done, and the roast would be perfect in fifteen minutes. Not knowing what else to do, she pulled plates, bowls, utensils, and cups from the cupboard and placed them on the end of the counter. She had enough food to feed an army. At least, she could provide a meal to thank them for spending their Sunday worrying about her safety.

Olivia walked back into the cottage holding her phone to her chest. "Excuse me, ma'am. Do you know these two people? They were outside looking in the window."

"Simon, Laura," Cassie said as she rushed over to them. "It's so great to see you. I didn't know you were coming." Olivia nodded and went back outside to continue her call.

"Evie's strict orders to get out here. She had me pick up groceries and things for you as well," Simon said as he looked around. "What's going on? Why is everyone here?"

Cassie leaned over to the pair and whispered. "They are upstairs working on some extra security for me. There have been some strange happenings around here."

"Good then. I feel better if you're protected," Simon said as he took Laura's hand. "Let's get the bags from the car."

Cassie smiled as she watched them go out the door together. She added two more plates to the counter. She hadn't been with this much company on a Sunday since she was a young girl visiting her Gram's house for dinner, but it felt very nice.

Simon and Laura walked into the cottage with several bags filled with fresh groceries and Cassie's favorite foods. Simon ran back out to the car and returned carrying a large cardboard box filled with liquor. Evie gave me strict instructions on multiple bottles and brands of single malt as well as some wines and beer."

Cassie shook her head and laughed as he placed each bottle on the counter. "Yes, it has turned out to be an important commodity around here."

Laura gave her a nice hug and unpacked the groceries as Olivia walked into the cottage and Alex and Miles returned from the upper level.

"Oh my, we now have a party," Alex said as he looked at the activity.

Cassie caught everyone's attention. "Yes, and dinner is ready to be served. I'd love for us all to eat together if you're able to stay?"

"Is it okay with you, sir?" Miles asked with a hopeful look. Anything was better than the stale sandwiches at the station.

"As long as you don't have anything to attend to," Alex said with a shrug. "This is quite a surprise."

"I've put plates, bowls, and utensils on the counter. Why don't you serve yourself and then take a seat at the table. There's Broccoli Cheddar Beer Soup with a beef roast, mashed potatoes, and vegetables."

Miles was excited. "The food smells delicious." He grabbed a plate and bowl and started off the buffet line. He carried his food to the table and sat down while the others gathered near the food.

"Evie had me bring some other items too. Where do you want them?" Simon asked as he held up a paper bag.

"If they don't require refrigeration, then please put them over there and come eat. We'll go through the bag later."

Simon did as he was requested. After a few minutes, everyone was seated at the table with a delicious dinner before them. "Does anyone want wine with dinner?"

"Not while they're on duty," Alex said looking at his detective sergeants with a stern nod. The table laughed.

Cassie offered wine to Simon. "No thanks. I have to drive back to London this afternoon.

Cassie nervously clinked her glass. "If I can have your attention for just a second."

All eyes were on her. "I want to thank you all for helping me get adjusted to England. You've all helped me in a special way. This is the best Sunday dinner I've had in a very long time."

The group cheered when they heard Cassie's words.

"Thursday night should be a lot of fun, too," Miles said as she smiled at her.

"Thursday? What's happening on Thursday?"

"Didn't anyone invite you yet?" Miles asked. "They're having a small party for you at the pub, so everyone gets to know you while you do their interviews the next couple of weeks."

Cassie looked at Alex. "Did you know about this?"

Alex shrugged. "No, they don't routinely consult me on things of this nature."

"I think Arlene set it up," Olivia added. "I'm sure she meant to tell you."

"I'm sure she did," Cassie said as she looked at Alex over her teacup. "Do you think you could check for more information?"

"Of course, I'll let you know what I hear," Alex said as he smiled at Cassie. He missed the questioning glance between Miles and Olivia.

Cassie's cell phone began to ring. She looked at the number ID. "It's Evie. I'll get back to her in a bit." The phone stopped ringing.

"I think she'll call back and you'll want to pick it up," Simon said excitedly.

Cassie shot him a questioning glance as her phone rang again. She picked it up. "Evie?"

"Are you with Simon and Laura?"

"Yes, they're here," Cassie said.

"Then put the phone on speaker, please."

"Evie, I also have Alex Knight and his two sergeants here as well. We're at the table."

"That's fine as long as everything is okay."

"Yes, we were having a little dinner."

"Even better. Put me on speaker, please."

"Okay," Cassie said as she put the phone on the table and hit the speaker button. "Everyone can hear us."

"Simon, did you get them?" Evie asked excitedly.

"Yes, I did."

"We got as many as we could," Laura added.

"Fantastic. Bring them to the table. Hello to Alex Knight. My name is Evie and I'm Cassie's literary agent and friend."

Alex looked at Cassie. "Hello, Evie. So nice to make your acquaintance."

"You, as well. Cassie has told me so much about you."

"Has she now?" Alex asked, a playful grin on his face.

Cassie immediately frowned in her teacup.

Simon handed Alex and Cassie several newspapers. "I'm thrilled to tell you two that you made the society page of all the London newspapers. Well done."

Cassie's face registered shock. "What? What are you saying, Evie?"

"Open the papers and look. The entire publishing company is buzzing about you two."

Alex frowned and opened his paper as Cassie did the same with hers. The others crowded around to get a look as well.

"Oh my," Alex said while Cassie still turned pages, her hands starting to shake.

"What is it?" Cassie asked.

Alex quickly read through and started to chuckle at what he read. "I hope this is good news. Otherwise, I'll have to apologize and seek revenge. That would be awkward considering the people involved."

Laura reached over and helped Cassie open the proper page of the newspaper. There she saw several photos. The main photo was of her and Sir Charles Effingham with his arm around her shoulders. He was quoted as saying how much he enjoyed meeting Cassandra Ashcroft and was eagerly looking forward to her next novel. The article then went on to recount his appearance and his talk about his new book. There was mention of the Books by the Sea Bookshop and Alex's cousin, Thomas Knight. There were several more photos. One was of Sir Charles, Cassie, Alex, and Thomas. One was of Sir Charles sitting on his throne chair during his speech."

"Cassie, are you there? What do you think?"

"I think I'm speechless at the moment," Cassie murmured.

Simon and Laura hugged her about the shoulders.

"Your sales have grown already as well as requests for interviews in America and abroad. Don't be nervous but please do be careful of any requests that come to you directly. Let us handle it, please."

"Of course," Cassie said in a small voice. Evie understood that this type of publicity made Cassie want to hide under her bed. It clearly made it difficult to stay under the radar and write.

"Alex, I owe you a dinner and a drink. I'll be in London in a couple of weeks, and I hope to meet you then."

"That would be lovely," Alex said with a nod to the phone.

Miles and Olivia glanced at each other again, now understanding where their boss was the day before. Although they had worked with him for years, this was the first time they had a peek into his private life.

Evie spoke again. "Please go back to your dinner. I'm sorry for having interrupted you but I thought you should hear it from me instead of seeing it online for the first time. It is being posted all over."

"Yes, of course. Thank you, Evie, and thank you for all the things you sent today," Cassie said quietly.

"You are most welcome, my dear. Have a great day and week everyone. See you soon." Evie hung up and Cassie's cell went silent.

"I'm sorry about all the excitement," Cassie said as she stood up and retrieved a chocolate cake from the counter. "If I can have your dinner plates, please help yourself to dessert." Alex was the only one who noticed Cassie's hands were shaking.

Simon and Laura helped to clear the table and serve the cake. Tea and coffee were available and after a short while, the guests all got up to leave.

"Do you want me to stay and help with the dishes?" Laura asked as she smiled at Cassie.

"Absolutely not," Cassie said. "I want you and Simon to go back to London. It's a bit of a ride."

"Are you sure?" Simon asked.

"Of course. I like doing dishes. It gives me time to think."

"Okay then."

Sunday dinner was complete, and the group moved toward the door. When Miles opened the door, he noticed a group of villagers standing in the lane outside of Cassie's cottage. "Hello, what's this all about?"

Mrs. Peabody, James, Mrs. Witherspoon, and the vicar were standing there as well as some other villagers.

"Who are these people?" Cassie asked.

"You know most of them," Alex whispered. "That bloke over there is Granger Lowell. He's a farmer who helped William Blake with his livestock and crops. Next to him is Wyatt Smith. He worked with Granger and Mr. Blake." Alex discreetly pointed to another woman.

"Over there is Shelly Tolbert. She works in the pub. I'll tell you the other names, later."

Miles walked toward the group. "Can I help you?"

"We saw all the cars. We were worried there was a death or some-thing worse," the vicar, Mr. Witherspoon, said as the chosen spokesperson.

Cassie muffled a sigh. He was right. Being the center of attention was probably worse than death for her.

"No, no, everything is fine. We were having a small planning event for the research for Ms. Ashcroft's book. Everyone is healthy. You can be assured and move on." Miles waved to everyone outside including Cassie and Alex. They all waved as they got into their cars and left.

Cassie gave Laura and Simon an extra hug and kiss. "Be safe, you two."

When the villagers walked away, Cassie and Alex went back inside.

They walked to the table and in a subdued silence, cleared every-thing to the counter. Cassie started running water in the sink while Alex pulled out two glasses. After looking at the bottles of single malt, he finally chose one, opened it and poured himself two fingers. He then took out the brandy and poured a small amount for Cassie.

He walked to the table, pulled out a chair and guided Cassie to sit. He handed her the brandy and then took the chair next to her. "I owe you an apology. I wanted to thank you and instead I've created a bit of a mess this weekend."

Cassie sipped her brandy and shook her head. "No, not at all. I loved seeing Sir Charles and I would never give that back or dinner. I enjoyed having everyone here for dinner today. This was the best weekend I've had since coming to England. I don't like a lot of unex-pected commotion coming at me all at once. Everything was fine until Evie called."

Alex nodded. "My mum had anxiety."

Cassie laughed. "I can tell you recognize what's happening."

"Yes, it's okay. I know it can feel overwhelming at times."

"Quite frankly, I had an amazing weekend. It's been too long since

I allowed myself to relax. Thank you for helping me with that." They both sipped their drink. "That's one of the reasons I love to go to the sea. When I feel overwhelmed, I visit the ocean and the power of the water reminds me that everything is okay."

Alex nodded. "If you don't mind, I'd like to stick around for a little while. After the dishes, I'd like to look around the library, but I don't want to be a nuisance if it will impact your writing or schedule."

"I'm fine doing the dishes by myself. Please be comfortable and help yourself."

"And I'm afraid I'm going to have to ask you to take me to your bedroom once again."

Cassie looked at him with shielded eyes before he went on. "I need to show you how the new locks work."

Cassie smiled and put down her brandy. "Let's go."

They went upstairs and Alex demonstrated the new lock and deadbolt for her bedroom as well as the bathroom. "If you hear someone at the door, make sure the deadbolt is thrown. Run into the bathroom, throw that one as well and call me. I can be here quickly. Call 999 as well to get a constable over as soon as possible."

"I'll have to remember to keep my phone with me at all times, then." As Cassie looked at her phone, she could see there were numerous messages, but she didn't have the heart to go through them. Evie had predicted she would receive attention. "Thank you for giving up your Sunday. I appreciate your concern."

"My pleasure completely," Alex said. "The unexpected meal was worth it all. It was delicious."

"I'm glad you liked it. Please stay as long as you'd like."

36

The next morning found Cassie reviewing her notes, preparing for interviews. She had asked Alex to remind Miles and Olivia that they had interviews scheduled for today. She also had an appointment with Inspector Bryce Graham, Detective Sergeant Dennis Osborne, and Detective Sergeant Tim O'Hara. She scheduled appointments with several constables and had other appointments set up for the entire week. If she stayed organized and focused, she would have the interviews for the police station done by the end of the week. The next step would be to take the individual interview notes as well as her collective thoughts and send the information to the publisher. She would include copies of the organizational chart and training manuals as well as limited protocol. The publisher wanted some information, but the police force obviously couldn't hand their disaster response plans to potential criminals for review.

Next, she went through her email. She forwarded any request for interviews and information to Evie's office to handle. She read through commentary from the article online but didn't add any comments of her own.

Once she was done with email, she quickly scrolled through her social media to gauge the response to the article. Most of the comments were positive, with requests for advanced reader copies of her new book. The only issue was she hadn't finished writing it yet.

Checking the time, Cassie thought the next best step would be to take a quick walk in the open air. She hated sitting for hours on end although that was the length of time it took to perform the business of being a writer.

Cassie reviewed her notes for the next chapter and then left the library to find her hiking shoes. The day was warm, and the floral scent was strong. She could smell freshly mowed grass and hear the bleating of sheep in the distance.

Jamming her hands in the pockets of her thin jacket, she walked toward the back of the property. She crested the hill, went round the tree, and walked toward the small cemetery on the property. The tombstone for William Blake was front and center and once again, Cassie had to wonder who had arranged the burial, the stone and whether anyone attended a service for him.

She walked through the rest of the small cemetery and tried to read the stones. Many were worn and she was unable to see full names or dates of birth or death. Two of the headstones had the name Blake on them and Cassie assumed they were the gravesites of William Blake's parents, but she couldn't be positive. She didn't see any graves that would indicate William had a wife or children. Cassie was hoping she would find some answers when she spoke with Alex this week.

Walking back to the cottage, she hurried so she would be ready for the interviews scheduled for the day. Not wanting a parade of officers through the cottage, Cassie planned to interview the officers at a small park near the police station. That way, they wouldn't be distracted by the cottage or villagers.

After taking twenty minutes to freshen up, collect her laptop and notes, she went out to the lane and waited for James to pull up and drive her to the park.

37

Tuesday morning, Cassie followed the same routine. She quickly reviewed her notes and was ready to return to the park for another round of interviews. Thankfully, the weather was beautiful, and she was able to carry out the interviews without difficulty. After six hours of meeting with officers and asking questions, she returned to the cottage by late afternoon. She made herself a cup of tea, grabbed a piece of chocolate cake and allowed herself a small measure of time for a mental respite.

Fifteen minutes later, she began to heat up food for dinner. Thankfully, the deep freezer in the cottage had a lot of room and she spent the first weeks of her move making meals and storing them for the future.

She pulled out a container of roast chicken, stuffing and vegetables and placed everything in the oven. Hearing her phone, she checked the text and found the following from Alex.

Okay for me to stop by? I have the case file.

Cassie answered immediately.

Absolutely. Dinner is ready if you're hungry.

Alex responded to her.

Sounds great, but only if it is already done. Don't cook for me.

Cassie sighed as she wrote.

See you soon.

She immediately set the table and had everything ready for Alex's arrival. He pulled in twenty minutes later and greeted her with a warm smile and hug. He had a briefcase in his hand. Setting the briefcase down, he took off his jacket and walked to the table. He smiled when he saw the single malt and a glass waiting for him. He only poured a small amount and said, "I need to stay completely alert to discuss this case. I may have to run out. We just got a triple 9 call. Miles and Olivia went to scope it out."

"Of course. Have a quick bite and then perhaps we can review the case file. I'll take care of dishes and things later."

"Sounds great," Alex said. "Have you had any more issues with visitors in the night?"

Cassie shook her head. "No. I put the dead bolt on last night. I haven't heard or smelled anything strange, and all was well when I came downstairs this morning."

"Good, that's encouraging to hear."

They spent the next half hour discussing Cassie's thoughts on the interviews she had conducted with the detectives and constables. She then went over the list of interviews scheduled for the rest of the week.

"No one is giving you a problem, I hope."

Cassie shook her head. "No, everyone has been respectful. I've not asked for specific case details but more about why they wanted to be an officer. I've asked what the hardest part of being an officer was but no details whatsoever."

"Good. Then it should all go swimmingly."

38

After a quick dinner, Cassie cleared and cleaned the table while Alex retrieved his briefcase. He opened the case file for William Blake and pulled out marked documents. Cassie tried to contain her excitement but reached forward to measure her skills of reading upside down. Unfortunately, Alex had the documents shielded in such a way she couldn't read a full sentence. He looked up and said, "We'll talk about this case, but no photos and no details are to appear anywhere. Understood?"

"I promised," Cassie said. "Can I keep a few notes for myself to help keep track of information?"

"As long as you destroy them when this is over."

"I promise," Cassie said as she put a heading on her paper.

William Blake Murder

She underlined the heading a few times while Alex watched.

"See, now that is the first thing in police work you must learn. Never make assumptions. Learn the facts, follow the evidence, and always look for means, motive and opportunity."

Cassie shook her head. "What are you talking about?"

Alex pointed to her page. "See, right there. You wrote, *William Blake Murder*."

"Only for myself," Cassie said. "I promise."

Alex laughed. "The problem with that is Mr. William Blake dropped dead of a heart attack at the local pub in front of thirty people. Remember?"

"Was it poison?" Cassie asked with raised eyebrows.

"No, not at all. He had a bad heart; his autopsy was done, and the death was ruled completely natural. See, you assumed William Blake was murdered. If you were one of my sergeants, I would have called you on that immediately."

Cassie stared at him, mouth slightly open, but with no words coming forth.

"Here, rip that up," Alex said as he picked up the paper and tore it in half. "Get another piece of paper and let's start again. Do not write anything down until I present the case."

Cassie did as she was told and realized Alex was training her like one of his sergeants. She could only imagine a fraction of the scrutiny and level of detail that Alex used to solve his cases. No wonder his solve rate was so high.

"Okay, my paper is blank and I'm ready to listen."

"Okay, let's begin," Alex said as he cleared his throat, but then looked at her with a smile. "This process is good for me as well. Revisiting the file, helps to review all information from the very start."

Cassie smiled and nodded at him.

Alex began to read but then put the file down and decided to tell Cassie what happened in his own words.

"William Blake was an 85-year-old man who lived at Heather House his entire life. His parents owned the estate and when they both died, it was passed down to him. The dates and such are in the file, but at this moment, let's review the case with a bird's eye view. Their income was derived from farming and raising livestock which was sold at market. Heather House is a large estate and as far as we know, Mr. William Blake was never married and had no children. They were a wealthy family. Mr. and Mrs. Blake passed, and William continued working the estate. As he aged, he hired a couple of village men. One of them was Granger Lowell who was with the group gaping on your doorstep Sunday night. Another was Wyatt Smith."

Cassie nodded but didn't write anything down. "Go on, please."

"One night, many of us were in the pub for game night. You see, once a month we have quite a rouser of a competition."

"So, you were there?"

"Yes, indeed." Alex nodded at her.

"The competition was tight, but the last question was tough. William Blake jumped up and shouted his answer at the same time as did another villager. However, Blake's answer was the only correct one. He was very excited and as is the custom, the losers must buy rounds. Mr. Blake was having a great night and probably finished his third pint, which may be a bit much for a gentleman of that age taking medicine for a heart condition. At any rate, he stopped laughing, grabbed his chest, stated he was going to be sick and then keeled over and died."

"That's terrible and sad," Cassie said.

"Yes, yes it was," Alex said with a nod. "Anyway, we were at a loss. We followed procedure, the police were there. We called the medical examiner. I don't think you've met him yet. His name is Casey. He's a very nice chap. I think you would like him, and you should probably interview him to see how he interacts with the department when we chase a homicide."

Cassie couldn't help herself and let out a small laugh. "That is an excellent idea. So back to Mr. Blake, then."

"His death was declared a natural death, but then we had a problem since there was absolutely no family to collect him or arrange his funeral. It's one thing when we can't identify a dead person, but we know who he was. He had property and a private cemetery. What he lacked was family so our quandary was what to do with him."

"What normally happens when a body isn't claimed in Britain?"

"The body is referred to the local authority for a public health funeral. The local authority can bury or cremate them. They are given a coffin and the funeral director handles the details."

"I'm sorry, but I'm not understanding the crime here," Cassie said as she looked into his eyes.

"Ah, see, that is the next lesson of being a homicide detective. Always be patient and listen."

Cassie suppressed a grin and said, "Good advice. Continue."

"Of course," Alex said with a smile as he watched Cassie pour a bit more whiskey into his glass. Alex lifted the glass and said, "Many have tried to ply me with alcohol or other services, and many have failed."

Cassie made a face in mock horror. "I'm not plying you with anything. I just want you to get to the punchline before I die of old age."

"So noted," Alex said. "I warned you. I'm very complete and try to be attentive to detail."

"Yes, you did," Cassie acknowledged as she made a circular motion with her hand for him to continue.

"We decided to spend the money to bury Mr. Blake in his own cemetery, on his own estate. It was the correct moral and ethical thing to do. However, we had a problem getting the coffin up to that little graveyard. You see, his parents had an old car that broke down on the small dirt path that leads to the graveyard. Their approach was to simply leave it there. It sat for years in the same spot to the point that the wheels sank into the ground. The vehicle became rusted and quite an eyesore. Mr. Blake didn't bother to have it removed so there it sat. We decided to have the vehicle towed so we could deliver Mr. Blake to the cemetery in proper fashion."

Cassie pressed her lips together, not sure if Alex was purposely having fun at her expense, but she kept her comments to herself.

"When they went to collect the automobile, the rusted trunk lid popped open and that was where we found a body."

Cassie sat up straight. "Wait, you found a random body in a rusted car on this property."

"That is correct. He was mummified in the trunk. We called the medical examiner, and everything was towed to the station for analysis."

"Do you know who it was?"

"That is the part we haven't been able to figure out or who killed him."

"It was murder. Are you sure?"

"Casey was able to ascertain the victim was murdered by a bullet hole in his skull."

"Do you know for a fact it was a male?"

"Yes, we do. It was determined the body had been dead approximately eight years. From initial DNA analysis, we know it was a male but there was no match to anyone in the database."

"That's the case that's unsolved?"

"Yes, indeed it is."

"I saw headstones in the cemetery today that I believe to be William Blake's parents, but I couldn't read their death dates. Do you know when they died?"

"Yes, they both died approximately fifteen years ago. They died several months apart from natural causes. There is a record of both death certificates, and they were properly buried so we know our victim was not one of them. Our victim died years later. We don't know if William Blake was involved in that murder and at that point, we couldn't interrogate him."

Cassie giggled. "Not unless you used a medium."

"This is England. That was a suggestion made by some. Investigating a cold case is one thing, but we now have a cold case that's another year colder."

"Is that why the estate is in limbo?" Cassie asked as she leaned forward.

"One of the reasons, but the other is that we cannot find a will or an heir for the estate. Until we can find the will, it will remain in limbo or eventually be turned over to the Crown."

"Do you know if there is a will? Is there something on file? I'm sure you spoke to the local solicitors."

"That is correct. There is no will on file. However, we have a witness. One of the villagers in the pub stated that Mr. Blake was upset and specifically told him, after a pint or two, that he changed his will."

"But he didn't say why or to whom he was leaving the estate."

"Once again, correct. The investigators have been in and out of Heather House, but we've not been able to find anything and as you already know, there have been some strange things happening here. I can't help but think that we're missing something and that frustrates me to no end."

"What if the murderer took the will?"

"The murder and the will may have nothing to do with each other. For all we know, Mr. Blake was the killer of our victim in the trunk which may be a separate issue."

"Wow." Cassie felt she needed a few minutes to rethink the details.

"He may have committed murder, then dropped dead eight years later before he finalized his own business."

"What about people who worked on the farm? You said there were a few villagers who did a small amount of work. What did they say when you interviewed them?"

"No one claimed to know anything about the dead body, or specific information on the car or anything about a will."

"Did he have any close friends that he would have confided in?"

"None that we know of, and no one came forward with information."

"Fingerprints? Were there fingerprints on the car? The trunk or anything on the body?"

Before Alex could answer, his cell phone started to chime. "He looked at the number and jumped up. "I'm sorry, I'm going to have to take this."

"Of course," Cassie said as she watched him walk into another room.

Cassie leaned forward and would have loved to look through the documents from the case file, but Alex returned quickly. "I'm sorry, I must go. It looks like we have a new homicide to deal with in the region and I like to look over the scene before the crime scene technicians stomp all over it."

"Okay," Cassie said as she stood up. She pointed at the file. "Is there a possibility you may want to leave that here?"

"I'm afraid not unless I'm hell bent on ending my career on a very sour note. The investigation is still active at this point. As far as you know, you haven't seen this file."

Cassie laughed. "Technically, I haven't. You had it in front of you the entire time."

"Yes, of course," Alex said as he gathered all the papers and slipped them into his briefcase. He stood up straight and looked at her. "Thank you for everything. I'll try to stop by tomorrow after work if possible. Sometimes, we conduct interviews and such for days. If I can be here, we'll talk about the autopsy and subsequent investigation."

"Great, I hope you can make it but, in the meantime, please be safe."

Alex smiled at her. "You too. Make sure you lock this door and call me if anything happens." He reached out, squeezed her shoulder and was out the door.

Cassie went back to the table. She took some time to write notes about what she heard to gather her own thoughts. Next, she would write down questions she would ask when they talked again. In the meantime, she had dishes to wash.

39

Wednesday morning dawned and Cassie jumped out of bed and got dressed. She had spent the evening thinking about the case. She tossed, turned, and tried to review details as she relaxed in the dark. Her door was locked but she slid a piece of furniture across the door, just in case. She thought about the other bedrooms and wondered which one William Blake used. Perhaps he used one room as a study. She promised herself she would look around tomorrow.

Turning to her side, she thought she heard a noise, but after five minutes of lying completely still, she heard nothing else and fell asleep.

The morning was bright, and the day was already warm. Cassie got dressed but before she went downstairs, she opened the doors to the other rooms and peeked inside. She saw old-fashioned furniture, bookshelves, a scarred desk, and flimsy closets. She'd had no reason to go through these rooms up to now, but she was determined to start, right after she had a strong, rich cup of coffee.

After breakfast and two hours of searching the rooms, she found plenty of items from the previous owner. None of them looked to be precious, but things he used daily while he was alive. With no one to take over direct responsibility for the estate, Cassie assumed these items wouldn't be donated, tossed, or sold until a decision had been made. She found a box of personal items that must have been in the bathroom.

Cassie remembered that Evie had hired villagers to make the cottage attractive and livable for her, but there were probably strict instructions about handling Mr. Blake's personal items. She made a mental note to ask Evie if the contract had any such stipulations as there was an active investigation.

Cassie took a moment to stretch and decided to walk through the village. She hadn't been out and about much, but she ran out of milk with her morning coffee and needed more. It would be an excellent time to check the shop that sold groceries and other items.

She made sure her jeans and shirt were clean. Cassie took a moment to recheck her face for dust and then brushed her hair. Hopefully, she wouldn't be approached by a lot of villagers, and she had no idea if they would be welcoming if she was.

Cassie left the cottage and made sure she locked the door. Wearing her hiking shoes, she started down the lane toward the shops. There were tall hedges on one side and the field behind her cottage was full of pink and purple heather. As she walked, she passed the village green, farm animals, a fence, and the vicarage. Mrs. Witherspoon was working in her garden and offered a large smile and a wave when she saw Cassie in the lane. She beckoned her over for a chat.

"It's so good to see you out, dear. How are you?"

"Doing well," Cassie said. "I'm getting through all the interviews for my research."

"Yes, I've seen a lot of our police force coming and going. At first, we didn't realize it was a book. We were afraid something was terribly wrong." They both looked up when they saw Mrs. Peabody making her way toward them.

"No, nothing wrong. I'm getting used to the cottage and a few strange noises," Cassie said as she spoke to Mrs. Witherspoon.

Cassie welcomed Mrs. Peabody to the group and after a pleasant greeting she asked, "Did you both know Mr. Blake well?"

"He was a bit of a sod and full of himself," Mrs. Peabody said.

Mrs. Witherspoon clucked at her neighbor. "Let's just say he was a bit of a loner toward the end of his life. He was well into his 80's and may not have felt well. We don't know, really."

"We tried to visit and cheer him up," Mrs. Peabody said, "but he certainly wasn't welcoming."

Cassie wasn't sure if that was due to his health or Mrs. Peabody's approach or tendency to gossip. "I hear he died in the pub?"

"Yes, he did, poor soul," Mrs. Witherspoon said. "He's buried in the cemetery on the property. As he didn't have a wife or children, the village wanted to make sure he was with his parents. Their resting places are there as well."

"That's very nice of you," Cassie said with a smile.

"We try to watch out for each other, and we welcome all, especially to the service. Please dear, do come whenever you'd like. You're always welcome," Mrs. Witherspoon said with a smile.

"We saw that you were in the London papers with DCI Knight," Mrs. Peabody said. "We didn't know that you were acquainted with Sir Charles Effingham. What's he like?"

"Oh, well, he's a very nice man and an extremely talented writer," Cassie said as she started to be wary of probing questions. She had learned the hard way, that one inquisitive question led to many more.

"I should probably get going for my milk," Cassie said as she looked at her watch. "It was lovely seeing you this morning." She took a few steps before she heard Mrs. Peabody call out behind her.

"Can't help noticing the DCI is spending a lot of time at Heather House. Would that be police business?"

Cassie stopped in her tracks. She managed to lose her frown before she turned around. Mrs. Witherspoon was staring at the ground, apparently hoping a hole would open and swallow her, but Mrs. Peabody stood her ground, waiting for an answer.

"Yes, Mrs. Peabody. He's been assigned by the Chief Constable to ensure the accuracy of the book that's been commissioned by the police department as well as checking the cottage. Due to his schedule, he's not able to hold meetings until after work, but all is well. We'll be sending the first packet of information to the publisher soon. I'm sure they'll be very excited about the relationship between the local police and village. Thank you for caring, Mrs. Peabody."

Cassie turned round again and quickly set off for the store. She arrived in eight minutes, looked around and purchased her milk. She was pleased to hand over the proper banknote and she received coins in return. The store owner smiled and introduced herself.

"Pleased to meet you. My name is Cindy Mason. Me and my mum run this store. We're so excited to have you living here." Cassie could tell she was curious but polite enough not to ask questions.

"Thank you. It's so very nice to meet you and I'm sure I'll be back often. Please call me Cassie." Smiling to herself, Cassie was sure that Mrs. Peabody would be trailing her to deliver and collect any information she could, so she collected her milk and left.

Cassie increased her pace and took a small circuitous route around the village green to get back to the cottage. She slowed when she reached the stone bridge. The sun glistened off the water like jewels and Cassie watched the small river flow under the bridge. She'd have to check her maps to find the name of the river, but the breeze was refreshing and smelled sweet. Looking over the side, she wouldn't want to be on the muddy banks or under the dark stone. She noticed some trash down below and worried that a homeless person may be staying there. She made a mental note to ask Mrs. Witherspoon about it when Mrs. Peabody wasn't listening.

40

True to his word, Alex texted he would be able to arrive Wednesday evening to continue their discussion. She was glad as she wanted to get back to the mystery.

Cassie marveled at the difference in personality from some of the detectives she had worked with in Manhattan. She wondered how Alex would do if transplanted to a large city in the US. Being interviewed by a polite, respectful, British detective, speaking in quiet, but intense tones would probably throw off quite a few suspects and she smiled at the thought. He probably pulled the interrogation chair out for females.

Laughing, Cassie made sure the table was clean. Since it was late, she threw together a platter of cold sandwiches and added various salads that she had prepared earlier in the week. Her final touch was a small dish of pickles, relish, and condiments.

Thirty minutes later, Alex knocked on the door of Heather House. He offered a large smile when she answered. When she invited him in, he placed his briefcase on the coffee table, took off his jacket and sat at the table.

"I hope you don't mind. I made a plate of sandwiches today," Cassie said as she carried the food to the table.

"Mind? Please, I never expect you to cook for me," Alex said with a smile. "A visit doesn't mean you must offer a meal."

"Well, I have to eat, and I'd rather not eat alone or with someone watching me. So please, have a sandwich."

"This looks like a wonderful spread," Alex said.

"Would you like whiskey?" Cassie made her way to the liquor cabinet.

"No, thank you. Could I have a cup of tea if it wouldn't be too much to ask?"

Cassie stopped in her tracks. "Of course. Tea is perfect."

"I don't like to drink if there's a chance I may be called out," Alex said. "There are still a lot of interviews and evidence gathering happening with the current case."

"I understand completely. I don't drink much because I get sleepy. I can't write when I've had alcohol. I suppose you can't discuss the current case?" Cassie asked as she raised her eyebrows.

"No, I can't. We're quite sure it's a homicide but it's an active case. I don't believe it's anyone you've met or know."

Alex waited for Cassie to return with the tea before they started dinner. "Milk?"

"That would be lovely," Alex said.

"I bought it fresh in the village today," Cassie explained. "My greatest fears were answered. Mrs. Witherspoon was kind enough to say hello, but then Mrs. Peabody started grilling me. I walked around the village green on the way home so I wouldn't meet her again."

Alex laughed as he listened to her story. "You haven't met with the villagers then?"

"No, it's awkward. There are times I can't think of anything to speak with them about. Although, I suppose I could spend hours answering Mrs. Peabody's questions."

"That's very true," Alex said nodding his head. "Have you been to the pub yet?"

"No, and I'm not sure how I feel about this pub business tomorrow night. It's not like I would have popped in before today and asked for a beer."

"You would technically ask for a pint."

"Oh, see. It's awkward when you don't know where to sit or what to ask for. I made change for the first time today in the village."

Alex smiled as he sympathized with her discomfort. "I don't know who planned tomorrow night. But I did hear that it was a way of thanking you for doing all the interviews this week. It's also a good way for anyone who doesn't know you to be introduced."

Cassie shrugged. "If I stay on point, I should have all the interviews done by the weekend."

"Cheers to that," Alex said as he put his plate to the side. "Would you feel more comfortable if I escorted you to the pub tomorrow night? That way, you wouldn't go in cold and try to fit in."

"Would you? I would be so grateful," Cassie said with eyes wide.

"I will swing by and pick you up. We can walk from here."

"That would be fantastic," Cassie said as she stood and reached to collect the plates.

Alex stood as well. "Please let me help with that."

Cassie waved him away. "It's only a couple of plates." She then grabbed a towel and tossed it to him. "Perhaps you can clean the table. I'd like to get back to the case file as soon as we can."

Alex complied and soon had the case file back on the table. He opened it up and placed a few papers in order. "Let's see. Where were we?"

"We established that William Blake died of a heart attack in the pub. When the funeral was planned and the rusty car removed, there was a mummified body found in the trunk of the car. You have no identification on the body. The car had been there for thirty years, and we assume the body had been there for eight years. You mentioned the victim was murdered by a gunshot to the head, proven by the hole in the skull. The deceased was a male."

"Yes, that's all correct. You are very good at detail and as I recall you didn't take notes."

"Not after I made assumptions," Cassie said as she made quote marks in the air with her fingers.

Alex chuckled. "Okay, what do you want to know?"

"You want me to ask questions?"

"Yes, to get a fresh perspective. You seem to know your way around a crime scene."

"Right then," Cassie said. "Means, motive, and opportunity. First the victim. Was the pathologist able to give us an approximate age after looking at the bony structure?"

Alex consulted his notes. "He put the age of the deceased to be around 70 years old."

Cassie nodded as she asked, "What about forensic findings? Was there any hair left on the victim? Any identifiable clothing?"

Looking through the notes. "There appears to have been a few wisps of hair. I'm not sure if the DNA was done on bone marrow or the hair. Either way, the DNA analysis was not compatible with anything in any database that we accessed. We expanded to the Interpol database as well. There was no clothing, no identification, no billfold, no mobile. The body was loosely wrapped in a blanket."

Cassie arched her eyebrows. "I'm assuming there was no gun or weapon in the trunk that could be tested for fingerprints?"

Alex smiled as he shook his head. "Sorry."

"Fingerprints on the trunk? Car? Anywhere?"

"No and the victim's fingers were unable to be hydrated enough to pull those fingerprints."

"Were you able to get anything from the blanket? Fibers? Hair? Trace of any kind?"

"The blanket was deteriorated and there were insects and rodents in the trunk. We did find insect excrement."

"You interviewed the workers that were active at that time?"

"Yes, we could always reinterview to see if there is any new information."

Cassie frowned as she thought for a few seconds.

"Didn't anyone smell anything as the body was decomposing?"

"Not that was reported, however smells are not always appreciated on an active farm which it would have been years ago."

"Okay, so identification is an issue. Means is clearly a gunshot wound to the head. Opportunity was present, as someone shot him and stuffed him in the trunk. What would be the motive?"

"We don't know," Alex said spreading his hands apart.

"A prowler that was taken care of without the police?"

"I doubt it. Mr. Blake called the police all the time to report strange happenings. I doubt he would kill someone and try to hide the body. He wouldn't draw attention to the estate that way."

"So, it's likely he didn't kill the victim."

Alex shrugged.

"It's probably not a random killing."

"Probably not," Alex said clearing his throat.

"What would the property be worth today?" Cassie asked as she looked into his eyes.

"That's a good question. The property, although not a working farm, is large. It's worth a pretty penny, possibly millions to a developer if they could get the permits to build."

"You said the will wasn't found and I'm assuming no one put in a claim," Cassie asked as she looked at Alex.

"You would assume correctly."

"The victim wasn't killed to take the will from them otherwise someone would have claimed the estate."

"Once again, correct."

"We have a villager who swears that Mr. Blake stated he changed his will, but no will has shown up. We don't know who would inherit if it did. It's odd, don't you think?"

"What's odd?" Alex asked, tilting his head.

"I can understand a suspect killing someone to remove a beneficiary that would inherit before them, but to kill someone so they couldn't inherit knowing the outcome would be abandoned property doesn't make sense."

"I agree completely which is why I feel we are missing a piece of the puzzle and until we find it, we have nothing."

"Unless the abandoned property could be picked up for a song by a developer who was willing to wait? I don't know the laws in England."

"That would be a large risk and there's no assurance the property wouldn't be put into use by the local authorities. As a matter of fact, the reason they were happy to lease it for you was so that no one could squat here and claim it as their own."

"Glad to be of service. This is a difficult case," Cassie said chewing her inner cheek.

"Any other questions?"

"Yes, my last one. What did the DNA show for Mr. Blake?"

Alex raised his right eyebrow. "Mr. Blake?"

"Yes, do you have the DNA analysis for him?"

"We didn't do DNA on him. The police budget is very tight, and they normally don't do DNA on someone we are easily able to identify."

"But that could be important."

"Why?"

"What if it shows a connection of sorts?"

"I'm not sure we have Blake DNA on file."

"Can you find it somewhere in your budget? Do you have a fund for unusual inquiries? Something like that?"

Alex stared at Cassie for a long moment before he spoke. "Mr. Blake is buried, and I doubt anyone will pay to have him exhumed."

"That's okay," Cassie said excitedly.

"Excuse me?"

"I was thinking of our conversation last evening so this morning I took a tour around the upstairs rooms. There's a box with Mr. Blake's bathroom supplies. I'm quite sure I saw a hairbrush in there as well as a razor, toothbrush, and various other bathroom sundries. Would you care to go upstairs to the bedrooms with me?"

Alex remained stone faced for a moment. "We have to stop meeting like this."

Cassie started laughing. "C'mon, let's go." She stood up and waited for him to join her. She then led him up the staircase but to a room on the right. She opened the closet door and pulled out a box. "I'm assuming, as it was an active scene at one point, there were instructions not to remove anything from the premises. You can take it now for analysis. The investigation is still active. You said so, yourself."

Alex looked at her and the box with a bit of exasperation on his face.

"Please, what could it hurt?"

"You're right. It couldn't hurt. If the finances are a problem, I'll get a bill from the Chief Constable."

"Then let me know and I'll help cover it," Cassie said with a shrug.

Alex sighed, picked up the box and carried it downstairs.

"Did the analysis of the muddy hay or whiskey bottle that you took show anything?"

"Not yet," Alex said as he looked at her. "Would you mind if I took a turn around the library again? I still think we're missing something, somewhere in this cottage."

Cassie shrugged. "Help yourself. I'm going to start the dishes but tear the place apart if you'd like. Would you like more tea?"

"That would be grand," Alex said.

Thirty minutes later, Cassie looked into the library and found Alex sitting on the couch with a book in his hands and reading spectacles on his face.

"I didn't know you had reading spectacles."

"I do use them for some things," Alex said a bit defensively.

"They look adorable." When Alex frowned, Cassie added, "What are you reading?"

"I found a journal of sorts. I gather it was kept by Mrs. Blake. I thought it might add some insight to the family."

"That's a great find. I haven't had time to look over all these bookshelves yet, but I think I'll start soon."

"Do you mind if I keep reading? I'm glad for the opportunity."

"As long as you don't mind me writing. I've got to catch up on my WIP."

"WIP?"

"Work in progress," Cassie responded with a grin. "One of the many acronyms enjoyed by writers."

"Ah, I see. Of course, I don't mind you writing. Let's carry on, then."

Laughing to herself, Cassie sat at the desk, opened her computer, and reviewed her last words. It was the oddest feeling. The desk was facing the couch. She was comfortable writing, and he was perfectly comfortable reading. When she had finished reviewing her last 1000 words, she turned her back to Alex.

Pulling out her phone, she set the camera to take a selfie of the two of them. Though she tried to be surreptitious by putting the phone on silent, she heard him say, "I'd better get a copy of that and please do not share it anywhere."

She turned back and laughed. "I'll send it to you, and I promise I won't share with anyone else, if not for your sake, then mine. Privacy is sacred to me. I just had to memorialize this moment. I've had men ask for many things, but rarely a book to read, unless it was a free copy of my latest bestseller."

Alex laughed. "I'd better be going. Mind if I take this with me?" He held up the journal.

"Of course not, but I'd like to read it when you're through."

They walked to the front door. Alex packed up his briefcase and lifted the box of William Blake's toiletries. Cassie opened the door for him and smiled.

"I've had a lovely evening," Alex said. "Thank you for everything."

"So did I," Cassie answered, feeling herself blush.

"Pick you up at 7:00 p.m. tomorrow night for the pub?"

Cassie nodded but then asked, "Yes, what do I wear?"

Alex grinned. "Anything would look great, but in this case, jeans and a nice shirt will do."

Cassie's blush deepened as she nodded.

Alex looked as if he wanted to kiss her but walked out the door. "I'll be standing right here until I hear the door lock. Don't forget to send me that selfie."

Cassie closed and locked the door and watched him drive away as she retrieved the photo and hit send. As she went up to bed, she silently kept repeating to herself, *no relationships, no relationships.*

41

Thursday was a busy day. Cassie completed six interviews by late afternoon. She asked everyone the same basic questions about what motivated them to join the police force. She was interested in their reaction to various crimes and their future in the police force.

Once she was done, she went back to the cottage, grabbed a quick bite, and typed her handwritten notes. She only had a few interviews left and she planned to complete them on Friday. She had an appointment with the Chief Constable on the following Monday. She would then take a couple of days to put all the information together, redact any real names of victims or criminals, and then go to London to meet with the publisher.

Her next goal was to make serious headway with her current fiction novel. She felt it was more realistic from what she had seen of England to date. She had added a British detective as her main protagonist and reworked the book. Tonight, would be her first night in a British pub and she would use that experience to create a scene for a future book.

Cassie was looking forward to learning more about England. She made herself a light meal in case there was not enough food at the event. She had been to many book events that advertised light hors d'oeuvres and had nothing but a dish of olives, mostly for the martinis.

Racing upstairs, she showered and then dressed. She had a pair of favorite jeans that fit her just right. A brand-new silk blouse would pair very nicely with the jeans. She only needed to add a new pair of espadrille wedges. She then spent time on her hair and make-up. She wanted to look her best in front of a crowd and especially if the attention was to be focused on her.

Cassie made it downstairs with ten minutes to spare. She collected her purse and her phone and took several deep breaths. Alex was right on time, which surprised her. She fully expected him to beg off due to the recent investigation. She opened the door and he immediately smiled.

"You look lovely."

"Thank you," Cassie blushed. "And you're wearing a suit?"

"Sorry, I didn't have time to go home and change."

"Yet, you look perfect. Your shirt is crisp, your suit is pressed, and your silk tie is perfect." He smiled at her comment, pleased she had noticed. "And your cologne is still heavenly."

"Glad to please," Alex said with a grin.

"Do you want to come in or shall we start out?"

"We don't want to be late for pub night, so we'd better go." He held out his arm like a perfect gentleman. She hooked her arm through his as he escorted her outside.

"It's a ten-minute walk. Are you okay with that?"

"Perfectly. It will give me a few minutes to calm down."

"There's nothing to be nervous about. In all honesty, it gives them another reason to have a few pints. They'll toast you a time or two. No speeches and hopefully you won't add any post notes to anyone who has too much to drink. I'd better not see anyone drinking that's on duty. As their Chief, they generally don't stay late when I've been invited to these events."

Cassie laughed. "The taskmaster in motion."

They enjoyed a leisurely walk past the village green which held a lovely pond with a bench. Minutes later they approached the stone pub. Above the door was a sign which said Wexley Pub.

"This is it," Alex said. "Are you ready?"

Cassie blew out a breath of air. "As ready as I'll ever be. Please promise there won't be a lot of people coming at me."

Alex laughed. "I've been your protector since you've arrived in England. I'll beat them all off."

"Okay then, let's do this."

Alex pulled the heavy wooden door open, and the pair stepped inside. The people surrounding the bar looked up and cheered.

"Well, aren't we cozy? She has a personal escort." Arlene hissed to another clerk beside her.

Grayson Taylor, the owner of the pub, rushed over and led them to a table which had been reserved for Cassie. "So nice to meet you Ms. Ashcroft. We don't often have famous people visiting. It's an honor."

"Thank you," Cassie said. "The honor is all mine."

"What can I get for you?"

"How about a small glass of merlot?"

The owner glanced at Alex. "And for you guv'nor?"

"I'll take a pint, please."

"Brilliant," he said. "It'll be here in a moment."

Cassie sat against a stone wall with Alex seated across from her. The table sat four people. Within minutes, Miles and Olivia approached the table and welcomed her. "Please, sit with us." She gestured to the two seats that were available and after receiving an approving nod from their boss, they smiled and sat down. Cassie was happy as that gave her another layer of insulation from the rest of the crowd which was having a fun celebration.

Grayson brought their drinks and a variety of food to the table. A few people waved and Cassie waved back. She recognized most of the detectives and constables she had interviewed. Cassie made a point of waving to the two constables that almost arrested her. After a while, Cassie and the crowd relaxed. The officers sang a chorus of She's a Jolly Good Fellow and everyone cheered.

Cassie smiled when she realized she felt so much camaraderie with a group of people she had only known for six weeks. They kept shouting, "Speech," and she finally stood. "I want to thank everyone for your kindness since I've come to the village. It's been great meeting you."

The pub crowd clapped, and Cassie sat down. Alex noted her hands were shaking slightly. He grabbed her hand under the table and with his thumb he rubbed circles on the inside of her wrist until he felt her relax. All the while, they spoke to visitors at the table with smiles.

A short time later, Miles received a phone call and beckoned Alex and Olivia to follow him outside. Other officers filled their seats immediately and held pleasant conversation with Cassie. She was invited to several events which she promised to consider although she knew she wouldn't attend. It was easier that way. *No entanglement. No promises. No problems.*

Alex made his way back to the table to overhear part of a conversation between Inspector Bryce and Cassie.

"I'd like you to meet my family on Saturday. How about if I swing by around 2:00 p.m. to collect you?"

Cassie smiled and prayed her facial expression didn't begin to reveal her thoughts. As Alex sat down, she said, "That sounds lovely." When Bryce smiled, she continued, "But, I'm sorry to say Alex has already planned to show me part of a crime scene on Saturday. I have an upcoming meeting in London, so I need to have everything ready." Cassie used her elbow to poke Alex under the table.

"Oh yes, yes we have arrangements," Alex said. "On Saturday."

Bryce offered Alex a slight scowl, then turned back to Cassie. "I'll look forward to setting another date then, soon."

Cassie smiled in return.

"It's about time to get you home," Alex said as he held up his watch.

"Yes, thank you." Cassie stood up and gathered her things. There were many handshakes and pats on the back as they made their way to the door. She took a photo with the owner so he could hang it on the wall.

"Don't be shy and please come back often. We don't bite and we protect our own if anyone tries to bother you."

"I'd appreciate that," Cassie said with a smile. Minutes later, she was outside the wooden pub door with Alex at her side. She took a big breath and blew it out. "They were a lovely bunch of people but I'm glad that's over."

42

Cassie turned to Alex. "Thank you for shielding me."

"My pleasure," Alex said. "I volunteer to be your bodyguard anytime your body needs guarding."

Cassie blushed at his comment. "What was all that with Bryce? Why do I need to go meet his family?"

Alex let out a hearty laugh as they walked down the lane. "Bryce is a very proper British gentleman. Meeting his family is the start of a proper courting ritual."

Cassie's eyes opened wide. "Excuse me? It's the 21st century."

"As I said, he's a very proper Brit. If the family doesn't like you, he won't waste the time."

"Wow. Thanks for saving me there. I was hoping you would follow my lead."

"Yes, so now that we have a date for Saturday, there's something I want to show you. You've been asking about seeing the English Channel from the cliffs."

"Are you sure?" Cassie asked hurriedly. "I don't want to infringe on your time."

"Of course not. If I didn't want to go, I'd come up with a proper excuse. However, this is a small village and Bryce will know if you're home all day."

"Spare me," Cassie said with a lopsided grin.

"My pleasure. By the way, I had a busy day today," Alex said. "I reinterviewed several of the villagers that worked on William Blake's farm in the last five years. I also read more of the journal."

"Did you find anything new?"

"Not so much in information as in attitude. Several of them were quite annoyed to be questioned yet again."

Alex took Cassie's arm and stopped their walk. "Have you ever been to the village green at night?"

Cassie shook her head. "I haven't gone out at night by myself." She started to laugh. "To be honest, I'd feel more comfortable walking around Manhattan at night then this village."

"Come let me show you something." He pulled her in the direction of the green and up to the pond near the back. He then pointed upwards. "It's a beautiful sky tonight. You can see stars all over the sky and then reflected in the water. It's quite a sight on a good night."

Cassie looked up and was rewarded by a shooting star. "It is lovely, isn't it?"

"Did you know you can go on a guided tour of Exmoor, the national park, at night. They have very interesting programs for those that love that sort of thing."

"I do love that. How did you know?"

"I'm a detective," Alex said with a sly grin.

The pair turned and continued their walk toward Heather House. "The officers were very nice. I'm still very grateful that you accompanied me to the pub, and it turned out to be a fun time as well."

"You're quite welcome. The villagers are not always receptive to outsiders but once you're accepted, they surround and keep you close as one of their own."

When they reached Heather House, Alex said, "I'd like to check first if you don't mind."

"Not at all," Cassie said, turning over her keys.

He opened the front door and immediately stopped in his tracks.

Cassie leaned forward and whispered, "Do you smell it? I can smell it from here. That strange combination of hay and cigarette smoke."

"Yes, yes I do," Alex said. He took a small step inside the cottage. He stopped to listen and look around while gently telling her to stay outside. Cassie stayed on the doorstep but craned her neck to look inside. Alex went from room to room and returned to the front door. He put the lights on in the cottage. "I don't think anyone is here, but I'm going to go upstairs and have a look around. Why don't you stay here? There's a bit of a mess and I think it's very coincidental that it happened tonight, after we questioned several people, and it was known you would be out at the pub."

"At least, whomever it is doesn't seem to want to hurt me," Cassie said. "I think they're looking for that will."

"Most likely, but I'm not happy with the situation at any rate. Would you like to stay somewhere else tonight? You can stay with me or if you're uncomfortable with that, there's always an extra room at the vicarage." Alex shrugged. "We don't have any hotels in this area as I'm sure you've noticed."

Cassie swallowed. "Let's look around first before I decide. I need to check the library."

Alex walked her inside the library and turned the light on. He quickly looked around and said, "I'll be right back." He then went upstairs to have a look.

Cassie's attention was brought back to the room. Books were strewn on the floor and the writing desk was completely turned out. Drawers were emptied on the floor. Her computer screen was facing down. She reached out to pick it up when Alex walked into the room and said, "No, don't touch it. I've called it in. I want someone to document all this and check for fingerprints. How the devil are they getting in here? Do you think you've lost your work?"

"Ultimately, no," Cassie said. "It's all in the cloud. But if my desktop or laptop is destroyed or missing, then I'll be set back until I get it all righted up again."

The pair waited outside in the warm summer night for the constables and forensics team to show up. Cassie sat on a bench that had been placed in the garden years ago and continued to watch the stars. She was questioning why some level of misery always seemed to follow celebration.

After several hours had gone by, Alex approached her and told her she could go back inside the cottage and look around. He waited for her to notice whether anything specific was taken. She lifted the computer and plugged it in. Holding her breath, she exhaled when it booted up successfully. She was able to reach her files and the internet was active. She then picked up the things that were strewn around the rest of the library as well as her kitchen. She must have had the only vandal who insisted on drinking single malt and eating while he looked around. Apparently, the area around the fireplace was searched as well.

"I don't see anything missing, but it looks as if someone was intent on finding something."

"Are you sure you want to stay here tonight?" Alex searched her face for an answer knowing that Cassie was torn.

"As much as I'm not happy about it, I wouldn't relax in a strange place. It's late and I'm tired. It was a long day for both of us. Do you think they would come back tonight?"

Alex shook his head. "Probably not and I'll have a car stay here for the night which will also discourage further exploration, but I'm worried for you."

Cassie looked up at him and smiled. "Thank you, Alex. For being there when I need you and protecting me."

"You're most welcome. This is all very coincidental and I'm afraid our intruder is escalating."

"I know, but I think they're done for tonight."

"Are you sure?"

After a small pause, she nodded. "Yes."

"Okay but call me immediately if anything happens."

Cassie nodded. "I promise, I will."

"Is it alright if I text you to check?"

"Yes, of course. I'd like that." Cassie smiled and walked him outside. "Thanks again, Alex."

He waited until she was inside with the door securely bolted and then turned to get into his car. As he did, he looked up and noticed Mrs. Peabody staring out her window despite the late hour. He made up his mind to call her early the next morning. Perhaps she had seen something that would help.

43

Friday morning dawned warm and bright. Cassie rolled to the side of the bed and opened her eyes. The deadbolt remained on the door and the furniture was as she placed it before she had fallen asleep. Cassie quickly reached for her phone and found an unanswered text from Alex at 4:00 a.m. asking if she was okay. He had texted her 30 minutes earlier and she had answered she was secure in her room. He must have texted again, but she hadn't heard the chirp. She quickly sent a reply that although she hadn't been downstairs, all was well.

Rising and looking out the window, she noticed the police car was still there. Alex mentioned the car would remain until she waved all clear in the morning. She quickly pulled on jeans and a shirt and went downstairs. She cautiously looked around and all seemed the same as when she went to bed. She opened the front door of the cottage and waved to the constable. He got out of the car and entered the cottage. After a quick look around to make sure she was okay, the constable drove off for the day as the intruder was unlikely to return during the day when the house was occupied.

Cassie needed to clean the house, but first she made a pot of dark, rich coffee and thought about calling Evie. It was still early in

Manhattan, so she hung up before she completed the call. She opened her contacts and called Simon. When he answered, she explained what had happened.

"I know you're coming to pick me up for the meeting in London. What are the chances I could get security placed with a video cam either before that time or as part of our trip?"

They discussed the idea for a while and Simon promised to talk to Evie about it. Cassie was more than willing to pay privately if the publisher refused. If Simon couldn't arrange for a good installer, she would ask Alex.

Cassie then spent an hour cleaning the downstairs. She went from room to room, sweeping, cleaning, and vacuuming the floor. She wasn't sure if all the dirt was from the original incident or the crime scene investigators doing their job. Finishing the living room, the fireplace, the library, she then tackled the kitchen. She had some mud and hay on the floor and around the counter as if the intruder made a sandwich while there. Cassie took the time to sweep out the pantry and check the shelves. It didn't appear as if any food was missing, but the cans were moved on shelves situated on the back wall. Perhaps there was a search for a particular sandwich item. She was thankful they didn't search around the fireplace in her bedroom.

Once she was done cleaning, she quickly changed to a summer dress and matching light shoes and went to start her first interview of the day. She only had a couple interviews left and then would have completed most of the research she needed for the publisher.

44

Cassie woke Saturday morning after a decent night's sleep. She hadn't heard any noises during the night and Alex texted her before she went upstairs to make sure she was safe.

All okay there today?
Yes, cleaned up and no new visits. How was your day?
Busy with follow up.
What is the plan for tomorrow?
I'll pick you up in the afternoon. We'll go for a bite and a walk.
Okay, looking forward to it. Good night.
Sleep well. Call if you don't.

Cassie ended the text with a smiling emoji and a thumbs up. As usual she made sure the deadbolt was in place as well as placing a chair under the doorknob. She then slid into bed and slept like a baby.

After coffee, she spent the day typing up her notes until it was time to shower and get ready for her visit with Alex.

She dressed in slacks and a nice blouse with matching earrings and walking shoes. Alex apparently liked surprises, but she hadn't been disappointed yet and she was able to use the experiences in her novel.

Alex arrived, knocked on the door and waited for her to answer. When she swung the door wide, he offered a big smile. He was dressed more casually than normal in slacks and a dark blue button-down shirt opened at the neck.

"Ready?"

"Yes, I am," Cassie said. "Let me get my purse. Do I need anything else?"

"Not at all. We're having a picnic."

Cassie nodded as she tried to imagine where they were going. He opened the door for her, and she got into his car. He waited until she was belted in before closing the door and getting in behind the wheel. He started the car and they drove off.

"How are you?" Alex asked as he looked at her.

"Doing well," Cassie said. "No more visits. I was so tired that I slept well last night. I finished my interviews except for the one with the Chief Constable, but I have an appointment with Joe Duffy on Monday morning at the station.

"Great. Deep down he's a good fellow if he keeps his blood pressure down."

Cassie laughed. "I'll have to remember that. How about you?"

"I spoke with Mrs. Peabody. I saw her watching all the activity from her bedroom window on Thursday night and I was wondering if she saw anything or anyone around the cottage. She swears there was no activity all night and honestly, I'm sure she was watching."

"I don't know if that's comforting or disturbing," Cassie said with a grin.

"Of course, I think she asked me more questions than I asked her, but we got through it."

"Did you give anything away?"

"No, she knew as much as I did. I'm sure she reached out to her network first thing Friday morning."

"Maybe you should hire her? Does she often help you with leads?"

"Usually, she gives me the villagers' version which after a day or so has grown by leaps and bounds. I like to stick to the facts and not make assumptions."

"I remember," Cassie said as she made a face.

He grinned. "All in good police work."

As they drove along, Alex told her where they were and about the landscape they were passing. He gave her a little bit of history about Devon and the people who lived there. "Is there anything you would specifically like to know?"

Cassie shook her head. "I'm not sure. I start writing the book and it evolves on its own. Sometimes I don't know what information I need until I get to it. I realize that doesn't make sense."

"It's like police work. An investigation takes us where we need to go, but we don't know where that is until we start."

"Yes. And we often end in the last place we expected."

Alex nodded. "Very true."

"We understand each other's process which very few do."

Alex smiled as he slowed down the car. "Here we are."

"Which is where?" Cassie looked to her right and saw a large stone wall with black wrought iron gates at the drive. "Wow, one of the fanciest places I've seen since arriving at the village."

The gates were open, and Alex drove through. "This is the Moreland Estate. You can see the Moreland Castle up ahead on the right."

"It's gorgeous," Cassie said breathlessly as she looked out the window. "The grounds are beautiful as well. Look at those gardens. Is this a public place?"

"No, it's privately owned and does not receive many visitors."

"Are we allowed here?" Cassie asked with eyebrows raised.

Alex nodded. "Yes, I know the owner, and this is completely fine." Alex drove past the Castle and continued until he reached the end of the lane. He parked the car and turned to her. "This is where we get out and walk."

Cassie was excited. "I can't wait to explore the grounds. I'm already plotting a book in my head using this location." When Alex turned toward her with eyebrows raised, she hurriedly added, "Under an assumed name, of course."

"Just wait. There's more to see." Alex nodded and reached into the back seat. He retrieved a wicker basket and then pointed to a copse of trees near the car. "Off we go."

The pair made their way through the trees. When they emerged on the other side, they were on a stone path which wound up and around to the right. There was a low stone wall lining the path and Alex pulled her in that direction.

"I hear water," Cassie said as she tilted her head.

"You have very good hearing. We're near the English Channel."

They continued walking up the path for a half mile until Cassie had enough of an advantage to see more than the blue sky over the stone wall. She stopped and stared. Below her was an array of cliffs. The water was crashing onto the rocks below. She turned her face toward the breeze and the sun.

"It's beautiful, isn't it?" Alex asked. "Let's walk a bit more."

The pair continued up the stone path. When Cassie looked toward the end, she could see a chapel with a graveyard next to it.

"What is that?" Cassie asked with as much excitement as a child in an amusement park.

"That is the Moreland Family Chapel and their burial ground."

She looked at Alex. "Are you sure we're allowed to be here? It's glorious. Are we allowed to look inside?"

Alex grinned broadly. "Yes, and yes. I knew you would love it."

Cassie walked up the path until they reached the chapel. She turned and once again was in awe of the sight of the water from the chapel door. Bright blue skies, birds flying in circles overhead, green field sloping down to the small rock wall and nothing but the beautiful English Channel beyond.

"What a beautiful place to be buried, but I would want to sit here for many years, enjoying this view, before it came to that."

Alex laughed. "I agree with you completely."

Cassie turned once again and approached the chapel door. It

opened easily. "Can I go inside?"

Alex nodded. "I figured you would want to, so I had it opened for you."

"You know the owners that well?"

"Indeed, I do," Alex said.

They went inside the chapel and Cassie looked around. She noted the pews and a smooth stone altar. There were stained glass windows lining both sides of the chapel. She sat in a back pew and was still. She immediately felt like she did when she entered a quiet church as a child. There was an expectant yet powerful hush that enveloped her as she took breaths and looked around.

She sensed Alex sitting beside her, but they both remained quiet. Looking beyond the altar, she noticed two small doors that most likely were preparatory rooms for the celebrant. Along the side, and against the back wall, there were candle holders and some yellowed candles that Cassie realized had been there for years.

Not wanting to speak or whisper, she beckoned to Alex and together they stepped out of the chapel. "What a glorious place. Can you imagine the history and stories that must linger there?"

"I'm sure they are quite powerful," Alex said as he pulled her hand. "Come, let's go toward the cemetery." They walked through a few headstones, on toward the edge of the cemetery, where they found a lovely solid bench. From there, they could see the Channel, cemetery, and the Chapel. Behind them were trees.

"I can't imagine a more beautiful spot," Cassie said as she shook her head.

"I thought you might enjoy sitting here for a while and having a picnic." Alex opened the wicker basket he had with him. He pulled out a red checkered tablecloth and lined the bench between them. He then pulled out platters of cold chicken, cheese, and grapes. Next, were rolls. "Ah, the piece de resistance," Alex said as he pulled out a bottle of wine and two glasses. He uncorked the wine and poured a glass for each of them. Handing her a glass, he made a toast. "To the greatest best-selling novel ever."

"Thank you," Cassie said as their glasses clinked. "This is

certainly a phenomenal setting for a book. I can't wait to use it." She sipped her wine. "This is delicious." She then looked at the wine. "No wonder, that's expensive wine."

"Certainly, worth it for such a picnic and company," Alex said with a genuine smile.

Cassie blushed and smiled. "I'll have to remember to turn Bryce down more often."

They sat comfortably eating and talking for the next hour about all things. The atmosphere was light, and they seemed to have an unspoken agreement not to ruin the moment with thoughts of intruders, murders, or deadlines.

Once they finished, they packed up the refuse, the wine bottle and glasses and stood up to stretch. "The basket will be much lighter now," Alex said as he placed it on the end of the bench.

Cassie walked up to the small stone wall and looked out at the water. She closed her eyes and felt the energizing breeze and listened to the water below the cliff. She felt Alex walk up behind her and place his hands on her upper arms. After a moment, she said, "Breathtaking. Absolutely breathtaking from the first moment."

She heard him whisper, "That's my thought, exactly."

Turning around, she realized their faces were inches apart. She felt his strong arms around her and smelled his cologne. Looking up into his eyes, he lowered his lips to hers. An electric shock went through her, and she trembled slightly. Pulling back, he whispered, "I hope you don't find me too forward. I've been wanting to kiss you for a long time."

Cassie smiled in response, and he kissed her again. He then pulled her into a tight embrace, his strong arms wrapped around her, holding her.

She rested her head against his hard chest, listening to the sound of his heartbeat. Her arms were wrapped around him.

After a few moments, he loosened his hold, looked at her and kissed her on the tip of her nose. "We'd better go."

Holding her hand, he picked up the picnic basket in the other as they made their way down the path.

45

When they reached the car, Alex opened the door for her and then placed the picnic basket in the back seat. They were both quiet as he drove toward the cottage.

Alex finally broke the silence. "Do you have everything ready for London?"

"Almost. Once I have the interview from the Chief Constable, I'll update my notes. Simon is scheduled to pick me up for the meeting at the end of next week so I can hand everything over to the publishing team."

"And then what happens?" Alex slowed the car to wait for several sheep to return to their field.

"I still have work to do on my fiction novel. Evie's planning on being in England the week after next so I'll meet with her about the novel then."

"Good," Alex said. "There's more planning than I realized in publishing."

"Absolutely," Cassie agreed. "She also wants to fill me in on what's been happening since that photo with Sir Charles was in the paper."

"Ah, yes," Alex nodded.

"She asked if she would be able to meet you when she's here."

"Why not?" Alex said with a shrug. He slowed the car as they approached the cottage. They got out of the car after he parked. Alex put his hand out for the keys.

Cassie retrieved them from her pocket and handed them over.

Alex opened the door and stepped inside. Cassie slowly followed. There was no strange odor, and everything looked fine in the living room. After walking through the house, Alex returned to Cassie at the front door. "Everything looks fine today."

"Would you like a cup of tea?" Cassie asked, looking up at him. She felt awkward as she asked.

"I'd love to, but I must go," Alex said as he stood in front of her, holding her close to him. "I'd also love to drop by tomorrow, but I must be in court during the week, and I promised I would take a preparatory meeting tomorrow in Bristol. Is it okay if I text or call you?"

"Yes, I'd like that. Thank you again for the fantastic picnic. As you said, the company and view were gorgeous."

Alex smiled. "Good night, Cassie." He bent forward and lightly brushed her lips with his. "Please lock the door right away."

"I will," Cassie said as she watched him leave. He waited until she locked the door. She leaned against the door and waited until she heard his car drive away. Her hands were shaking, her heart was hammering, and she slowly exhaled to slow it down.

What was she thinking? What was he thinking? The last thing she needed was to get involved before moving back to Manhattan. It was a spontaneous kiss. He was very quiet on the return trip. Perhaps he already regretted his action.

46

C assie rolled out of bed late Monday morning. She hadn't slept well Sunday night thinking about the picnic with Alex. She reviewed the day in her mind repeatedly. Each time she did, she blushed.

Shaking off the brain fog, she put on a pot of rich coffee and made herself a light breakfast. She needed to get ready, and she was nervous. Her plan was to see the Chief Constable at 10:00 a.m. and finalize some questions.

She wasn't sure if she would see Alex at the station. He texted her twice during the day on Sunday to see how she was and then to make sure she was safe at night, but he wasn't sure if he would get through all the court preparations for him to be back in Wexley by Monday morning.

Wearing a pretty dress with matching heels, she made sure her hair and make-up was pristine. She collected a matching bag that was big enough to hold a writing pad for taking notes. She checked the time and waited only a few minutes before James pulled up to drive her to the station. Walking down the lane in heels was out of the question today.

James popped out of the car and pulled his cap up slightly. "Good morning."

"Good morning, James. How are you?" Cassie smiled at him.

"Fine," James said. "I hope you don't think me forward, but you look lovely today."

"Thanks. I'm meeting with the Chief Constable so I thought I should look nice."

"I know what you mean. I'd be a bit nervous if I was you."

"I met him the night you picked me up for the event at his home. He seemed very nice."

"Not for any special reason, but I try to stay away from officers of the law."

Cassie looked at him in the rearview mirror and laughed. "James, I'm sure you have nothing to be worried about."

"True that, and I don't want anything to come up either." James pulled to the front of the station. He ran around the car and opened Cassie's door for her.

"Thank you, James. I appreciate the drive. You don't have to always open the doors and such."

"It's the respectable thing to do for a lady. My missus would whomp me good if I didn't."

Cassie grinned and squeezed his hand. "You're an ace in my book, James. I'd like to pay you today."

"No, no. That's not necessary."

"But I don't want to take advantage of our friendship."

James smiled. "I'd be honored if you would give the missus and I a copy of your new book when it comes out."

"You got it! I'll make sure it's autographed. Do you have the other books?"

"I think she took one from the library one time, but I'm sure she brought it back."

"I see. I won't forget you, James."

He smiled and made his way back to the car. Before he got in, he tipped his cap to her. "Call me when it's time to come back."

Cassie waved goodbye. As she turned, she made a mental note to have the publisher send them a whole set of books.

She made her way through the small lobby and up to the desk. She didn't announce her name, sure that everyone knew her by now. "I have an appointment with the Chief Constable, Joe Duffy, this morning."

The desk constable nodded. "Of course. Please take a seat." He picked up the phone and within minutes, Joe Duffy's assistant appeared to collect her from the lobby.

"Good morning," he said. "Will you follow me, please?"

Cassie smiled and walked through a glass door with him toward an office in the back. He opened the door and announced her to the Chief Constable. Joe Duffy rose from his desk, greeted her, and guided her to a set of chairs on the side of the room.

"Thank you for meeting with me this morning," Cassie said. "I'm sure you have a very busy agenda given that it's Monday morning. I assume you need to sort out the weekend activity."

Joe smiled. "Hopefully, all my inspectors are doing that for me and preparing their reports."

Cassie couldn't help smiling back. He was a congenial man which was probably why he was well suited for his position.

"How is your research coming along?"

"I've completed interviews with everyone who was scheduled, and I've gotten a broad view of your department. I would like to ask a few questions about your position and responsibilities."

"Of course, ask away," he said.

"Thank you. Once I have those answers, I'll start to prepare the information for a meeting with the publisher in London at the end of this week. Before I do, I want to go over your expectations and objectives for agreeing to have this book published. I want to make sure I'm meeting all the objectives before I turn everything in. I'm sure there will be follow-up to do, which is completely normal. I'm not sure it'll be done by me, but there's always more questions and things to do for editing."

"Let's get started then, shall we?"

.   .   .

IN THE NEXT ROOM, Alex was seated at his desk reviewing reports that had been filed over the weekend. The room was crowded with sergeants and constables. Most were catching up on paperwork, finishing reports and arranging follow-up on investigation leads.

Alex had stayed late in Bristol so he could be back for Monday morning. He called Miles to his desk and asked multiple questions about potential witnesses.

Once Miles answered the questions to Alex's satisfaction, Miles said, "The medical examiner asked to speak with you later, this after-noon, sir."

Alex raised his eyebrows. "Did he leave a time?"

"No, he said he would call when he finished the last post of the morning. I believe he's had results from the last murder, and he wants to go over them with you personally before he releases his report."

Alex listened as he organized his desk. "He must have found something interesting then. I'll meet with him and if you're not busy, you can come along. Where's DS Olivia this morning?"

"She has the day off, sir. She worked the full weekend, so this is her off day."

Alex nodded as he continued to hold the reports in front of him. He handed the reports to Miles. "Please update the investigation board with this information."

"Of course, sir." As Miles walked across the room, the door opened, and DS Dennis Osborne entered with another DS.

"Morning," Dennis said loudly as he walked into the room.

"Glad you finally made it," Tim said. Their conversation was loud enough for all to hear. As he approached his desk, Arlene walked through the door with a pile of paper and handed it to him.

"You forgot these, and you have quite a bit to do this morning."

Dennis half bowed. "Why thank you, Arlene."

Tim laughed at him. "Did you just call it in this weekend, or did you do some work?

Dennis pretended mock anger. "Hey, I was busy with my interview with that beautiful writer."

Alex's head popped up straight as he listened.

"Oh, do tell. How did that work out for you?" Tim waited with a sneer as Arlene and others were now watching as well.

"The interview obviously went well as I impressed her with my natural talent."

Tim shook his head and laughed. "I'm sure you did. And did she agree to go out with you?"

"No, not yet" Dennis said, "but it's only a matter of time. She'll come around to my way of thinking and I'll have a perfect streak."

"What streak is that?" Another detective yelled out.

Dennis looked over, pleased with himself. "You know, having the ladies swoon over me. They all want to be with me sooner or later."

Alex sat up very straight and gripped the handles of his armchair. His face turned red, and he was about to stand and yell out when everyone in the room heard a roar from the back entrance. They turned toward the noise and noticed the Chief Constable standing there with Cassie at his side. From the purple color of his face and the ashen look on Cassie's, it was obvious they had heard the entire conversation.

The room went deathly silent as they waited for Joe Duffy to bellow. He managed to take a deep breath before he yelled. "That's enough. I walked Miss Ashcroft into this squad room to demonstrate what a professional, dedicated staff of officers we had working in Wexley. Instead, I find you boasting about your dating prowess?"

Alex's jaw and fists were clenched as he watched the encounter unfold.

Joe Duffy continued. "As it is, we already owe Miss Ashcroft a major apology." While it didn't seem plausible, Joe's facial color deepened.

Cassie wasn't sure if the staff in the squad room took a few steps away from Dennis or it just seemed that way as he swallowed. Cassie needed to remind herself to breathe.

Dennis shrugged. "Harmless stuff, sir. We were wondering if Miss

Cassie would be interested in dating anyone while she was in England."

Cassie's eyebrows rose as high as they possibly could.

"Was there a wager involved?"

Arlene held back a grin as she nodded in the corner.

Joe could barely contain himself when they all heard Cassie's voice.

"Chief, if you'll allow me a moment." Alex could see she was trembling.

Duffy turned to her as he shook his head. "I am mortified, Miss Ashcroft. I have no words right now. We have policies in place for this nonsense, but that doesn't change this situation. I can only apologize for the stupidity of these officers."

Cassie answered tersely, "I'd like to say I don't know the details of their discussion, but you can be sure that I've not gotten involved with anyone and now it's obvious why it would never happen." As she spoke, she glared at Alex, daring him to contradict her. "Chief, if there's any money on this bet, may I suggest it all be donated to the children's hospital because I can guarantee you that no one in this department would ever be taking any of it home."

"I think that's an excellent idea," the Chief said, his voice rising. "And I'll be happy to collect it all in my office right now as we discuss who will continue to work in this department."

"I'll take my leave, then," Cassie said. "I have no further need to speak with anyone in the department and I'm sure the publisher will contact you by other means if they want more information."

"Sergeants and Inspectors in my office now," Duffy yelled as he pointed.

Cassie frowned at Alex as she strode past his desk.

"Cassie," Alex called out, swallowing hard.

"You too, Knight! On the double," Joe roared as people moved toward his office.

Cassie bolted out of the side door and hurried down the drive. She made it to the lane before she started to cry. She was embarrassed in front of the entire room. She was supposed to call James but didn't want to be with anyone right now. She turned to walk through the field to get back to the cottage. She kicked off her heels so they wouldn't sink in the soft dirt. She picked them up in her hand as she walked home, chiding herself the whole way. She stopped by a tree to rest for a moment. Her anger was beginning to grow at Dennis and Alex. Was Bryce in on it too? *I trusted him. I let my guard down and now I don't know if anything was real or just a laugh for them.*

47

Cassie reached the cottage, opened the door, and went inside. She locked the door and went upstairs to her room. Her head hurt, she felt dizzy and was angry. She threw her bag on the dresser and threw herself on the bed.

A short time later, the chime went off on her cell phone, but Cassie ignored it. She then heard a text coming through which she also ignored. After another thirty minutes, she decided to take a hot shower and change. She stood under the hot spray and washed her hair. As she toweled off, she realized she felt more relaxed.

Pulling on jeans and a T-shirt, she pushed her hair into a knot on top of her head and went downstairs. Her stomach growled, which was a surprise to her, so she made a sandwich and ate slowly in front of the television.

When her cell rang again, Cassie looked at the caller ID. It was Evie, so she hit accept. "Evie."

"Are you okay?" Evie sounded harried.

Cassie took a deep breath. "I've had an aggravating day."

"So, I heard," Evie said sharply.

"From whom?"

"Your friend, Alex Knight, called me. He said I should reach out to you immediately. He couldn't connect with you."

"I'm sorry. Did you say my friend?"

"He was very worried about you. He said he's tried calling and texting many times."

"If you must know, I haven't looked at my phone until just this minute so I'm not aware of what he's tried to do, but even if I was, I wouldn't answer."

Evie was quiet for a moment. "Cassie, he sounded very worried about you."

"Are you more worried about him or me?" Cassie's voice rose.

"I'm just trying to understand what happened, which no one has told me yet. He was driving to the cottage when he called. He said I should call you right away because he couldn't get hold of you. What's going on? Do I need to fly over there? Or have Simon pick you up?"

Cassie blew out a breath. "Okay, here's the story." She started with catching Evie up to date on the interviews and then told her about the picnic on Saturday but left out the kiss.

"Interesting, go on," Evie said. "What happened today?"

Cassie spent the next hour telling Evie about her meeting with the Chief Constable, and then the meltdown at the station. "Evie, I feel like a fool. I should have remembered Alex Knight's cardinal rule. What was I thinking? I want to return to Manhattan. I've finished my part of that book and I've seen enough of England to write my novel."

"Cassie, can you hang in there until Friday? Simon will be picking you up and bringing you to London for the meeting. I'll be there shortly thereafter. When he comes to get you, pack a bag for the weekend. I'll put you up in the hotel so you can get away for a few days. We can plan next steps then."

"Okay, I will," Cassie said as she held her emotions in check.

After speaking with Evie, Cassie felt restless. She didn't want to sit in the cottage, and she was too wired to write. Pulling on her hiking boots, Cassie locked up the cottage and set out to take a walk. She started down the lane and then headed into the woods. She had avoided them since her first outing when she got lost. Now, she followed a well-worn path, so she wasn't worried about direction, but she kept alert for hunters.

Traveling several miles, she stopped to rest and then turned around and went back to the cottage. She was at the end of her fifth mile when she approached the stone bridge that led to the edge of William Blake's property. She stopped to look over the side and watched the river flowing past. The water was clear, but as before the area under the bridge looked dark. Cassie leaned over the bridge as far as she could and shuddered as she looked at the area.

She was surprised to see Granger Lowell looking back up at her. Cassie stood still as she watched him climb the bank. He looked back and saw she was still watching him. He then gave her a salute and Cassie half-heartedly waved back before she continued across the bridge and back to the cottage.

48

When Cassie neared the door, she spotted a large bouquet of flowers on the stoop. Her first instinct was to pick them up and throw them in the trash, but it wasn't the flowers fault that some men were assuming. She took them into the house and placed them in a large vase. The card was from Alex.

Please talk to me
Alex

CASSIE DUMPED the card and envelope and then placed the flowers near her desk. At least she would have something pleasant to look at as she spent time with her WIP. She worked for several hours and then shut down her computer and decided to go to bed. She went upstairs, locked the door, moved the hope chest in place and started to change. Her cell phone rang, but Cassie didn't get there in time.

She then heard it chirp and checked the incoming text, thinking that Evie was checking on her. It was from Alex.

Are you at the cottage? Are you safe? I haven't been able to get hold of you. Worried about you.

CASSIE DIDN'T ANSWER HIM.

I'm going to send a constable to make sure you're safe in the cottage but will wait five minutes for you to text back.

CASSIE GROANED and knew he would do just that if she didn't answer to make sure her intruder had not visited. She had no choice.

I am fine. NO need to send anyone.

Glad to hear you are safe. Can we talk tomorrow after court?

No, not in the mood for company. Concentrate on your case. Stay in Bristol.

Can we please talk about this?

Good night, Alex.

CASSIE THEN TURNED the volume down on her phone, turned the lights off and went to bed. She didn't see that Alex was texting her from outside the cottage. He was hoping they could talk, but when he saw the lights go off, he started the car and drove off.

49

The next day, Cassie continued to spend time on her WIP. The day was gloomy, like her mood, so she was not able to take a walk. When she took a break from writing, she pulled out a piece of luggage and started to pack what she wanted to bring with her to London. She would feel better, even if she simply spent time in the hotel room, reading or watching the world go by.

Early afternoon, the doorbell rang, and Cassie checked to see who her visitor was. She still didn't want to speak with Alex. She spent hours overthinking what had happened on Saturday and assumed his relative silence on the way back from the Moreland Estate was his reluctance to admit he made a mistake or felt guilty.

Cassie smiled when she saw James at the door. He was holding a large vase with a beautiful bouquet of flowers. She opened the door and James lit up. "Miss Cassie. These are for you. I was asked to deliver them. They're from the Wexley Police Department. I assume they're thanking you for all your research."

"I'm sure they are," Cassie said as she opened the door wide enough to allow James to come inside.

"I'm sorry about yesterday. I hope I didn't miss a call about coming to pick you up," James said with a worried look as he placed the vase where Cassie indicated. He pulled his hat from his head and looked at her with wide eyes.

"No James, I didn't call. It was such a lovely day, I decided to walk home through the field."

"In those heels?" James asked, surprised.

Cassie grinned and leaned toward James with a conspiratorial whisper. "I took them off and went through the field in my bare feet. Just like a child."

"Oh, well, if you wanted to, that's fine. I was worried I messed up."

"James, you are very sweet. No, you didn't mess up at all and I will still be sending something to you and your wife."

"Thank you," James said. "Well, I'd better be getting out of your hair unless there's anything else you need?"

"No, thank you. I'll call if I do." As Cassie walked James to the door, she decided to tell him that she would be gone for the weekend. "I'm going to London for a couple of days at the end of the week to meet with the publisher. I'm sure certain villagers will have questions, so I wanted to make sure you knew I wasn't kidnapped or anything."

James laughed. "I see you're getting to know everyone. Have a good trip, then." James waved to her as he left the cottage.

Before Cassie stepped back inside the cottage, she saw a car drive up. After a moment, Miles stepped out of the car with an envelope and walked up to her with a shy smile. "Hello," he said as he walked toward her.

"Hi, Miles, how are you?" Cassie was honestly happy to see Miles. He was always a pleasant respectable young man.

"I'm doing well. The Chief Constable said you were waiting for some papers from him. He asked me to deliver them to you personally."

"Ah, yes. James dropped off flowers from the department."

"Yes, well I'm sorry you had to hear that," Miles said, embarrassed as he looked down. "I'm not sure if you heard the outcome?"

"No, Miles, to be honest, I haven't spoken with anyone from the department."

"Oh." Miles seemed surprised. Knowing the person Miles was, he wasn't about to talk about anyone without prompting.

"Can you tell me what happened?"

Miles blushed and swallowed hard. "Arlene cooked up one of her schemes and Dennis, with his ego, was all too eager to help. The Chief Constable has them both on suspension now. They'll have to wait to see if they'll be fired." Cassie nodded her understanding as Miles looked at her. "Can I speak freely?"

"Of course, Miles."

"I want you to know that what they said in there and what they did, doesn't have anything to do with the rest of us in the department. It's been a pleasure to speak with you and help with the interviews. And I'll always remember how kind you were when we had Sunday dinner. I know the other officers all feel the same. Dennis has always been a bit of a sod and Arlene is jealous."

Cassie smiled. "Thank you for saying so, Miles."

"I wanted you to know. I must go, now or my boss is going to let me have it." Miles smiled, handed her the envelope, and then quickly got into his car and drove down the lane.

Cassie went inside and looked at the beautiful urn of flowers. She removed an envelope from the top and opened it. Inside was a handwritten note from Joe Duffy.

Dear Miss Ashcroft,

Once again, I can only apologize for the embarrassing display and lack of professionalism you witnessed yesterday. I assure you, the officers responsible for the issue are being dealt with as we speak. I hope you can understand they, in no way, represent the opinion or behavior of the entire department. It's been more than a pleasure working with you and I look forward to our paths crossing again in the future.

Enjoy the flowers. You deserve more!

All my best,

Joe Duffy

50

Alex continued to call and text, making sure she was safe. He continued to ask to come to the cottage and to speak with her, but all things considered, Cassie thought it was best to stay apart. She continued to think back about his cardinal rules and the fact that she would be leaving England soon.

Cassie was mollified by the flowers and the apology note, but still was not up to having an emotional conversation with Alex only to tell him she was leaving. She blamed herself for being anxious and allowing an emotional attachment to someone. He was different from so many of the men she had met in the past and seemed to truly understand her, but the situation was quite impossible. He had his cardinal rules as well.

Friday morning finally approached. Cassie had her report and her luggage ready. Her flowers were still in beautiful bloom, so she gave them to James the night before and asked him to take them to Mrs. Witherspoon at the vicarage.

Cassie assumed she would receive another visit from her intruder while she was gone so she either packed everything that was dear to her or locked it into a small area that hopefully wouldn't be searched or touched. She heard a chime and checked her text messages to see that Simon was five minutes away. She promised to be ready as they were to leave immediately so she could be in London on time for her first meeting.

She rolled her luggage to the front door of the cottage, collected her phone and bag. It was a hot day, so she wore a light dress and had her hair pinned up in a chignon. Her make-up was done so she could run right into the meeting.

Cassie opened the door, pulled the luggage outside, and locked the cottage door. She pulled everything to the gate so she could jump in the car. Cassie pulled the gate closed and when she turned around, her breath caught when she saw Alex walking down the lane toward her. His suit jacket was off and flung over his right shoulder. His white shirt and blue silk tie were crisp as always. He saw that she noticed him and held his hand up. He had a sad, longing expression on his face and took another step toward her when Simon came down the lane and drove straight up to her gate, inadvertently placing the car as a barrier between her and Alex.

Simon popped out of the car and opened the trunk. He didn't notice Alex as he ran to her side, picked up her luggage, threw it in the trunk, and ran back to the driver's seat. "We've got to go or we'll be late."

Her eyes still locked with Alex; she broke contact when Simon called her. With one last look toward Alex, she got into the car and felt bad when she saw disappointment cross his face as Simon drove away.

51

Cassie was quiet for the first ten minutes, which was fine as Simon chatted away. He told her about her schedule of meetings for the day and then extra meetings that were arranged when she agreed to stay in London for a few days. They had scheduled dinner for her as well as made reservations for entertainment at a London theater with the president of the publishing company. Cassie listened but as Simon kept listing each item, Cassie started to hear a small roaring in her ears. She felt overwhelmed and for a moment, wished she was back in the cottage with Alex. She had felt so safe, he sipping his whiskey and she making dinner. She realized she had created a dream world that couldn't last, but it was comforting, and so very safe while it lasted.

After a while they arrived in London. Simon dropped her directly at the publisher. She needed to go to her meeting right away and he would take care of the check-in and her luggage at the hotel.

Cassie went inside the building and was greeted by Laura in the lobby. "Cassie, how are you? I'm so excited to see you. I would have come out with Simon, but I had an assignment to get done before Evie comes out next week."

"Hi, Laura. How do you like working in London?"

"I love it. I'm going to ask Evie if I can stay. If not, we're going to ask if Simon can return to America with me." Laura guided Cassie to the elevator and pushed the button. "The team is looking forward to meeting you and discussing the research. Also, they have a few of your other books here for signature if you have time."

"Of course," Cassie said as she let Laura lead the way.

Cassie spent the remainder of the afternoon presenting the material and interview summary to the publishing team. They discussed their thoughts and promised to let her know what else they needed while she was in Wexley. She was then ushered into another area with books piled high on a glossy table. After a few promo shots of her signing her books, she was able to get through the pile. She made sure to give James's address to Laura and told her to send a complete set to the couple. Next on the schedule was a stop at the hotel to change clothes and a quick rest period. The limo would then pick her up to go to dinner.

Cassie made her way to her room after receiving her key card from an assigned hotel liaison. She opened the door, let out a sigh, and sat in one of the plush seats in the living area. The day was hot, but the room was comfortable, and Cassie eyed the bed in the darkened bedroom. Although sorely tempted to drop down for a nap, she realized she didn't have time. She hopped in the shower, then changed clothes and redid her hair and make-up for dinner.

Hurrying down to the lobby, she was in time for the car's arrival. The president of the publishing company was waiting for her inside the limo. When she was ushered to the car and comfortably seated, the bell person closed the door and tapped on the roof.

A silver-haired gentleman introduced himself as he took Cassie's hand in both of his. "Hello, I'm Mr. Portman. I'm so happy to meet you."

Cassie nodded with a smile. "Happy to meet you as well."

"Evie Thompson tried to be here with us, but unfortunately could not make it in time."

"I understand," Cassie said. "I'm sure we'll have a lovely evening."

As the evening unfolded, Cassie found that Mr. Portman was a gracious host and an excellent conversationalist. The restaurant was top-notch, and the play was excellent. They had perfect seats in the theater and Cassie realized she was given the royal treatment. When she returned to the hotel, she was escorted to her room. She extended her gratitude and told Mr. Portman she looked forward to their meeting in the morning.

Although everyone she met was pleasant, and the venue glorious, Cassie couldn't help comparing the night to her day in Plymouth. Spending time at Books by the Sea with Sir Charles and the Sea Treasure Pub with Alex seemed more personal and real. The experience she had this evening felt a bit superficial. If anything, she knew Alex's thoughts, opinions and time were genuine. If he didn't want to be somewhere, he surely wouldn't be for the sake of appearances.

Cassie undressed and wrapped herself in a soft, silk robe. She took advantage of a small glass of Amaretto and sat near the window staring down at the nightlife in London. The city was hopping despite the hour. This was the closest she had been to Manhattan in months, but she didn't miss the city as much as she thought she would. Feeling tired, she turned off her phone and went to sleep.

The next morning, Cassie slept late. The stress of the last couple of weeks finally caught up to her. She ordered room service, including a large pot of coffee and relaxed. She was through her second cup when she had an incoming video call from Evie.

"Good morning, Evie," Cassie said. "It must be 7:00 a.m. in New York."

"Yes, I think the only other creatures that are up are the birds," Evie said in a dramatic voice.

Cassie laughed at her distress. "It's noon here. I'm only on my second cup of coffee and still in a robe. Do you want to speak later today?"

"I would love to, but I can't, dear. I have a hectic schedule if I want to get through all my meetings and contracts. I fully intend to be in England by the end of next week."

"That's great," Cassie said. "I'm looking forward to seeing you."

"So sweet. Did you have a good time last night?"

"Yes, although I would have been as comfortable sitting in this beautiful suite. I'm curious why I got the royal treatment. You, of all people would know."

Evie laughed. "Ever since you had your photo taken with Sir Charles Effingham, your profile has skyrocketed. Book orders, interview requests, book signing requests, you name it. The publisher was very impressed. Besides the fact that you're a young, attractive, single woman, the president is smart enough to create more publicity opportunities for you. I'm glad you dressed. I've already seen a few shots that were taken by paparazzi at the theater last night. You're in the London papers again, my dear. I'm sure everyone from London to the village are talking."

Cassie groaned. "Wonderful. I suppose today will bring more opportunities?"

"Yes, I'm afraid that is the case. Someone will be bringing you some fresh clothing choices. Pick what you want. You have two meetings today. One has to do with the non-fiction book about the police in Wexley and the other will go over your upcoming fiction novel. They would like to have an idea of timelines and plot so the publicist can start promoting nine months in advance."

Cassie groaned again as she drank her coffee.

"Did you finish your coffee?" Evie asked a minute later.

"Yes, why? More fun news?"

"I want to discuss your decision to leave Wexley."

"Evie, it's strange because it's been wonderful, but it's been stressful. Now that I'm back in London, I think I miss the quieter times in the country. I don't miss having an intruder trash the house every time I'm out. I don't miss everyone knowing my business although I am getting fond of some of the villagers. As a matter of fact, I need to send an entire signed set of my books to a man named James and his wife."

"That's fine. Send me the details or better yet, give them to Simon and Laura and ask them to send them."

"Already did. Thank you," Cassie said. "I told Simon to cancel the video security as I won't be staying in Heather House much longer."

"So, about that, here's my question."

"Oh no, what?"

"Do you think you could go back to Wexley for a few more weeks?"

"Why?"

"I'm coming in next week and I'd like to see the village and Heather House for that matter. I still would like to meet Alex Knight. Cassie, I know you're not going to be happy when I say this, but he's our only connection to Sir Charles right now."

"Oh no! I am not going to ask him to exploit that relationship. I was shocked when Sir Charles wanted to meet me, and I did promise to send him my next book. I have the publicist's name. We don't need Alex Knight for that."

"All right, we'll do it that way. I'd still like to meet him. Plus, you must go back and pack anyway. Hang in there for a couple more weeks. Wait until I get there."

Cassie sighed. "I suppose I can do that."

"Do you despise the man that much? Or is it, as I suspect, quite the opposite?"

"It doesn't matter, does it, Evie? The man has a cardinal rule not to get involved. That was our deal. The whole incident at the station was about another DS, who has quite the ego, but it made me realize I wasn't thinking straight about anyone."

"Then listen to me, young lady. I'm older than you and the closest thing you have to a mother so please take my advice. Regardless of what happens, you need to, for your own peace of mind, go back and get some closure. Otherwise, it will sit there with this ugly stain on it forever. Go back, make peace with him and yourself so you're not emotionally in a state, although it might make some good fodder for writing. You shouldn't leave the country without talking it out. By then, I'll be there. I want to see this bookshop in Plymouth and a few other things and then we'll plan for whatever you need."

Cassie was silent. "Has he reached out to you again?"

"Not since Monday, when he was beside himself that he couldn't reach you. Has he reached out to you?"

"He's texted and called but I haven't answered. I feel bad about yesterday. He was walking to the cottage when Simon swooped in, threw me in the car and left before Alex could reach the door."

Evie giggled. "You know that's not right. You must have closure to be at peace. At least do that for yourself, if not for him. It's the decent thing to do. At least, hear his side of the story. You'd want the same chance. Oh, and by the way, I tried to investigate the Moreland Estate. It's one of those things that you can't get information on unless you're highly classified which apparently, I'm not."

"What do you mean?" Cassie asked as she poured another cup of coffee.

"All I could find out is that the estate belonged to Lord Moreland when he was a member of the House of Lords. He has since passed. I believe Alex has a connection to the estate, but I can't find out what it is. He's the only one who can tell us."

"I see," Cassie said. "You want me to spy for you?"

"More good fodder for a book, right?"

"Evie, I can't. He's a very nice, polite, respectful type of guy."

"All the more reason to go back to Wexley, speak with him, and put this matter to rest. He deserves a conversation at minimum. I'm not asking you to have a relationship, just treat him with the same level of respect."

Cassie nodded as she looked at Evie over the phone. "You're right."

"Good. Now speaking of rest, go get some before your schedule starts for the day. You're staying in London for two more nights. Simon and Laura will drive you back to Wexley on Monday. If there's anything you want or need while you're in London, have them take you shopping."

"Will do. Thank you, Evie."

"Love you, dear." Evie blew Cassie a kiss.

Cassie smiled into the phone. "Love you, too. See you soon."

52

The rest of the weekend flew by. Cassie spent time shopping with Simon and Laura, visiting a few landmarks and then quiet time in her hotel room. She reviewed a subplot for her upcoming novel with her literary team and then rested. Her favorite activity was to open the drapes as wide as possible, turn the lights down low and watch the city at night. Before now, she never looked up at the stars but since living in Wexley she looked up as much as she looked down. She doubted that would make sense to anyone but her, but there it was.

By the time Monday morning rolled around, she was packed and ready to go back to the cottage. She had a last meeting with the publisher. At the end of the meeting, they gave her a manilla envelope and asked her to personally deliver it to the Chief Constable, Joe Duffy. Cassie groaned inwardly as she knew it meant she would have to return to the station, but Evie was right. Cassie had nothing to be ashamed of and better to move on with her head held high.

Simon and Laura sat in the front, while Cassie watched the world go by in the back seat. They hit a lot of traffic, so the trip took longer than they planned.

Back at Heather House, Cassie opened the door and stepped

inside to find everything in order. She was afraid that she'd find books, or her kitchen scattered all over, but everything was clean.

Simon and Laura walked in behind her carrying several boxes. Cassie had indulged in a few more outfits and food to restock her pantry.

"What beautiful flowers," Laura said as she placed one of the boxes on the dining room table.

Cassie put her luggage near the stairs and walked to the dining room table. There was a beautiful vase of fresh flowers on the table. There was no card.

"Did you leave the key with someone?" Simon asked as he looked around.

"No, but several people have the key to the cottage, including the police. There is a tendency for visitors to let themselves in when you live in a small village." Cassie laughed. "Took me a bit to get used to that."

"Is there anything else we can do for you?"

Cassie shook her head. "No, but would you like something to eat before you go back to London? I can make something."

Simon shook his head. "No, thank you. It's late afternoon. I know a place we can stop on the way and it's better if we get back before too late."

"Thanks again for all your help. Evie will be here soon."

"I'm sure we'll be driving her out here, so we'll see you then. If you think of anything you want us to bring, call or text and we'll be happy to shop for you."

"That's for sure," Laura echoed with a smile.

Cassie couldn't help but laugh. "I certainly will. You two had better get going."

She walked them to the door and watched as they drove away. She turned and brought her luggage upstairs and when she placed the bags on her bed, the sealed envelope fell to the floor. There was another hour before dinner and she needed fresh milk, so Cassie decided to walk to the station before everyone left for the day.

She changed her clothes, put on her hiking shoes, picked up the envelope and headed to the lane. She took time to look more closely at the fields, the beautiful fragrant flowers, the cottages, and the sky. It was different than the city. She crossed the stone bridge and watched the small river for a moment. Finally, she arrived at the heart of the village. She continued to the station as she wanted to drop the envelope off before she went to the store for the milk.

Opening the glass door, she went into the police lobby and up to the desk. "I'd like to leave an envelope for the Chief Constable. It's imperative he get it as soon as possible."

"Yes, we'll see to it immediately. Thank you." The constable extended her hand for the delivery.

IN THE ROOM next to the lobby, Miles was walking past the door to bring papers to Alex. He handed his boss the report and said, "Cassie's back. She's out in the lobby."

"Oh, does it look like there's a problem?"

"I don't think so. More like she's dropping something off at the desk."

"I'd better check," Alex said as he grabbed his jacket and headed toward the door. He saw her leaving so he quickly went out the side door to intercept her by the time she reached the steps.

Cassie walked down the steps and saw Alex waiting for her on the sidewalk. He was watching her and smiling. Her stomach clenched and she initially felt awkward.

"Cassie, how are you? How was your trip to London?" Always the gentleman.

She walked up to him and smiled. "It was hectic. Lots of meetings and whirlwind publicity events."

"A writer's life? I saw the publicity page."

"Yes, fun for some."

Alex pointed to the station. "Is everything all right?"

Cassie nodded. "Yes. The publisher asked me to drop an envelope off to Joe Duffy. I thought I would get that done since I needed milk."

Alex quieted and looked at her with that intense gaze. "Cassie, can we talk?"

Cassie hesitated for a moment.

Alex smiled and tried again. "I'm glad you're back and I know you haven't had time to cook. Please, have dinner with me? We could go to the pub for something light." His smile was hopeful. "Besides, there's been a break in the case. I want to tell you about that."

Cassie looked into his eyes, then smiled as she remembered Evie's words. "Alex, that sounds great."

Alex's smile was wide. He stepped back and guided her in front of him. Together, they walked to the pub and sat at a table in the corner.

Shelly appeared instantly. "What can I get for you?"

Alex looked at Cassie. "Would you like a glass of wine?"

"Sounds perfect," Cassie said, thinking it may cause her hands to stop shaking.

"A glass of white merlot and I'll have a pint. We'll order the food in a bit."

"Very good," Shelly said as she turned away.

They spent the next few minutes selecting something to eat. Alex looked at Cassie. "I'm glad you're back."

Cassie blushed and nodded. "I'm sorry about Friday morning. Simon was in a rush, and he didn't see you. I don't want you to think I purposely snubbed you."

Alex was gracious and nodded. Shelly came back to the table with their drinks. "Do you know what you'd like to eat yet?"

They both ordered the Shepherd's pie which was on a special that evening. "This will be my first official Shepherd's pie in England," Cassie said to break the silence.

"Now that's worth celebrating." Alex picked up his drink. "Cheers."

Cassie took a few sips of wine, which tasted delicious, and leaned forward so she couldn't be heard. "What's up with the case?"

Alex grinned and leaned forward as well. "You were right. I had to listen to some squawking about the budget, but they did the DNA test on Mr. Blake's hairbrush and there was a familiar match to the victim."

"Really? Were there any specifics?"

"It appears to be a half-brother probably on the paternal side."

"Now that's interesting," Cassie said as she took another sip of wine. "Do you have any other information on William Blake's father?"

"Such as?" Alex asked.

"Are you able to track birth certificates by the father?" Cassie asked.

Alex was pensive for a moment. "William Blake's birth certificate would have been recorded 85 years ago. His half-brothers would have been over 70 years old. I'm sure if we went to a specific town or church, we might be able to track something but it's very possible we might not. Things weren't digital as they are now." Alex took a sip of beer. "However...,"

Cassie waited a few moments. "However, what?"

Alex looked at her. "I've been reading the journal I found in your library. I seem to remember there being a mention of the senior Mr. Blake going off for a while. Maybe there's some information in the journal. Or there may be a mention of when he came back. I'll have to have a look, but I wouldn't hold my breath."

Cassie took a sip of wine. "You mentioned that a villager stated that Mr. Blake was unhappy about something and was going to or did change his will."

"Yes, he said that the week before his death, William Blake mentioned he had changed his will but didn't go into details about why he was unhappy. Something was bothering him."

"So here is the million-dollar question," Cassie said. "Did William Blake kill his half-brother or did someone else kill him and hide him in the car. If so, why? What was the motive?"

Alex took another sip of beer. "We could possibly discover the answer if we found that will."

"And I'm sure that's what the intruder has been looking for. He's only been downstairs as far as I know. There's nowhere to hide anything like that in my bedroom. The fireplace is not that extravagant. No desk, no bookcase. Just the toilet and I don't think it's in there."

Alex laughed as he imagined that scenario. "Are you sure there's nothing in the loo?"

"Would you like to examine it?" Cassie asked as she laughed.

"Perhaps, I'll send Miles."

"You'd better not if you know what's good for you."

They looked up when Shelly appeared with their food. She put the plates down, asked about more drinks and then walked away. Alex and Cassie picked up their forks and ate their dinner in peaceful companionship.

53

When dinner was over, they left the pub. "I'm sorry but it's too late to get your milk."

"That's okay. Perhaps I'll get some tomorrow. I'll have tea instead of coffee in the morning."

Alex nodded. "Let me walk you home." They started down the lane. The weather was pleasant, and the sky was still light despite the hour. As they walked, they made idle chit chat.

"Do you mind if we walk around the village green?" Alex asked her with a lift of his eyebrow.

"No, of course not, if that's what you'd like."

They walked through the green and to the pond near the back. There was a bench there, but they both stood looking at the water. Alex finally broke the silence.

"I want to talk to you about last Monday at the station."

Cassie looked straight ahead. "I'm trying to forget about it and move forward."

"You know that Dennis is on suspension?"

Cassie nodded.

"Arlene started the whole thing off. She has a habit of eliminating potential threats with humiliation."

"Except, she has no competition. No expectations, no obligations, no relationships, right? Cardinal rules and all that."

Alex looked at her but didn't speak for a moment.

"Cassie, I need you to believe I had nothing to do with what happened."

Cassie looked into his eyes. "Did you know about it? Did you know that Arlene had challenged him or anyone else?"

"Me? Do you think they would tell the boss that something like that? If they had, their ears would be ringing for months."

Cassie blew out a breath and turned back to the pond. "Arlene got her way, didn't she? Managed to embarrass me in front of the whole station."

"Except that everyone was uncomfortable including the other officers. No one thought it was funny or respectful. I want you to know that."

Cassie looked into his blue eyes and nodded. "Thank you. I appreciate you telling me."

She was quiet for a moment as they walked around the pond. "This type of thing is always easier in Manhattan."

"Why is that?" Alex asked wondering what she meant.

"Because many people are rude all the time. But you're very polite, very respectful, which makes it harder."

"For what?" Alex asked again as he stopped to look at her. When she didn't answer, he said, "To cut and run? Set up a barrier to ease anxiety? Have another excuse to end a friendship? That won't be happening here."

"I told Evie I wanted to leave immediately."

"And what did she say?" Alex asked with a raised eyebrow.

"She would always support what I asked, but she wanted me to come back and work it out."

"Good advice," Alex said. "I would have found you if you didn't come back."

"Oh, really?" Cassie smiled, amused at his persistence.

"I have it on the very highest authority that I'm a good detective. I would have found you."

Cassie smiled at his words. "Why?"

"I enjoy our talks, our walks, our dinners. Not that I want you to cook for me, but I enjoy intelligent conversation and knowing someone who thinks the way I do." Alex looked at her with that quiet intense gaze and whispered, "I missed you while you were gone. I missed you all last week. Weren't you curious about the case or anything else?"

Cassie's smile was awkward before she stammered. "I thought it might be better to just leave it than to make a bigger issue. No sense in having people hurt in the end."

Alex looked at her without speaking. He let the subject drop, but he held her shoulders and asked, "Are we good?"

Cassie looked up at him. She smiled and nodded. "Yes, we'll keep working on the case. We're so close."

Alex nodded and then guided her out of the green and back to her cottage. He went inside for only a few minutes to make sure the house was secure.

"Thank you for your flowers," Cassie said.

"You're welcome. You deserve beautiful flowers."

"Two bouquets from you are quite enough." Cassie smiled.

"I only brought one," Alex said as he narrowed his eyes. "I'll be more than happy to bring another."

Cassie frowned and pointed to the dining room table. "Did you drop these flowers here?"

Alex looked at the flowers and shook his head. "Was there a card?"

"No. It looks like they were handpicked. There was no note or at least not when I returned here."

"Curious," Alex said with a frown. "Very curious. Please let me know if you find a note."

"I will."

Cassie walked Alex to the door. "Good night, Alex. Thank you for dinner."

"Thank you," Alex said with a respectful smile and a nod.

Cassie locked the door while he waited outside. She then watched him walk away as a tear dropped down her cheek.

54

The next morning, Cassie woke up to her phone chirping. She checked the text and saw a message from Alex.

Good morning. Check your stoop.

CASSIE GOT UP, pulled on her robe, and went downstairs. Outside the door, she found a fresh quart of milk and a newspaper. Smiling, she picked them up and brought them in. *Only in the country.* She could have had room service in London, but this was very different and nice. She grabbed her cell and texted Alex back.

Thank you very much! Stopping to discuss the case tonight?

SHE RECEIVED a reply from Alex that he would be there right after work if it was okay with her. She told him she would be ready with dinner. Next, she made a pot of coffee and looked through the freezer and pantry to see what she would make. She found a couple of steaks in the freezer. A garden salad would pair very nicely.

Cassie spent the remainder of the day unpacking and updating files at her desk. She made sure her internet was intact as well as her computer files. She updated the notes for her novel. Very often, a change in scenery provided a powerful boost to creativity and Cassie wanted to make sure she put everything down before she forgot the flow.

When she was up to date with her file, Cassie turned off the computer to start dinner. She had marinated the steaks earlier in the day. Gathering the vegetables for the salad, she spent the next fifteen minutes washing and chopping. She placed the salad in the refrigerator and set the table. Cassie smiled when she set out the bottle of single malt and a glass for Alex. It would be sad when she returned to Manhattan.

She had the grill warming so she could throw the steaks on when he arrived. She went to the cabinet to check for condiments and once again had to move the pot that was sticking out of the brick archway. She reminded herself to ask Alex if he could help her fix it, but not tonight.

A small time later, she heard a knock on the door. She opened it to find Alex smiling at her. He held up his right hand which contained the journal. "I thought we might do some reading tonight after dinner."

"Sounds great. Please come in," Cassie said lightly as she pulled the door completely open. "Does steak sound okay for dinner?"

"Okay? It sounds great," Alex said as his smile widened.

"I'm glad. I'm going to start grilling then. Make yourself comfortable."

Cassie walked out the back patio door to the grill with a covered plate she took from the refrigerator.

Alex took off his jacket and hung it on a peg. He noticed the single malt on the dining room table and poured whiskey into his glass. Although it was the same bottle, the single malt tasted better than usual. It may have been because it was his first visit to Heather House in ten days, and he was very happy about it. Hopefully, none of his sergeants would surmise that he was beginning to enjoy a mild version of domestication for the first time in twenty years. To add to that feeling, he walked to the kitchen, found a full apron on a peg, and put it on. He then walked outside to help Cassie with the grill.

"Can I help with the steaks?"

Cassie turned to look at him and burst out laughing when she saw the apron. He was holding up a grilling fork while wearing an oven mitt. "This is one of the times I wish I'd brought my phone with me to take a photo."

"Thanks, luv," Alex said as he moved his fork in an arc like a sword. "I'm sure there are other things that need to be done to prepare for dinner."

"I do have to toss the salad," Cassie said as she tilted her head.

"Then allow me a run at the steaks, so you can do the rest."

Laughing, Cassie went inside and readied the rest of the meal for the table. A short time later, Alex walked into the kitchen with the platter of steaks in one hand and his whiskey in another. The pair sat down and while Cassie served the steaks, Alex opened a bottle of wine and poured.

"This steak is absolutely delicious," Alex said. "Don't let anyone at the pub know or we'll have more problems to deal with."

"Flattery will get you everywhere," Cassie said.

"Oh, really?"

Cassie's face reddened. "Well, not there."

Alex nodded as he chewed.

They talked over dinner about their day and her trip to London. "Evie will be arriving in Wexley at the end of the week. She's still hoping to meet you."

"I'll make it a point to be available," Alex said. He was quiet for a moment. "Can I make a suggestion?"

"Of course."

"This Saturday, Plymouth is having a large festival. I know some of the officers are going and some are working private duty for extra money. Perhaps we could make a day of it. I'm sure Tom will have the bookshop open for business. We could take her there and then perhaps have a late lunch at the Sea Treasure Pub?"

"You would do that?" Cassie asked, feeling flattered.

"Of course. I think it would be fun. I'm not used to fun, but it's becoming more familiar. They have a real carnival with a Ferris wheel and all."

"Sounds like fun," Cassie said. "I'll call Evie to make sure her schedule is free."

"Perfect and I'll let my cousin know. We'll give her the works."

Cassie nodded. "I appreciate that, Alex. It's very kind of you to offer."

"My pleasure."

Cassie stood to collect the plates and Alex helped to clear the table. She realized the two of them working together seemed completely natural, which was strange. Alex cleaned the table and when all was dry, retrieved his briefcase as well as the journal. He pulled out the case file. For the next two hours, the pair discussed the facts they had uncovered and went through the journal for clues.

"It says here that William Blake, Sr. left the estate for almost a year. It doesn't say exactly where he went or what he did, but you can see from this entry, he returned to his wife and his son, William, who was 15 years old at the time."

"Did Mrs. Blake write anything later in the journal?"

Alex shook his head. "No, I went through most of it, and I didn't find any more details that we could use."

"So, the timing is right, but we're back to square one unless we find the missing will," Cassie said.

"And at this point, we've looked all over as well as the intruder, I might add, whomever that would be."

"Then we'll have to keep looking," Cassie said as she decided to look further into the closets and other areas of the house in the daylight. "Is there anywhere else Mr. Blake would have hidden the will? Were there any outbuildings or businesses he owned in the village? Are you sure there was no solicitor that would keep it on file?"

Alex took a deep breath as he finished his whiskey. "No outbuildings on the property that I'm aware of. I've worked here for over ten years so nothing has been removed or fallen in that time except the car and we went over that with a fine-tooth comb. As far as I know, there was nothing in the village that he owned or frequented."

Cassie poured herself a cup of tea and stirred in a small amount of sugar. Her head popped up. "What about Mrs. Witherspoon and Mrs. Peabody?"

"What about them?"

"Did Mr. Blake get on with them in the sense that he may have given the vicar a copy of his will or a letter in case of death?"

"If he had given something to the vicar, I would hope he would have enough sense to send it along to the station without being asked. I doubt he would give anything to Mrs. Peabody. If so, she would have read and distributed the information to the village immediately."

Cassie laughed. "I agree, but perhaps she heard snippets of gossip about a will or something."

"The police force doesn't investigate gossip," Alex said in a formal voice.

"No, I didn't think it did, but there are times one can find a clue that could lead to something official to investigate."

Alex gave an exasperated sigh. "You know if I approach Mrs. Peabody, our conversation would be all over town."

"What if it wasn't you?"

Alex turned toward her. "I don't think I like what you're suggesting. We're already trying to keep you safe from intruders. If someone thinks you're getting too close, our friendly intruder may not stay so friendly."

Cassie tapped her cheek as she thought. "What if I asked Mrs. Peabody about the strange vase of flowers to see who might have sent them? You can ask Mrs. Witherspoon if they have anything to add."

"I don't like it, Cassie." Alex's voice was firm.

"We're out of ideas."

Alex stiffened and his voice turned cold. "First of all, you and I were supposed to be discussing how a case is handled and trying to keep you safe. Asking questions may flush out more than we want. There's no we in this investigation. That's why I formed my cardinal rules to begin with. I don't want anyone to get hurt."

Cassie turned toward him with a stiff reply. "Your message has been noted, Detective Knight."

The pair continued with casual discussion for a short time until Alex thanked her for dinner and left for the evening. Once again, he waited for her to lock the door before he got into his car and drove away.

55

On Wednesday, Cassie attempted to walk to the store again for a few things. She hadn't traveled far into the lane when she spotted Mrs. Witherspoon and Mrs. Peabody. Mrs. Witherspoon called out and waved as they made their way over to her. "Cassie, how are you? How was London?"

"It was a nice break from writing but almost all business. Publicity photos and dinners and such."

"That sounds rather exciting," Mrs. Peabody said with a turn of her head.

"It sounds exciting, but it's not always that way," Cassie assured her. "By the way, I'd like to thank the person who left a beautiful vase of flowers on my dining room table. There was no card. Would that be either of you?"

"A new vase?" Mrs. Witherspoon asked. "We enjoyed the flowers you sent before you left for London. They looked lovely during the church service last weekend."

"I'm so glad," Cassie said. "Yes, there were more flowers on my table. The vase is mine, but it looked like someone placed fresh cut flowers in there."

They both shook their head before Mrs. Peabody spoke, "No, I have no idea who did that."

"Did you ladies happen to see anyone go into the cottage? It would have to be someone who had a key or access."

Once again, they both shook their heads. "Some strange happenings at that house. That's for sure. Are you sure it wasn't from the police?"

"No, I don't think so. They would have left a card and I don't think they would leave fresh cut flowers there."

"It's that house," Mrs. Peabody said. "There's nothing good going on there."

Cassie's eyes widened.

"Thelma," Mrs. Witherspoon said. "Let's not talk about things we don't know."

"I'd better get on for my shopping. It was nice seeing you ladies." Cassie said as she started down the lane. She was afraid to look back and see Mrs. Peabody wagging a finger as she talked about her.

LATER THAT DAY, Alex stopped by the vicarage to check whether the vicar and Mrs. Witherspoon had any information about Heather House and the estate. They assured him there was no will or papers on file at the vicarage.

"I was assigned to Wexley about eight years ago," Vicar Witherspoon said. "There were several men working there at the time and I believe there was a cook who also did some housekeeping for Mr. Blake. As he got older and more demanding, they left one by one and, of course, were never replaced. Granger Lowell was the farm manager back then so he may have the best recall of the lot. You'd probably find him at the pub."

"Did Mr. Blake ever mention any family?" Alex asked as he looked at them.

"Other than his parents, we've never known the Blakes to have any other family," Mrs. Witherspoon said.

"We checked into all that when we had to bury him last year.

Wanted to make sure we didn't do anything wrong. As a matter of fact, we're still waiting on the estate to settle the matter," the vicar pointed out.

"Yes, thank you for that," Alex said with a nod. "I'm sure they are working on it." Alex wished them a good day and left the church.

56

The weekend as well as Evie Thompson arrived with a flourish. A car pulled up at 6:00 a.m. Saturday morning with Evie sitting inside. The driver opened the door for her, and Evie spilled out as Cassie stood at the door of the cottage. Once the limo pulled away, Cassie and Evie hugged as Cassie pulled her inside.

"It's so good to see you," Cassie said as she squeezed her agent, friend and closest person Evie had as family.

"You too, my dear." Evie looked Cassie over. "Country life agrees with you. I think I see a glow around you."

Cassie laughed. "I'm sure it's from getting up early. Speaking of which, what time did you leave London?"

"Oh, some dreadful hour. I arrived from New York yesterday afternoon, had dinner and a drink and went straight to bed so I could be up early enough to arrive here on time. I wanted some time alone before Alex Knight comes to take us to Plymouth."

"It's a shame you couldn't stay for a week with me. I believe we have a great day planned, but I'd love to visit with you longer." Cassie hugged Evie again.

"Don't worry about visiting. You and I shall be in London in a couple of weeks. We'll catch up then," Evie said with a smile. "Do you have any coffee?"

Cassie laughed. "Of course. Please come in. Sit down. Would you like a tour of the cottage first?"

They sat at the table once they had toured the cottage. Cassie served scones with tea as well as strong coffee per Evie's request. Evie tasted one of the scones. "You do seem to be settling in nicely."

"I like it. It's quiet, very little drama or display."

"It is quite lovely but let me get this straight. You've had an intruder several times and you're still here by yourself?"

"Yes, we think whomever it is wants the will. I don't think there's any harm meant for me. Alex has asked me to relocate but I'm happy here."

Evie arched her eyebrows as far as they could go.

"Alex was here one Sunday and insisted on special dead bolts for my bedroom and bathroom to be safe. We still can't figure out how the intruder is getting in."

"And your cottage isn't haunted?" Evie asked with a grin.

"As far as I know, ghosts don't drink single malt and help themselves to the pantry."

Evie shook her head. "I think we need to discuss this further."

"Not right now," Cassie said. "What else is going on? How is Mrs. Roberts?"

Evie sipped her coffee. "She's fine. She misses your cooking, but she's wrapped the entire Manhattan apartment building around her little finger so she's not missing out on anything. She insists you are the best cook of them all, restaurants included."

Cassie smiled. "She used to listen to me read some of my draft if it wasn't sitting right. She had some good suggestions."

"Wise, she is," Evie said with a laugh. "She's lived a long, rich life. She's always been an influence on your career. By the way, your books are skyrocketing in the UK as well as America. You're even more popular. You said you wanted to return to Manhattan, maybe now is the time. Talk shows, interviews, book signings. You're in demand."

"That's the last thing I care about. You know I hate living in the public eye. I like living in the country, in a nice quiet village. I'll admit I did want to come back," Cassie said slowly. "I was hurt by the incident at the police station, and I wanted to run from my embarrassment. But you were right, Evie. I came back to the village and spoke to Alex. We're back on a friendly basis."

"Speaking of Alex Knight. Tell me about him. You're the only female he's been close to for a long while and believe me I've heard many have tried."

Cassie laughed at her words. "Especially a particular clerk at the police station." Cassie sat down and picked up a scone as she spoke. "He and I have established a working relationship. Let's see, what adjectives would I use? He is an extremely attractive, charming, dashing, witty Brit. He's authoritative, but very polite and respectful. I think that's also a shield for him though. When he questions you about things, he gets this very quiet, intense look. It makes you want to confess to something even if you haven't done anything."

Evie laughed. "Please continue."

"He has a cardinal rule that he does not get involved with anyone, so they can't be a target because of his work. Therefore, no relationships."

"Interesting," Evie said. "Keep going."

"We discussed his solve rate for the book. He's very detail oriented and agonizingly dogged about a case. He's only ever agreed to discuss one case with me but that's because I'm involved in a way."

"Excuse me?"

"It involves Heather House. He's not been able to solve the mystery that happened here. We have a work arrangement where he comes by after work. We discuss possibilities and have done a bit of searching but nothing has been solved."

"Is it possible he comes by for another reason?" Evie suggested with a Cheshire smile as she sipped her coffee.

Cassie blushed. "He does like my cooking, and he so appreciates your assortment of whiskey. But there are times that I wonder if he wants access to the house to look for clues and such."

Evie burst out laughing. "I doubt he's going to go through all that effort. I'm sure he has other cases to attend to."

Cassie's cell phone rang. She looked at the caller Id. "Speaking of which, here he is."

She picked up the phone. "Alex, good morning."

"Good morning, Cassie. How are you?"

"Fine, thank you. Evie's here."

"Wonderful. I'm calling to say I'll be by around 10:00 a.m. to pick you both up. We'll go straight to Books by the Sea. Thomas will be waiting for us. Afterwards, we have reservations at the Sea Treasure Pub. It should be a nice day."

"Sounds wonderful," Cassie said. "We'll be ready."

"Brilliant. I'll see you both soon."

Cassie put the phone down when Alex rang off. She looked at Evie. "He'll be here soon."

lex was prompt and arrived on time. Cassie was ready when he knocked on the door and invited him in with a flourish.

"Evie Thompson," Cassie said as she pointed at her friend.

"Alex Knight," Cassie pointed the opposite direction.

Alex reached forward and grasped Evie's hand in both of his. "Pleasure to meet you. Cassie speaks of you often."

Evie turned toward Cassie. "Oh, she does, does she?"

"Yes," Alex replied. "I believe she thinks very highly of you."

Evie's smile was wide and genuine. "Thank you. That's very kind of you to say."

Alex smiled and nodded. "Are you ladies ready to go to the coast?"

"I can't wait. It sounds like such a nice place to visit," Evie said.

"Indeed, it is," Alex said. "I think you'll love Books by the Sea."

The trio walked to the car. Cassie went to sit in the back and Evie pulled her forward. "Absolutely not, my dear. I need to sit in the back. I may have to answer some emails and texts."

Alex opened the back passenger door and Evie got in. He then opened the front passenger door for Cassie before he settled himself into the driver's seat.

They spent a comfortable time chatting while on their way to Plymouth. "I have a car picking me up in Plymouth to take me to the Exeter Airport tonight," Evie said as she tapped away on her phone. "I'm going back to the States, but I'll be back in London and then I'll look forward to seeing you there. Alex, I'd love to have you join us if you're free."

Cassie turned to her. "That's a long plane flight. Are you sure Evie? You could stay with me tonight."

"No, I really must go. I'll have a stop in Dublin, but I need to be in New York by tomorrow."

Cassie looked at Alex who shrugged and continued driving.

When they neared Plymouth, many streets had been closed in anticipation of the festival. Alex was able to get close enough to Books by the Sea for Thomas to move a barricade and allow them entry to the parking lot. He then replaced the barricade so no other cars could follow.

The trio got out of the car. "Evie Thompson, this is Thomas Knight, my cousin."

"Hello, Thomas. I'm so happy to meet you."

"My pleasure, my dear," Thomas said as he took her hand. He turned to Cassie next. "And it's always a pleasure to see you as well."

"Thank you, Thomas," Cassie said with a wide smile.

Thomas pointed to the door. "Why don't we go inside. I have tea waiting."

A small feast was waiting as Thomas led them to a back conference room. It was very well appointed and had brunch waiting on the conference table. "Please, help yourself and we can sit down and chat."

"Everything looks delicious," Cassie said as she helped herself to a small plate of food to be polite. Thomas poured her a cup of tea from a beautiful Royal Doulton tea service. Evie and Alex followed.

When they finished, Evie said, "Please, tell me about your bookshop. I'd love a tour."

Thomas did just that as he toured them around the shop when

they had finished their tea. He had hired several extra people for the day to help interested tourists find books while in Plymouth. He showed Evie where they set up the small stage for Sir Charles and a few private back rooms for VIP guests when they visit. There was an area with a back deck overlooking a beautiful view of the English Channel where one could sit with a drink and a good book while enjoying the day.

"It's gorgeous," Evie said. "I'd never leave."

"If that was only true," Thomas said flirtatiously. "We have many special book signings here."

"I imagine so, if Sir Charles was here," Evie said with a smile.

"And Miss Cassie has agreed to hold a book signing here as well," Thomas said with a grin.

Cassie nodded. "Indeed, I did, and I shall."

"That brings up an interesting point," Evie said. "Cassie's novel will be all the rage when it's released, but the non-fiction book about the Wexley Police may be a great opportunity to attract a crowd as well. It could be combined with a crime con or something like that."

"Great idea," Thomas said with a nod.

Evie turned to Alex. "I'm sure you'll receive many invitations for speaking engagements from universities and writer's conferences once the book is released."

Alex politely smiled at Evie without commenting. Cassie looked away to hide her expression as she guessed he wasn't interested in public events on any level. Not unless he retired as a DCI within his own district.

"Does the festival bring in many clients?" Evie asked politely.

"It sure does, although we have a busy shop to begin with."

"I'll bet," Evie said looking around once more.

"Why don't we all walk through the street to see some of the festival?" Alex asked, trying to change the venue.

"I think that's a great idea," Cassie said. The four of them walked out into the streets. They walked past various stalls selling crafts and food.

"We have many festivals here throughout the summer months," Thomas said. "We have famous entertainers, films, crafts, food, firework competitions, and cars. We have a 5K as well. You name it, we can probably find it."

"This is amazing," Cassie said as she looked around. "Such a great turnout."

They walked through Plymouth, taking in the sights and watching the crowds grow. Alex looked for officers from Wexley. He knew several had signed up for extra duty. The group had a fun day as they enjoyed the festival.

Alex looked at his watch. "It's almost time for our reservation at the Sea Treasure Pub. Shall we go?"

They all agreed and walked toward the restaurant. When they went inside, they were shown to a VIP line and given a table on the main floor. Other diners without reservations waited in a different line and were eventually led to small tables in the back of the room.

Alex and Cassie were unaware that Miles, Olivia, Dennis, Arlene, and several constables waited in line on the side of the building.

They received menus and were told of the specials for the evening. They each ordered their meal and shared several bottles of expensive wine before eating. They had a wonderful conversation as if they had known each other for years.

Halfway through the meal, Evie asked a question. "Cassie was very impressed with a trip she had taken to the Moreland Estate. I've heard it's an impossible place to visit and I was wondering if there was a connection there?"

Alex and Thomas passed an imperceptible look that was caught by Cassie and Evie. Finally, Alex spoke. "Archie Moreland was a member of the House of Lords. He passed away several years ago. The Moreland Estate, where he grew up and lived, is part of our family estate now."

Evie's eyebrows raised and she nodded. "So that's where the connection to royalty, prestige and power lies."

Thankfully the server appeared at their side to collect dishes and get ready for the next course. In the corner, the band set up to play music for the dinner guests. Once dessert and coffee were served, Evie put her cup down and said, "I have to say, this meal was excellent. I have never had fish as fresh as this and the rest of the meal was scrumptious."

They all agreed as they enjoyed their after-dinner drinks. The restaurant's lights were turned down low while the guests listened to the band.

After 30 minutes, Alex looked at Cassie with a strange expression. "Dance with me?"

Cassie felt nervous but smiled as she looked at him. Her nod was barely perceptible. He stood and reached out for her. Without speaking, Cassie stood and took his hand. They walked out to the dance floor but there was no awkwardness this time. They came together for the first song, moving in perfect rhythm. After a few songs, the band began a classic slow, romantic number. Alex gently pulled her to his chest and wrapped one arm around her tightly. Their hands clasped together as they moved. She closed her eyes and laid her head against his hard chest. All else disappeared and it was just the two of them pressed together in the dark. She felt the beat of his heart, the strength of his arms and noticed that he wore her favorite cologne. This time, she didn't want the song to end. When the saxophone solo began, she tilted her head upward. Their lips were inches apart as they gazed into each other's eyes.

EVIE AND THOMAS watched them as they danced. Eventually, Evie arched her eyebrows and started to smile. Next to her, Thomas chuckled. "I think we're going to be seeing each other quite often and I'm glad."

IN THE BACK of the room, the officers from Wexley were sitting at a table. Dennis looked up and noticed Alex and Cassie on the dance floor. "Isn't that our DCI?"

"He's got moves," Miles said as he smiled at Olivia. "Good for him."

Arlene's jaw clenched as she watched them dance. "Could they get any closer?"

"I don't think so," Dennis said as he put his hand around Arlene's waist. "But we can."

"Give it a break, will you please?"

"Arlene, they're not doing anything but moving."

"When you dance like that, you don't need to do anything else." Arlene slammed her glass down on the table.

One of the constables used his cell phone to film the dance and sent it to a few other officers working at the station. Within minutes, Joe Duffy received an incoming text as part of an officer's group. He opened the video and watched Alex and Cassandra dance. Normally he'd be enraged about personal items in the chat but instead he shook his head and laughed. "You old bastard."

When the song ended, the band announced they were taking a break and Alex and Cassie made their way back to the table. The group was quiet for a moment until the waiter appeared to take their plates and Evie's cell phone chimed. "This phone is driving me crazy." She picked it up and looked at the text and uttered a curse.

"What's wrong, Evie?" Cassie asked.

"My driver cancelled. I need to be at the Exeter Airport tonight."

Cassie looked at Alex with a questioning glance when Thomas cut in. "Evie, would you allow me to drive you to the airport? It's about an hour from here. That will give us more time to make plans for book signings and such." He then winked at her.

"I think that's a grand idea," Evie said with a smile.

The group got up and left the restaurant. "I have a sweater in the car," Evie said.

"No problem. We must go back to the bookshop to retrieve my car as well."

"Perfect," Evie said. "Cassie, walk with me so we can go over our schedule." The two women walked behind Alex and Thomas. Evie hooked her arm through Cassie's. "You mentioned Alex was attractive and dashing. You didn't tell me he was an absolute dreamboat."

Cassie laughed. "A Brit with cardinal rules. As I said, we have a working relationship."

"Honey, wake up. That man has a pheromone trail around you that's ten feet wide. We were getting hot and bothered watching you dance."

Cassie burst out laughing. "Oh Evie, that's why I love you so much."

"And there's more to the whole Moreland Estate. There's an interesting story there."

"One they don't want to tell," Cassie said. "Let's mind our business and worry about meeting in London."

The women reached the men in the parking lot. Thomas had his keys ready, and Alex opened his car so Evie could retrieve her sweater. Sharing hugs and a goodbye, Thomas and Evie drove off toward Exeter.

Alex turned to Cassie. "Would you like to walk a bit more? The night is young. They have a smashing Ferris wheel and there will be fireworks."

"Sounds lovely," Cassie said. Alex took her hand through his arm, and they walked off.

They spent the next couple of hours listening to music, looking at the waves roll to shore, enjoying the warm ocean air and having ice cream. Alex then purchased tickets for the Ferris wheel, and they climbed aboard. They had gone around several times when it stopped, at the top, to allow additional riders to enter. Cassie was in awe of the sight of Plymouth and the ocean from high above the ground.

"It's so gorgeous," she said as she shivered.

"You're getting cold," Alex said. "It's beautiful but the ocean winds are strong up here." He immediately removed his jacket and wrapped it around her shoulders. He kept his arm around her for a while to help her warmup and then leaned forward to kiss her temple. Eventually, the Ferris wheel started moving again and they were let out when they reached the bottom. They went to a small booth and Alex won a teddy bear for Cassie. He handed it to her and said, "What do you say? Ready to go?"

Cassie nodded. "Yes, it was a lovely day. It's sad that it must end."

58

The ride home was pleasant. Cassie felt like a kid again after she went to the boardwalk with her parents. Exhausted, but warm and content. Alex and Cassie made small talk about the day and how Evie liked the bookshop. They discussed their dinner, however Cassie purposely avoided mentioning the discussion on the Moreland Estate and their dance.

"I'm sorry if Evie appeared a bit pushy at times. She's lovely when you know her. Her grit is what makes her a successful businesswoman."

"No, she was fine. She and Thomas hit it off. They can make all the business plans they want to."

Cassie laughed. "I think I saw them exchange phone numbers."

Alex neared the cottage and pulled into the drive. He turned off the ignition and pointed to the cottage. "I'd like to go inside and make sure everything is in order."

"Of course," Cassie laughed, handing him her keys. He opened her car door, and she followed him to the porch. She waited there until he had gone inside and looked around the rooms, making sure the intruder had not paid a visit.

"All clear," Alex said as he opened the door for her to come inside.

"Thank you," Cassie said. "Would you like a night cap?"

Alex paused for a moment before he answered. "I'd love to, but I think it would be better if I go. It's been a long day."

Cassie nodded. She had been up before dawn awaiting Evie's arrival.

"Alex, I'd like to thank you again for a fantastic day. You were so welcoming to Evie, and I appreciate that. We had a lot of fun, but you made it all happen."

When Alex smiled, Cassie leaned forward and kissed Alex on the cheek. He stood for a moment with an imperceptible look on his face.

Cassie stepped back immediately and shook her head. "I'm sorry. I shouldn't have done that. I wanted to thank you for a great day. I know what you want. Cardinal rules and all."

He was silent for another moment as he looked at her and whispered, "No, I'm afraid you have no idea what I want."

Noting his husky voice, Cassie looked into his eyes, held her breath and felt her whole body start to tingle.

"I've been trying to tell you that I've known, for a while, that I'm madly in love with you." He gently held her by the shoulders as he spoke in that quiet, intense voice. "I've tried to show you, but I haven't told you because I knew your first instinct would be to cut and run. I'm not going to let that happen. I'm not interested in your fame or your money. As you can see, I have enough of my own." He paused to take a breath. "What do I want? I want us to be a couple. An official couple, in private, in public, everywhere. I want to announce to the world that you and I belong together."

Cassie took a breath. "And how do you plan to do that?"

Alex laughed. "That part is easy. I plan to kiss you full on in front of Mrs. Peabody next time we're on the village green. She's better than any social media. I'd estimate it would take about ten minutes for the news to spread worldwide."

Cassie looked up at him. Her eyes were wide, and her breath caught.

He held her tighter, his gaze traveled over her lips. He leaned closer, pushed a strand of her hair back behind her ear and whispered, "Bloody hell." His lips caught hers as his strong arms held her close against his chest. When he pulled back, he said, "I know you have a million questions and a million reasons why you want to run. Let's not think about that right now. We'll work everything out. I have a lot of holiday due to me and my papers are in order. My passport is ready. We can go wherever we need to and work on us. Just think about it for now."

Cassie didn't respond but she put her arms around his neck. They kissed again, more deeply but tenderly. Cassie pulled back. "But I'm moving back to Manhattan and....,"

Alex put his finger to her lips. "Let's talk about it tomorrow. I'll come by and pick you up for brunch. Don't cook anything. Let's go out to the pub or green so we can simply be together." Alex could see the panic welling up in her eyes. "Please? Let's talk about it." He smiled as he asked and continued to stroke her hair.

Cassie took another breath and whispered. "Okay, I'd like that."

"Great," Alex said with a wide smile. "I'd better go. Are you sure you're okay for tonight?"

"Yes, I'm fine."

They walked to the door. Alex paused and gave her a kiss on the cheek as he hugged her once more.

"Good night, luv."

"Good night."

Alex strode to his car after Cassie locked the door. She waited until she heard his car drive away before she went upstairs.

59

Cassie slept late the next morning. She spent half the night tossing and turning. She relived the day over and over in her mind, especially when they were in the cottage and kissed. Every time she thought about his words and his lips, she tingled. She wasn't sure if she was nervous or excited. He was right. Her first instinct was to run. She couldn't call Evie since she was flying home for most of the night. Cassie knew what Evie would say so she would meet Alex today and go from there. No decisions, just talk. Maybe after a good night's sleep, Alex would rethink his words. Yesterday had been that kind of a fairy tale day. Today may be different.

He arrived a little after noon. He was wearing slacks and a dark button-down shirt with an open collar. He looked great in a suit, but even better today. His tan complimented his eyes, and he wore her favorite cologne.

"Good morning, Cassie. You look beautiful today."

Cassie smiled. She went out of her way to put on one of the new dresses she had bought in London and spent extra time with her hair and make-up. The dress she wore had a lovely matching jacket. She was overdressed for a walk around the village or the pub but wanted to look extra nice.

She found her purse and locked the cottage door. Alex took her arm in his and they walked slowly down the lane. As they walked, they made small talk and didn't directly address the conversation from the night before. Cassie was shy, and Alex didn't want to force the issue.

They neared the pub and Alex turned to her. "How about we go inside and see what they're offering today. To be honest, I'm a bit hungry."

They took a table near the back, and both ordered a nice breakfast of eggs with bacon, buttered toast, and a pot of tea. There were more people in the pub than Cassie would have expected. All were talking and sharing stories about exciting games they had watched that weekend. She saw Wyatt Smith, Granger Lowell, two constables, James and his wife and others. James waved to her when they sat down.

Their food arrived, and they began to eat. After ten minutes or so, Grayson came to the table to chat. "It's nice to see you here." He turned to Cassie. "I've been hearing so much about your cooking; I was afraid you'd be putting me out of business."

Cassie laughed at his comment. "I don't think there's any chance of that. Your breakfast is wonderful."

The group jumped when they heard a noise from a nearby table. A man was leaving the pub and Shelly cursed as she bent over and picked up a brick. She brought it to the owner. "The brick near the fireplace has fallen off the wall again. I think it's time to get the wall fixed."

Grayson turned to her and said, "Where am I going to hide all the keys I collect from the drunkards at night if I fix the wall?" He turned back to Alex and Cassie and whispered, "Everyone knows I hide the keys behind the loose brick so they can come back and collect them in the morning without having to get embarrassed and ask me."

"That's kind of you," Cassie said before he waved and walked away. Alex and Cassie continued to eat their breakfast, but Cassie was quiet and looked pensive as she ate.

"What's wrong? Are you feeling all right?"

Cassie looked up at him. "I think I know where the will could be. I can't believe I didn't think of it sooner, but it all makes sense now. Let's finish and get back to the cottage and check."

Breakfast took another ten minutes to finish, and neither of them tasted much of it. Alex threw some bills on the table before Grayson reappeared. "What's the matter then? You act like I'm trying to poison you."

Alex leaned over. "It was wonderful, but we realized there's somewhere important we need to be. The food and tea were excellent."

Several villagers commented on their hasty departure and the words they overheard.

Cassie and Alex hurried down the lane toward the cottage. "I'm not sure if it's the right spot, but it's worth a look. It hit me as soon as I heard Grayson talk about the brick. I've had a loose brick in the kitchen archway since I arrived and it's driving me crazy. I was going to ask you to have a look, but it was never the right time."

They reached the cottage, unlocked the door, and went inside. Cassie pulled Alex to the kitchen area and pointed to the copper pan that was covering the brick sticking partly out of the wall. "This brick, here." She removed the pot and tried to pull the brick without success. Alex then tried and it moved a bit. Cassie reached over the stove and grabbed a paring knife. Alex used the knife against the side of the brick and had some success. He handed the knife back to Cassie who stuck it in her jacket pocket while watching Alex shimmy the brick from the wall. When it came loose, he reached inside and came out with a handful of papers.

Both leaned forward to read the papers as Alex opened them in full. There was a will but attached to it was a letter explaining why Mr. Blake wanted to change the will. Alex pulled out his cell, took a photo, and texted Miles.

Please come to Heather House immediately. We need to locate and charge someone.

ALEX AND CASSIE continued reading when they heard a loud noise and then a voice behind them.

"I'll take that, thank you."

Turning around, they saw Granger standing there, pointing a gun.

"You?" Cassie asked as she looked at him. "But why?"

"Because Heather House and the estate should belong to me. I worked hard for Mr. Blake all these years and he promised me. I asked for a copy of the will, but he never gave it to me."

Alex stood up straight and frowned. "According to this, you're not to inherit anything."

"No one will know that once I destroy the letter. Let's go," Granger said as he reached forward and ripped the will out of Alex's hands.

"Where are we going?" Cassie asked wide-eyed.

"I can't very well leave you two around to tell everyone about the letter."

Alex clenched his jaw as Granger grabbed Cassie and pushed her near the pantry. He looked at Alex, "I may not be able to kill you immediately, but I'm pretty sure I'll be able to kill her. Now, let's go."

Alex followed Cassie into the pantry and was surprised to find the back wall had been moved forward to reveal a tunnel behind.

"Is that how you've been getting in here?" Cassie asked, drawing his attention. Alex turned to hit him, and Granger jumped back, placing his arm around Cassie's throat. Alex saw he had no leverage and stepped back.

"Yes, and that's where your bodies are going to be stored for a while," Granger said with a hiss. He gestured with the gun towards the tunnel and pushed them forward.

Cassie grabbed Alex's hand. "I don't want to go in there. It's all dirt and it smells. I can't see a thing because it's dark."

"You won't need to be seeing anything. Let's go." Granger pushed

Alex forward with the gun.

Alex paused for a moment as he squeezed her arm. "It will be fine."

She continued to hold his hand as they entered the passage and as soon as they were in the dark, she quickly removed the paring knife from her jacket pocket and pressed it into his hand.

He leaned forward and whispered in her ear. "When I push you forward, fall to the ground and stay down."

Within moments, she felt Alex push her. She went down to her knees and flattened herself as close to the ground as she could. Alex spun around and sunk the paring knife into Granger's stomach. Granger screamed out and the gun went off. The bullet hit the top of the tunnel causing dirt and debris to fall on top of Cassie's head. Alex and Granger struggled as Alex sent the gun flying. Cassie felt the cold metal of the gun near her hand and pushed it further down the tunnel. Alex punched Granger in the stomach directly over the knife wound and Granger fell to the floor as he screamed out in pain.

Cassie couldn't see anything in the dark but heard other people yelling out and realized one of the voices belonged to Miles. "We're in the tunnel. Please hurry."

There were small bits of light that rushed into the tunnel and Cassie looked back in time to see Granger lying on his stomach with Alex pinning him down and holding Granger's hands to the floor. Miles took over as he and the other officers got hold of him.

"Are you all right, sir?"

"Yes, but he'll need a medic."

Alex ran to Cassie, pulled her up and wrapped his arms around her. "Are you hurt?"

Cassie buried her face in his chest. "I'm okay, I think." They both stayed that way for a few moments, clinging on to each other. He smoothed her hair and held her close. She looked up and said, "I pushed the gun down the tunnel. It's on the ground somewhere."

Alex swallowed and hugged her tighter. "If anything had happened to you...."

Cassie bitterly thought to herself, "Thus, the cardinal rules."

60

————

Hours went by. Alex and Cassie both emerged from the tunnel full of dirt, shaky but unharmed. The police had been in and out of the cottage all afternoon. They brought heavy duty lights to illuminate the tunnel and collect any evidence they could find.

When Alex left to accompany Granger to the hospital, Cassie was asked to leave the cottage as well, but she refused and sat in the library. Mrs. Witherspoon was called to sit with her and keep her company until Alex came back or the police were done with their investigation. Cassie was not good company as her thoughts continued to return to Alex and his cardinal rules. *It was sweet while it lasted although that must be a record time for the book of relationships.*

Eventually, Alex returned and immediately found Cassie. Both were still smudged and covered with dirt.

"How is Granger?" Cassie asked when Alex walked into the library.

"He's alive and talking. They had to give him blood and he may yet have to go into surgery."

Alex turned to Mrs. Witherspoon. "Thank you for staying with Cassie. Do you mind if we talk privately?"

"Of course, not. I'll be going. I'm glad you're both all right and the mystery is solved."

"You and me both," Alex said.

When Mrs. Witherspoon left the library, Alex turned to Cassie. "Let's take a walk and get out of here. We need to talk."

Cassie felt a lump in her stomach but nodded and they both walked out the door. Alex held her hand as they walked around the back of the village, so they had some privacy. "Thank you for grabbing my hand and slipping me the paring knife. You're good. I was going to tackle him, but the knife was crucial to our survival."

Cassie smiled. "All in a mystery writer's work. Were you able to talk to him?"

Alex nodded. "We did. Granger and Mr. Blake were close at one time and Mr. Blake did promise him the estate after his death. About ten years ago, Mr. Blake's half-brother, Dylan Blake, showed up. Dylan had found out about William from his dying mother and wanted to meet him. Dylan was a simple man and was not working at the time but wanted to be with family. They shared stories of their childhoods and memories of their father, Archie, but then Dylan didn't leave, and Granger got angry. One day, William shared his thoughts of splitting the property between both his brother, Dylan, and Granger. The reason was that Dylan probably wouldn't be able to manage the estate by himself, but since he was younger, he would have somewhere to live until his death. William Blake thought Granger could help manage both halves until then.

"It turns out that Granger had other plans about the property and when he shared that with Dylan, they fought. Granger admitted to killing Dylan. He shot him in the head one night after drinking too much and hid the body. He couldn't drag him through the cottage into the tunnel, so he hid him in the old car and covered it with the tarp because he knew no one bothered with it. He was going to leave his body there until he could eventually bury him or hide him elsewhere, but a couple of years went by and then William Blake died."

"Wasn't William curious?" Cassie asked.

"He was. He asked Granger if he knew where Dylan was, as he

had just disappeared one day. Granger denied knowing anything but told William he had seen Dylan packing as if he were going on a long trip. And then, Granger kept asking for a copy of the will. Apparently, William got suspicious. He couldn't prove anything, but he didn't like Granger's attitude and wrote the extra letter stating he had changed his mind and didn't want Granger to inherit."

"I didn't get a chance to read the letter. Is that what it said?"

"The will stated the property was to be split between Granger and his brother, but the attached codicil said that Granger was not to inherit anything. If Dylan was ever found, the estate was to go to him and if not, the local authorities were to decide what was best. His intention was that the estate would not be sold or turned over to a housing developer. Granger wanted that part of the will and letter destroyed especially if he could mount a court fight."

"What about the tunnel?" Cassie asked as she turned to Alex. "That was creepy."

"Yes, apparently the tunnel was built long ago to be an easy route to bring goods into the house from deliveries by boat in the river. The tunnel leads from the pantry to the river with a hidden opening under the bridge."

"I saw Granger under that bridge one day. It was one of the days our intruder visited. I'll bet I just missed him in the house."

"Yes, he mentioned that. And he mentioned that he was the one who brought you the bouquet of flowers when you were in London. He was happy to have the cottage to himself for a couple of days."

"That is so creepy," Cassie said with a grimace. "And he enjoyed the single malt and my cooking, no doubt."

"Apparently, he did," Alex said. "You'll notice the field right next to the bridge is filled with hay. That's where your muddy hay came from. The tunnel will be boarded up as soon as all evidence is collected so it won't be accessible anymore. You won't have to worry about staying there." Alex gave her a glance from the side as they approached the village green. "You haven't said anything about staying there after all this is done."

"So much has happened," Cassie said with a sigh.

"I would be beside myself if anything happened to you," Alex said to her as they stopped walking and looked at each other.

"Now, I understand the cardinal rules." Cassie acknowledged with a sad smile.

Alex leaned forward and pulled her toward him.

"Rules were made to be broken," Alex whispered as he studied her face, her eyes, her lips and waited for her to say something. "If I have to be your bodyguard for life, then so be it."

Cassie looked away for a moment. She sighed and then pointed. "Look, isn't that Mrs. Peabody on the green?"

Alex looked toward where she was pointing. "So, it is." He looked at Cassie and smiled, wound his arms around her tightly and kissed her full on for several moments. When he pulled back, he smiled again and said, "I want to be completely sure she saw us." He leaned forward and kissed her full on again. When they broke apart, Cassie and Alex looked at each other and then across the green to see Mrs. Peabody running at full speed toward the vicarage. Cassie leaned her head against his chest. They laughed, held each other and before they kissed again, whispered, "I love you."

ABOUT THE AUTHOR

Linda Rawlins is an American writer of mystery fiction best known for her Misty Point Mystery Series, including Misty Manor, Misty Point, Misty Winter, Misty Treasure, Misty Revenge, and Misty Retreat. She is also known for her Rocky Meadow Mystery Series, including The Bench, Fatal Breach, Sacred Gold as well as an independent novel, Midnight Shift.

Linda loved to read as a child and started writing her first mystery novel in fifth grade. She then went on to study science, medicine, and literature, eventually graduating from medical school and establishing her career in medicine.

Linda Rawlins lives in New Jersey with her husband, her family and spoiled dog. She loves spending time at the beach as well as visiting the mountains of Vermont. She is an active member of Mystery Writers of America. As a member of Sisters in Crime, Linda was the President of the Central Jersey Chapter for 2022, 2020, 2019 and the VP in 2018.

You can visit Linda at:
   lindarawlins.com

ALSO BY LINDA RAWLINS

The Misty Point Mystery Series

Misty Manor

Misty Point

Misty Winter

Misty Treasure

Misty Revenge

Misty Retreat

The Rocky Meadow Mystery Series

The Bench

Fatal Breach

Sacred Gold

The Elizabeth Brooks Mystery Series

Midnight Shift

Made in United States
North Haven, CT
18 July 2023

39217824R10152